Rebecca Stowe

Rebecca Stowe was born in Port Huron, Michigan. She is the author of *Not the End of the World* and of *The Shadow of Desire*, published by Sceptre in 1996. She studied at City College in New York and has published stories in various magazines and anthologies. The recipient of several American fellowships, including one from the New York Foundation of the Arts, she currently lives in New York State.

Also by Rebecca Stowe

Not the End of the World
The Shadow of Desire

Rebecca Stowe

ONE GOOD THING

SCEPTRE

Copyright © 1999 Rebecca Stowe

First published in 1999 by Hodder and Stoughton
A division of Hodder Headline
A Sceptre Paperback

The right of Rebecca Stowe to be identified as the Author of the Work
has been asserted by her in accordance with the Copyright, Designs
and Patents Act 1988.

10 9 8 7 6 5 4 3 2 1

All rights reserved. No part of this publication may be reproduced,
stored in a retrieval system, or transmitted in any form or by any means
without the prior written permission of the publisher, nor be otherwise
circulated in any form of binding or cover other than that in which it
is published and without similar condition being imposed
on the subsequent purchaser.

All characters in this publication are fictitious and any resemblance
to real persons, living or dead, is purely coincidental.

A CIP catalogue record for this title is available from the British Library.

ISBN 0 340 67191 2

Typeset by
Palimpsest Book Production Limited
Polmont, Stirlingshire
Printed and bound in Great Britain by
Mackays of Chatham PLC, Chatham, Kent

Hodder and Stoughton
A division of Hodder Headline
338 Euston Road
London NW1 3BH

To Jenny and Jules

'Now go and brag of thy present happiness, whosoever thou art, brag of thy temperature, of thy good parts, insult, triumph and boast; thou seest in what a brittle state thou art, how soon thou mayest be dejected . . . how many sudden accidents may procure thy ruin, what a small tenure of happiness thou hast in this life, how weak and silly a creature thou art . . .'

Robert Burton, *The Anatomy of Melancholy*

One

Everything was falling apart. The world, the economy, his apartment building. The entire city was crumbling to pieces in big noisy chunks. The only thing that wasn't falling apart, Harry Butler thought happily, was himself.

It was Harry's forty-seventh birthday. He refused to consider forty-seven the beginning of middle age, even though it was, mathematically, probably more than middle. It was unlikely he'd live to see ninety-four, but still, middle age was the beginning of old and old was something Harry Butler would never be. He'd had a premonition; a feeling he'd had since he was a teenager, that he'd die dramatically and young. He had a vision of himself burning out in a blaze of blue light, living his life so intensely and fast that the sheer momentum would hurl him to an early, tragic, and much-poeticised death. Spontaneous combustion. The only way to go. Anything else was settling for the ordinary and ordinary was something Harry Butler was not.

He jumped out of bed and began running in place. In the human life span, he thought, there are only two phases. Youth and Old Age. Since he refused to be old, he must still be young. What was age but a bunch of numbers, anyway? You're only as old as you feel, they say, and he felt twenty, fifteen, as happy and energetic as a ten-year-old playing hooky.

He whooped a Tarzan King of the Jungle wail and pounded his tight belly. 'Go ahead,' he told himself, 'hurt me.'

A rock, he thought gleefully, steel. This is not the body of an old man, this is the body of a god. Middle age is aches. Pains. It's arthritis and all that shit. I never get sick, he thought, I'm in better shape than Cher.

He thought about Cher for a minute, closing his eyes and seeing her dressed in tight black spandex, sequins glittering like sweat. He watched her slither across a lighted stage, like a charmed snake. If she could see me, he thought, she'd love me.

That would be something. He'd dump his flabby wife and go live in Cher's California mansion. They would work out together and then screw. She would support him – she had plenty of money, she was a Super Star, she wouldn't mind. She had supported that bagel guy, why not Harry Butler, starving artist?

Clark had left him half a grapefruit and a rose. HAPPY BIRTHDAY she had scrawled in red lipstick across the cover of the *Daily News*.

Harry grinned. He would never dump Clark, not even for Cher. She wasn't a goddess, but she did support him, and while no one could accuse her of doing it in style, she did it in her own way and that was good enough for Harry Butler.

He looked around their apartment. 'Squalid,' his

middle-class Midwestern mother would call it, if she saw it, which she wouldn't. Downscale, definitely, but rent-controlled. Clark had been living there since the beginning of time, practically, and even though she made a hefty salary, now, she wouldn't dream of leaving. For one hundred and sixty-two dollars a month they got two small rooms, with a hole cut out between the kitchen and the living room. One whole wall of books, with pride of place going to Clark's collection of junk-shop first editions, Clark's collection of plastic snowballs dangling around the hole in the wall: Mount Rushmore and Miss Liberty and Graceland swaying in the slight breeze from the kitchen window. What wall space they had was covered with papier-maché masks from Clark's performance art days: leering, bird-like faces covered with feathers and glitter, cheerfully grotesque. Nary a closet, although Harry had built, with his own hands, a kind of alcove where they kept their clothes in plastic milk crates and shopping bags.

Some people might call this a dump, he thought.

And they'd be right.

He laughed aloud at his own joke and thought about how good it was to be alive, to be healthy, to be happy enough to laugh at something someone else might cry about, like living in a dumpy two-room bathtub-in-kitchen tenement apartment. Like living at all.

'Kerouac died when he was forty-seven,' Clark had reminded him last night, but Kerouac had been a drunk. A fat, out-of-shape, raving nutcase drunk and Harry was, well, Harry. Kerouac had squandered his talent, belching it out at every two-bit bar he stumbled into, but Harry was holding on to his. He clung to it, savoring it, keeping it to himself as long as possible. He wasn't going to end up at the bar of some Blarney Rock, eyeing the door for some bum he could rope in and pummel with his tales of glory. Not he. Not Harry Butler. He had a masterpiece in him: he knew it, Clark knew it, everyone knew it. Parts of it had been circulating in the East Village for years. He had three publishers waiting for it. That made him a legend, of sorts. While everyone else was scrambling, begging, pleading, tooting their own horns in an endless horrisonous bleat, Harry just sat back and wrote. While everyone else was pissed off and depressed, Harry was happy.

He didn't understand depression, but he was working on it. Not for himself – he had never been depressed a minute in his life and he had no intention of starting now – but he needed to get *inside* it. It was the malaise of the late twentieth century and how could he hope to leave behind a lasting testament of his life without reflecting the world around him? And the world around him was depressed.

> *When you wake up in the morning*
> *And you wish you were dead*
> *You know you got that feeling*
> *Kierkegaard called dread . . .*

That was as far as he'd gotten. Harry was a multi-talented sort of guy – in addition to his book, he was developing a new kind of music, combining elements of rap with Gregorian chant. Raptor Music. Brutal. Assaultive. Scavenging. Picking the bones of a decaying society. And above all, depressed.

It was hard for him to get the depressed part. Just thinking about Raptor Music elated him – he felt powerful, strong, eagle-like, King of the Sky soaring above a city full of potential meals and it was hard to get depressed about that.

But he was trying. He was three-quarters of the way through *The Anatomy of Melancholy*, which he'd read to Clark in bed at night. She'd sit there, pull her foot up toward her chest and begin picking at her toes – a habit that disgusted Harry at first but that had grown bizarrely erotic: there was something so obscene about it, something down and dirty, something that made him want to rut. 'You read,' he'd say, handing her the book while he scooched down the bed, toward Clark's beckoning toes – long and white, prehensile, the nails painted with chartreuse glitter paint. Monkey toes. 'Listen to this,' she'd say, giggling while he licked her littlest piggie, '"Love is madness, a hell, an incurable disease; Seneca calls it an impotent and raging lust,"' and she'd toss the book aside, pull him up by the hair, and they'd shriek with laughter while they screwed.

He grabbed his bongo drums from under the kitchen table and headed for the loo. Couldn't very well call it a bathroom – there wasn't a bathtub in there, not even a sink. Just a runny toilet behind a warped plywood door, a toilet and five thousand of Clark's magazines. She got them free, one of her perks for being a Research Director.

He sat on the toilet and lightly tapped the taut drum skins, trying to get the beat. The depressed beat. Slow, monotonous, heavy. Thud. Thud. Thud.

Raptor Music. The perfect come-back vehicle for the Four Lornes. There were only three of them now, since Jimmy Houser sold out and moved back to Chicago to trade pork bellies and pea futures on the commodities exchange. Jimmy was rich, rich beyond belief – he lived in a mansion on Lake Michigan and had a skinny overgroomed wife and a Range Rover full of snotty kids. It mystified Harry – how could he give up New York, the East Village, being the star of a bongo band? Even though they hadn't performed in years, still, people remembered them, respected them, bought them drinks. Being one of the original Four Lornes gave Harry a capital more valuable than any amount of money – it gave him fame, admiration, and most importantly, women. It had given him, in fact, Clark.

'Harry Butler?' she had gasped the night he introduced himself to her at the Where?House. Lorna had dragged him there for one of those evenings of interminable performance art, the kind of thing where women complained about being sex objects and then took off their shirts. Harry liked that part, but the stuff leading up to it had been excruciating. Clark's piece had been different, about a twelve-year-old girl whose notions of sex and relationships came from watching *West Side Story*. Harry could still see her, standing on the plywood platform that served as a stage, dressed in a leotard and a starched pinafore. She was hilarious – especially the way she'd shiver and collapse in a heap every time she said 'Ber-NAR-doe.' The writing was minimalist: short, sharp bursts of words stretched taut over her ideas, like a surgical glove.

For Harry, it had been love at first sight, even though she was a little on the weird-looking side: short, kind of squatish and scrunched down, with a lime-green buzz cut. It looked like someone had melted a popsickle on her head, but she was good and her face, at least, was pretty: round, with glowing white skin, white as Siberia. Her eyes were a stunning gray, almost silver, with the eyelids drooping lazily downward. 'Harry Butler?' she had asked again. 'Of the Four Lornes?' 'In the flesh,' he'd said and she had grabbed his arm. 'I can't believe it!'

she had cried, 'I've been a Four Lorne groupie since I was twelve! I was the President of the Avoca Four Lorne Fan Club!' She had, she told him, worn out six 45s of 'Bongo Boogie'. 'I just can't believe it,' she said again, 'I would have thought you guys would be dead by now.'

They were far from dead and even though there were only three of them, the time was ripe for a revival. The other Lornes weren't nearly as enthusiastic as Harry was, they were perfectly happy resting on their laurels and living their comfortable lives. Paul had had the prescience or foresight or just plain dumb luck to get into the singing telegram business at the very beginning and now he had a co-op on East 10th, overlooking the Park, the whole fourth floor, all his own, with no letters or numbers carving it up. He had a wife, a big black bear of a dog and a Lincoln he kept at his in-laws in Queens. Harry worked for him off and on, delivering an occasional Tarzan-A-Gram, taking phone orders, covering for him when he and Bettina went hunting at their house up in the Adirondacks. Lenny, too, had been smart: he'd gotten his CPA and worked like a demon, from December 'til April, doing everybody's taxes, then took the rest of the year off to be a hypochondriac.

Harry wondered what time it was. He never wore a watch, didn't want that little strap around his wrist, confining him, limiting him, keeping him earth-bound. He liked being free, soaring above the limits of time and space.

He got up, put the bongo drums back under the kitchen table, did a few jumping jacks. He could think about Raptor Music later, right now he wanted to work on the book, wanted to see where he'd fly today. *Butler by Butler*. His magnum opus. He thought, with great satisfaction, how he had anticipated the memoir craze by at least a decade. 'And at the rate you're going,' Clark often said, 'it'll be over by the time you're finished.'

Not to worry. Harry was creating a new form, the form of the future: the Fictoir, the memoir of his imagination. Why not? What difference did it make if he lived his adventures in his mind or in the 'real' world? He was still living them and that made them as true as if he'd actually done them.

He tossed his head, pulled his thick grayless hair back in a ponytail and secured it with one of Clark's frilly elastic things, pink with silver threads running through it. Garter belts, Harry called them, and he reminded himself to remember to take it off before he went out, replace it with a manly rubber band.

He turned on the computer and waited for it to boot up. It was ancient, from the stone age, Lenny said, but Harry liked it. He was used to it. He knew exactly what he needed to do to work on his manuscript and that was good enough for him. He didn't want to learn how to do anything else, he only wanted to tax one side of his brain while he was working.

Life is good, Harry thought as the computer chugged and whizzed. He thought about how lucky he was, living exactly the kind of life he wanted to live, remaining true to his bohemian nature, devoting himself to Art, being married to a woman he not only adored, admired and respected, but who made a salary in the high five figures. And who was his greatest fan, to boot. It had been Clark, in fact, who had published his first story, back when she and Polly and Jana were putting out *Bad Ass Girls*.

God, those were the days. The girls had a storefront on Avenue A, back when even the beginning of Alphabet

City was the Danger Zone, and Harry would sneak over there at night – he was still living with Lorna at the time – and help out at the magazine: sorting through the slush pile, proof-reading copy, typing up mailing lists. It became a kind of local hang-out and there were art shows and readings and once a month they put on a Feminisation of some classic or other and Harry would get to play all the female parts. People still talked about his Ophelia.

"'There's rosemary, that's for remembrance,'" Harry peeped in his Ophelia voice, standing up and mincing around the living room, "'Pray you love, remember. And there is pansies, that's for thought.'" The pansies brought down the house.

'Butler,' he said, walking back to the desk and sitting down, 'You are one lucky son of a bitch.'

He looked out of the window, at the building on the other side of the courtyard. A derelict, falling apart, windows boarded up. Squatters were living there, crack addicts and bums, along with some rich kids from NYU, communing with the proles before moving on to Wall Street. Harry didn't mind their being there, as long as they didn't throw their garbage in the courtyard, which they did periodically. He'd go over and scream at them and the crackheads and bums would just ignore him and the rich kids would swear at him and act tough, but they usually cleaned it up.

He leaned forward, cracked his knuckles, and began:

Butler stood leaning against the stone wall. Central Park. 99th Street Entrance. It was late, too late for anything human to be in the Park. Why did she want him to meet her here? He heard an eerie buzzing, a jungly wing-rubbing sound, like a thousand horny urban insects shrieking in the trees, warning Butler to Stay Out.

He liked the 'horny urban insects'. He'd been waiting over a month to use it. It had come to him while he and Clark had been sitting on a bench outside the Park, waiting for a bus. They'd been to see the Van Gogh show at the Met, and Harry was thinking about swirls and whorls of color, of madness, and he heard the insects, crickets or whatever they were, shrieking away in swirls and whorls of sound. It was almost as if he could see the sound, see it hovering over the Park in thick whirling circles. 'Is that what it's like?, he kept asking Clark, 'Is that what it feels like to be insane?'

She got all huffy. 'Why ask me?', she snapped, 'What makes you think I'm an expert on madness?'

But Clark was an expert on everything. She was a genius; what she lacked in muscle tone she made up for in brain power and if she was sometimes a little testy, well, what could one expect from someone with so much going on in her mind?

It was amazing, what went on in that brain of hers. He'd like to get inside, to slither around in the tunnels of her corpus callosum, watch her neurons firing like a light show at the Planetarium. Harry loved to watch her, while she was reading, or going over his manuscript with her sharp blue pencil, and imagine her head filled with tiny little copy boys racing through the corridors of her mind, panting heavily as they passed the information along. What's going on in there? he would wonder, filled with awe that her little head, which he could cup in his hands, could contain so much.

The phone rang. It was probably for Clark, one of her thousands of friends. Clark was a Renaissance woman – actress, writer, musician, Director of Research for a magazine chain. She did volunteer work, served on committees, canvassed on behalf of the huddled masses yearning to break free. She had all kinds of friends – as many circles as hell, Harry always said.

He thought about letting the answering machine pick up, but then he thought it might be someone calling to wish him Happy Birthday.

As he turned to get the phone, he saw something, something large and white, fly past the window, followed by a muffled thud.

What the hell? he thought, if those damn squatters are throwing out their mattresses again . . .

He stomped over to the window and looked down into the courtyard. There was what appeared to be a big crumpled heap of clothes down there, somebody's laundry or something. He reached for his glasses.

'Sweet Jesus,' he said. 'Sweet Jesus.'

There, lying splayed on the broken concrete, was a body. A body, a dead one.

'Sweet Jesus,' he said again and ran for the door.

Two

He ran upstairs, to Martin's. Not that he'd be much help, but at least he had some kind of medical training; he'd been tossed out of Cornell Veterinary School and while that wasn't much, it was more than Harry had.

'Martin!' Harry shouted, pounding on the thick metal door, 'Open up!' But there was no answer, just the yelping of the dogs.

Harry ran through the building, pounding on all the doors, but nobody answered.

Shit, he thought, Shit. Where could everybody be?

What if the body wasn't dead, what if they could save him? Her? It? What if it was lying there, eking out its last breaths? Harry was wasting time, precious seconds, and if there was a chance the person could be saved, and wasn't, it would be Harry's fault. And that would be murder, sort of.

He ran back to his apartment and looked out the window. No, the guy – at least he thought it was a guy –

was definitely dead. He hadn't moved. Harry strained his eyes. Was that a puddle of wet, dark stuff around the body's head, or just a shadow? Harry shuddered. There it was – Death – staring up at him. This was his chance – he could go down there, face it, look it straight in the eye, check it out, gather some verisimilitude in case he ever bumped anyone off in *Butler by Butler*.

Bumped off. OmiGod, Harry thought, what if it *had* been a murder? What if it had been a mob hit or something? It wasn't out of the question, some Gotti or Gambino was trying to buy up half the Lower East Side. Those guys didn't mess around – they didn't like witnesses and even though Harry hadn't seen anything, except a flash of white, or heard anything, except a thud, how did they know that? 'Get the goombah,' they'd say and come after him with a sawed-off shotgun and that wasn't the kind of blue light he'd imagined himself going out in.

He had to *do* something, but what? Call 911, that was what it was there for.

He ran to the phone but began to worry about the call being traced. He imagined hordes of cops banging at his door. And the press. He saw his face on the cover of the *Daily News*: WITNESS TO TRAGEDY. Wouldn't that be something, waking up to his own face on the cover of the morning paper? He picked up the phone. But if he was on the cover of the paper, he would be identifiable. He imagined himself duct-taped to a chair in a dank warehouse, trying to convince some Rocco or other that he didn't know anything.

He'd call from the street. Make an anonymous tip.

He grabbed his keys, stuffed a five dollar bill in his sock, scooped up a handful of quarters from the change jar, and ran down the stairs, out the door, to the phone on the corner. Dead. Of course. He ran up another block, to the phone outside the bodega. One of the crackheads was using it, standing there scratching himself and crying, probably begging some disgusted relative for more money.

Harry kept running, up to 5th Street. He could just turn the corner, run into the precinct house, report that there was a body in his courtyard. It would be the right thing to do, the moral thing to do, the stand-up thing to do.

He turned toward the precinct building, then stopped.

'*Get the goombah*,' Rocco said.

The phone was better, if he could find one that worked. Anonymous was better. He thought for a second about Clark, about how disgusted she would be if she could see him now. She would accuse him of being no better than those cowards hiding behind their curtains, watching while Kitty Genovese got murdered. 'That's different,' he told himself. 'They could have saved her. This body is already dead.'

'Chicken-shit,' he imagined Clark sneering and he ran faster, up to St Mark's, to the phones by the bus.

He dialed 911 and waited. And waited. Good God, he thought, a person could bleed to death waiting for them to answer.

'Come on, come on,' he shouted into the phone, 'What are you *doing*?' He imagined a bunch of fat switchboard operators, sitting at their consoles eating and gossiping and laughing at the red lights flashing like crazy all over a digital map of the city. It wasn't fair, he knew it, he knew the emergency operators were overworked; he'd just read somewhere that there was an emergency of some sort every ten seconds in New York.

Right now, while he was standing on the corner, waiting for a person to attend to his emergency, there were six, maybe ten more emergencies happening, getting in line for attention. Someone was getting mugged, someone was getting raped, someone was having a heart attack. Add to that all the fires, the water main breaks, the gas leaks and the nutballs who called just for kicks, and that made for some stressed out operators.

They'd heard it all, Harry imagined, and it occurred to him that being an emergency operator might be a good job for him. Think of all the material I'd get, he thought. He could hear the troubles of the world, the secrets lurking down the dark alleys of Manhattan, be a part of the throbbing pulse of the City . . .

'What's your emergency?' an angry voice asked.

'Uh,' Harry said, lost in his vision, 'Uh, body. There's a body in a courtyard on Second Avenue.'

'What kind of body?' the voice, female, asked. Female, but not a woman. Not even a person. Too hard to be human. He'd have to remember that.

'Dead,' he said.

The operator wanted to know who he was but Harry wasn't telling. 'This is an anonymous tip,' he said, 'I don't want to get involved.'

She was disgusted; he could hear it in her horsy, phlegmy snort, and that irritated him. It wasn't her job to judge his character, it was her job to send somebody over to pick up the body. Who the hell did she think she was?

'Look,' he said, 'I'm just being a good citizen, reporting a body. It's lying in the courtyard behind the abandoned building on Second Avenue, east side. I don't know the address, but you can't miss it. It's the one with the People's Republic of the Bowery banner.'

He hung up. They'd send someone over, they had to check out all the calls, even the ones that sounded as nutty as Harry's. For good measure, he decided to call the precinct as well.

He'd have to disguise his voice. He called over there often enough, to complain about the squatters' garbage, to complain about the landlord turning off the heat, to have them remove some street person who was camping out in the vestibule, whatever. Although it was unlikely the desk sergeant would recognise his voice, still, it was a possibility. They were, after all, cops: it was their job to put two and two together.

'Anonymous tip!' Harry screeched in a high falsetto when the sergeant answered, 'Body in the courtyard behind the squatters!'

He hung up instantly, before he could be asked any questions. He'd done his duty, acting the part of the good citizen. He felt that he'd done enough, but he was glad he didn't have to explain himself to Clark. 'You didn't check?' she would scream, 'You didn't check to see if he was *alive*?' If Clark had been there, she would have instantly called the ambulance, then run down to the courtyard to practice her CPR. She was forever taking First Aid courses, disaster relief and that shit, volunteering at the Red Cross, preparing herself. 'For what?' Harry always wanted to know, 'New York doesn't *have* natural disasters,' but she said, 'Just wait. Manhattan is full of potential disasters and when one hits, I'll be ready.'

The truth was, he didn't want to know. He'd never seen a dead body before, except in a coffin. He didn't want to see it close up; didn't want to give it a gender or an age; to make it human. It wasn't that he wasn't curious; he didn't think he'd mind visiting a morgue, in fact that might not be such a bad idea, someday. But that would be different, those bodies were long since dead and their deaths had nothing to do with him, Harry. They were anonymous, and while this body was anonymous as well, it had died outside his window, within Harry's orbit, and that gave it a personal element.

He wondered who it was. Or rather, who it had been. *Butler looked out his window. There was a body crumbled in the courtyard, lying there like a large discarded doll.*

He couldn't tell Clark, but he'd have to tell someone. This was a major *thing*, it wasn't just something you'd tuck away and pull out at a dinner party, this was life and death, *it*, the whole point. He tried to remember what the body looked like, falling past the window, the sound it had made upon impact. Christ, he thought, just like that. One minute you're a person, the next you're a sack of laundry.

He decided to run up to Lenny's. The day was shot anyway, there was no way he could get back to work after this. What a way to start your birthday, he thought, everything's going just fine and then somebody takes a leap past your window.

Harry shuddered. It hadn't occurred to him that it might have been a suicide. The idea of *wanting* to die was inconceivable – what could possibly make someone want to jump off a roof? Probably a crackhead, Harry thought, probably so fried he didn't know he was dying.

But what if it *had* been a murder? Some crackhead dealer who smoked up all the profits and was too far in hock to live. Or some big-mouthed Marxist student who threatened to go to the cops when the mob guy came around.

He had the sinking feeling that the body was going to get him in a world of trouble. Why me? he thought. 'Life is in the right, always,' Rilke says and Harry wondered what could possibly be 'right' about a body falling past his window. He wondered if life was giving him a test. If so, he didn't think he passed.

Two girls – young Amazons, it was amazing how tall girls were these days – were standing in front of a deli up ahead, watching Harry as he approached. He hadn't dressed; he had on his spandex bike pants and a short tank top, his writing clothes. He looked good, and he'd built up just enough sweat to glisten, to give his body a nice sheen. He glanced at the girls and thought about Frank O'Hara's line. He couldn't remember the beginning, something about meter or form, but he remembered the part about wearing your pants tight enough so everyone will want to go to bed with you. O'Hara had been queer, of course, but it was true enough for straight guys, too. He wanted to watch the girls' eyes travel down to his crotch, watch them blush and turn to each other and giggle. Harry loved being looked at, loved the catcalls, couldn't understand Clark's fury when some guy smacked his lips and said, 'Nice tits,' as she bounced by in her sports bra. What did she expect? If she didn't want guys to notice her tits then she should wear a burlap bag or something. They were just appreciating her, but she didn't appreciate being appreciated. She called it harassment and spat fire.

After he passed, the girls started giggling, and Harry smiled.

'Hey!' the blonde bold-looking one called and Harry slowed to a trot.

'Nice scrunchie,' she said and they both shrieked with laughter and ran away.

Shit, he thought, and pulled the garter belt from his hair.

Three

At 24th Street, he stopped to get some wheat grass juice. He thought about saying something to the girl at the counter, something like, 'New York! Can you believe this place? This morning I saw a body fall past my window,' something like that, something world-weary with a tinge of shock.

She was good-looking, despite the ring in her nose. Harry couldn't fathom the body-piercing craze – an ear lobe, that was reasonable, he wore a small diamond himself, a gift from Clark. But the rest of it, he didn't get. Whenever he saw a girl with a nose ring, he wanted to stick a piece of twine through it and lead her down the street, like a cow.

The girl brought his juice and placed it on the counter. Harry flashed his most charming smile.

'New York,' he said, 'can you beat this place?'

She shrugged.

'The first thing I saw this morning was a body falling past my window.'

The girl didn't respond, so he continued. 'Whoosh,' he said, raising his hand and dropping it in an arc, 'plop.'

'Ummmm,' she said and turned away.

What's with her? Harry wondered, did she think he was trying to pick her up or something? Was she on drugs? Or just callous? All he was doing was trying to establish a little human contact, tap into the one thing all New Yorkers have in common: the siege mentality, the sense that no matter how horrific things get, the City will keep right on chugging along, and the inhabitants will keep right on living.

She didn't deserve it, but he left her a tip and headed uptown again. Normally, he enjoyed this run: north of 23rd Street, there weren't many people on the sidewalk; he could run up First Avenue unimpeded by women with strollers, or old geezers with grocery carts, or by punky kids hanging out on the corners or by junkies wanting a handout. There was an encampment of homeless people living across from the UN, but he could avoid them by keeping to the east side of the street. They never asked for money anyway – this was their home, not their office. They had discarded TVs plugged into the bases of the street lamps, little space heaters in winter, one guy in a wheelchair even had a small fridge. In a way, Harry admired their ingenuity. They were pioneers of a sort, pioneers of the last frontier – the street – and he avoided them more out of respect than anything else. It was like running through someone's living room and Harry didn't want to do that.

He had forgotten his glasses, but he could see the blurry skyline of the boxes and blanket tents up ahead. He should forget his glasses more often, he thought, it was like looking at the city though the slightly out-of-focus lens used for close-ups of aging actresses.

There were some things in life it was better not to examine too closely, Butler thought.

Like that body, Harry thought. He ran as fast as he could, pushing himself to the limit, trying to run the sound of that thud out of his memory, but the harder he ran, the harder his heart pounded, and each beat echoed in his head like the sound of the body hitting the concrete.

A guy could go nuts thinking about this, he thought. It had nothing to do with him. It was just something that happened, horrible for the person it happened to, but he couldn't let it get to him. He felt a vague discomfort, a rumbling in his chest, as if something was running up and down his ribs. His conscience, probably, trying to work him into a lather of guilt. He supposed he *should* feel something, something other than what he *was* feeling, which was a kind of combination of excitement – it wasn't every day a body flew past your window – and irritation at having that body ruin his concentration. He wasn't quite sure what it was he was supposed to feel, what would be the proper thing to feel, the thing Clark would approve of. Something that incorporated a love for one's fellow man that Harry simply didn't possess; something that included grief and sorrow.

He entered the park at the UN, and ran over to the river. He ran in place, watching a barge chug its way south. To his north, some guy in a full-body wet suit climbed over the railing and lowered himself into the mucky water, probably scavenging for sunken treasure. It was amazing what those guys found – just a couple of weeks ago, somebody pulled up a Persian rug with a body wrapped in it. Ugh, Harry thought, more bodies, and he ran back, around the sculpture of St George or Don Quixote, he could never remember which, back out to First Avenue. *Should* he feel something?

No, he thought. People died horrible deaths every day in this city, in this world, and if you let yourself think about it too much it could really mess you up. It wasn't as if he could *do* anything about it. And worst of all, thinking about somebody else's death led to thinking about your own and that was nothing but trouble.

This is how people get depressed, he thought. They start thinking about all the terrible things that are happening, and that they can't do a damn thing about, and they start feeling impotent, wormlike, crawling their way through the dirt of life rather than standing up straight, shaking it off, and living. It occurred to him that this could be his opportunity, his chance to get inside depression. All he had to do was let the weight of that dead body push him down, all the way down to sidewalk, get a little cheek-to-concrete action going, if only in spirit.

It would be in the service of Art. Give a depth to Raptor Music, give it the mournful element it was lacking, the wail-like refrain for the melancholy to howl along with in the middle of the night after they'd had a few too many drinks.

The thought of transforming himself into a worm, if only for a few minutes, made him shiver. It was too repulsive. And why should some faceless body falling off a roof make *him* feel like a worm, anyway? It wasn't his fault. In fact, if he'd stayed in the loo a few minutes longer he wouldn't even have known about it, it would have lain down there in the courtyard, covered by the squatters' garbage, for weeks before anyone noticed the stench.

He wondered if the EMS people had picked it up yet. The cops would be coming around, looking for witnesses, and when they did, he'd just play dumb, say he'd been out running.

But what about Clark? She'd know he was lying – she could smell a lie on him, even the simplest, stupidest, whitest little fib; she'd sniff it out, dig it up, prance around the apartment with it like a dog with a dirty sock.

Jesus, he thought as he turned on 63rd Street, to run up the Esplanade, what a jerk I am! It had been stupid – really stupid – to go the anonymous route. What did he have to be afraid of? If he was going to give in to his baser instincts, why couldn't he have given in to the lust for celebrity instead of giving in to fear? Why did he give in to that momentary panic about the Mafia coming to get him? He'd been hanging out in Theatre 80 too much, watching too much *noir*. What was Pascal's theory of risk assessment? If I believe in God and He doesn't exist, I'm no worse off; but if I don't believe in Him and He does, I'm in deep shit. Something like that. If I believe the Mafia were involved and they weren't, I'm an idiot. But if I lie to Clark . . .

Shit. He'd rather take his chances with Mafia hit men than spend the rest of his life having Clark sneering at him like some weak, wimpy coward.

Why hadn't he thought about this before? Now, it was too late. To turn round, go back to the precinct house and confess that he'd been a witness, sort of, would look suspicious. Why didn't he come forward immediately, they'd want to know and he'd have to tell the truth: that he'd been afraid. They'd laugh at him – 'what?' they'd say, 'Big tough guy like you, afraid? Afraid of what?'

No way. No way was he going to have those jerks at the 9th sniggering at him. He could just see them, falling all over the place when he told them he delivered Tarzan-a-Grams for a living.

Harry didn't waste his time looking at his life from the outside, why should he, what did he care what anyone thought of him, of the way he lived his life? He thought about his mother, whose entire life had been spent worrying about what people thought, what they'd say. She thought the entire world was just sitting around, waiting to pass judgement on her every move. It was stifling, living like that, and he wondered how she breathed, how she managed to get through life. As a kid, she had dragged him into that eggshell world with her, monitoring his every move, rating it for the repercussions it might cause her, as if she were some Confucian, terrified of losing face. She was constantly wringing her hands and wondering what 'people' would think, dissolving into a big gray puddle of shame every time Harry came home with a black eye or a 'C' in Citizenship. As if anyone cared, much less knew, what Harry was doing. His father was no help – he was mostly on the road and when he wasn't, he hid down in the basement with his eyedroppers and his bottles, mixing scents.

Harry felt a twinge of guilt. He should call them. He hadn't talked to his mother in a couple of months. Not that there was much point in it, it was always the same conversation. 'One step closer to the boneyard,' his father would say when Harry asked how he was, and his mother, who literally couldn't breathe any more, would wheeze and hiss in the background while she wondered what 'people' would think about a forty-seven-year-old son who dressed up like Tarzan and didn't have any children.

'Ma,' he told her. 'Don't worry. I'm married. I'm not a queer,' but she had her doubts about Clark, too.

'A grandson,' his mother said every year when Harry asked her what she wanted for Christmas, no matter how many times Harry told her that was out of the question. No kids, Harry and Clark had agreed, although at times Harry regretted the decision. He'd occasionally feel what could only be a biological drive, pure instinct, a *need* to impregnate her, to pass his genes along, to put another little Harry in the world. 'It will pass,' Clark always said and she was right, it went away, for a while, but it seemed to be coming back more often these days, stronger than ever. He'd find himself ogling young girls, much too young for him, seeing not a person, not even a mate, but simply a nice little receptacle for his genes. He wasn't ashamed of it – it wasn't as if he actually thought about *doing* anything about it – it was just an interesting little biological fact.

It was, he thought now, as he panted up the steps leading to Carl Schurz Park, just another aspect of life, asserting itself, wanting to continue, to go on, to not stop.

Four

'Thud,' Harry told Lenny, 'just like that. You couldn't even tell it was a body, it looked like a laundry bag or something.'

'Who was it?' Lenny wanted to know.

'Damned if I know,' Harry said, 'I couldn't even tell *what* it was.'

'Jeez Louise,' Lenny said. 'What did you *do*?'

Harry shrugged. 'Called the cops,' he said. 'What else could I do? The guy was dead.'

'Ugh,' Lenny said, 'you need a drink.' But no he didn't, all he needed was to sit there, in Lenny's dark overcrowded railroad apartment, surrounded by the cluttered chaos of Lenny's life. The mess, the dirt, the books stacked up the entire length of the hallway – it was comforting, embracing, it said, 'Someone *lives* here,' and it didn't matter to Harry if that person was a slob.

Lenny padded down the hall and Harry collapsed in a chair, *leather or naugahyde – Butler could never tell the difference*. Fake or real, it felt good to Harry, smooth and cool on his skin, refreshing.

Lenny came back with a cold beer and Harry rubbed it over his sweaty forehead and then clutched it, unopened, waiting for the pounding of his heart to quiet down.

'Did you read that thing about Beethoven?' Harry asked.

Lenny shook his head. 'Did he jump off a roof?'

'Naw,' Harry said, 'it was this thing, this medical thing he had or something. It was in the *Science Times*. Some scientist speculating that Beethoven didn't really go deaf, that actually his hearing became so intensely acute that he could hear everything – hear his blood flowing in his veins, all his organs working away, pumping and secreting and doing whatever they do, like a little factory inside him, and he could *hear* it all. It became so loud he couldn't hear anything else.'

'Cool,' Lenny said.

He sat hunched forward in his tweedy armchair, staring at Harry, listening eagerly, hungrily. He seemed so little and gray, old-mannish, with his wire-rimmed glasses slipping down his nose. He was wearing one of those nubby cotton cardigan sweaters, the kind Harry's dad wore, retirement sweaters, and beltless polyester pants. Lenny was what? Forty-eight? Forty-nine? What was with the nursing-home get-up?

'You should get out more,' Harry said.

'Huh?' Lenny asked. 'What are you talking about?'

Harry shook his head. He didn't know what he was talking about, it was just that suddenly Lenny seemed so old, elderly almost, sitting there sucking up Harry's words as if they were giving him some kind of nourishment. As if they meant something. They didn't. He was just babbling, he didn't even know if he had the information right. He hadn't really read the article, he'd just skimmed it, and it wasn't Beethoven he was thinking about, it was himself, it was his heart, thumping away like gloves on a punching bag: whop, whop, whopeta whopeta whop. Why wouldn't it slow down? He'd been sitting there what? Ten, fifteen minutes? Time enough for his heart to have slowed down to normal. It wasn't as if he had a regular old forty-seven-year-old heart – he had Harry Butler's heart: the heart of an athlete.

Death, he thought, I've never been that close to death before. He'd heard, or read, that a person who takes a leap generally dies before they hit the ground. Or water, if they jump from a bridge. Their heart gives out. So maybe that person died the instant he passed by Harry's window: a person one second, a corpse the next, and what happened to the life that was inside him? Was it still there, clinging to Harry's window sill, refusing to drop down and join the heap of broken bones at the bottom of the courtyard?

Harry shuddered.

'You OK?' Lenny asked and Harry nodded.

'Crappy way to start your birthday,' Lenny said. 'Kind of makes you think about your own mortality.'

'Oh no,' Harry said, 'I'm not going there. As far as I'm concerned, death is interesting as a concept, not a reality.'

'Yeah, well, it *is* a reality, man. Like it or not, you're gonna die.'

They stared at each other in terror.

'How about those Mets?' Harry asked, and Lenny nodded.

'Yeah. How about those Mets?'

It wasn't a good choice. Neither of them cared a fig

about baseball and between them couldn't name more than a handful of players – Dwight, Darryl, Mookie – despite the fact that the Mets had won the World Series the previous fall. Then, back in October, everyone in New York had known the whole team, including the base coaches and bat boys and bat girls, but that was no longer useful information, at least for Harry or Lenny, and had been tossed out of the filing cabinets in their brains.

Harry heaved a great sigh and ran the beer can over his forehead again. 'Do you believe we have a soul?' he asked Lenny.

'How about those Mets?' Lenny asked again and they both laughed, wanly; nice try.

'Really,' Harry said, 'do you think there's some thing – some energy or life force or being-ness – that goes on after we die?'

Lenny didn't know. His parents had been atheists. 'Nothing,' his father had answered when Lenny asked him what happened after you die. 'You get buried. Your wife remarries. Your kids spend all your money and then forget you.'

He shrugged. 'What about you?' he asked.

'Yeah,' Harry said, nodding, 'yeah. Yeah. Why not? If you believe you have a soul and you don't, so what? If you believe you don't have a soul, and you do, you might get punished or something.'

Lenny burst out laughing. '"Punished or something?" You mean like karma or something?'

'Yeah,' Harry said, 'why not? Why not karma? Why not God? Why not Allah or Buddha or Siva? Why not?'

Why not indeed? Harry hadn't thought about God since college, when, like all his friends, he dismissed the idea as so much superstition. They'd stay up all night, arguing about whether or not the table they were sitting around would exist if they weren't there to see it, whether, in fact, they themselves existed or were simply a figment of someone's or something's imagination. Was God dead? Had God ever been alive? Who knew? Who cared? Why think about something that wasn't there? And, at twenty, what did God have to do with anything? God was about what happened after you stopped living and who thinks about that at twenty?

'What about Clark?' Lenny asked. 'What does she believe?'

As far as Harry knew, Clark didn't believe in any organised religion, anything that even remotely smacked of patriarchy.

'Maybe some goddess stuff,' Harry said. 'For a while she was going to some kind of Good Witch thing. You know Clark; she believes in doing the right thing.'

Shit. And Harry hadn't done the right thing; she'd be furious with him.

'Hey, Lenny,' he said, 'do me a favor.'

'What?'

'If I need an alibi, say I was here this morning, OK?'

'Alibi?' Lenny's accountant's eyes narrowed. 'Why would you need an alibi? I thought you already told the cops.'

'It's not the cops I'm thinking about,' Harry said, 'it's Clark.'

'What about her?'

Harry's legs made a squishy noise as he squirmed in the chair, squishy and wet. Wormlike. How could he tell Lenny what a gutless wonder he'd been, about his visions of duct-tape and sawed-off shotguns and bruisers named Rocco? But Lenny was the world's biggest coward; if anybody would understand his rationale, it would be Lenny. His best pal. His bud.

'I didn't want to get involved,' he said sheepishly, 'I made an anonymous tip.'

Lenny gasped. 'You did *what*?'

'There wasn't anybody else in the building,' Harry explained. 'I didn't want to be the only witness, so I called from the street.'

Lenny shook his head. 'Are you out of your mind?' he asked. 'That's fleeing the scene of a crime.'

'What crime?' Harry asked. 'For all I know, the guy took a jump because his girlfriend left him.'

'It's still a crime,' Lenny said. 'Suicide is illegal in New York.'

'How medieval,' Harry said. 'What do they do? Put the corpse in jail for ninety days? Bury it at a crossroads?'

Lenny shrugged. 'I don't think they keep the law on the books to punish the dead person,' he said, 'I think they keep it around to have leverage over idiots like you. And probably for the insurance companies, too.'

'Leverage?' Harry asked, 'what are you talking about, leverage?'

'Suicide is a crime,' Lenny explained. 'It's a crime to flee the scene of a crime. So you're a criminal, get it? And if it wasn't suicide, if it was murder, then you're really in trouble.'

'What if it was an accident?'

Lenny shrugged again. 'I think that's a misdemeanor.'

What a bunch of baloney, Harry thought. He was nuts to sit there listening to this stuff – after all, where did Lenny get his information? From all those stupid cops and lawyers TV shows. Who knew if any of that shit was real, and even if it was, who cared? This was *real* real life. Most of the time, it didn't bother Harry that it was getting to the point where real life seemed less real than fake life – he wasn't above mixing the two in a blender for his own work and whatever sounded best was true, as far as he was concerned. But right now, he wanted real facts, not fake ones.

'I thought you were my friend,' Harry said petulantly. 'All I wanted was for you to say I was here, and you come at me with all this accessory after the fact bullshit.'

Lenny sat back in his chair. 'I *am* your friend,' he said, 'and this isn't accessory after the fact bullshit. It's fleeing the scene of a crime bullshit.'

'Whatever,' Harry said.

'Look, Harry,' Lenny said, 'you're asking me to lie – to commit *another* crime – to perjure myself! To risk jail, where I'd get raped and get AIDS and *die!*'

Lenny jumped up and began pacing the room, pulling on his graying curly hair. Harry had always loved that about Lenny, the hair-pulling. He found it rather endearing, and since endearment wasn't something guys could feel for each other a whole lot, without seeming faggy, especially in Lenny's case, since he *was* queer, Harry cherished it. But now he began to wonder if all that hair-pulling over the years, which Harry had found so cute, was actually a sign of madness. After all, in all the cartoons of 'madmen', they were always depicted pulling their hair. Harry firmly believed in stereotypes: they existed for a reason, he always said, and while he prided himself on never judging a person according to them, if the shoe fits . . .

'Lenny, for God's sake . . .' Harry said, 'you're acting as if I had something to *do* with the guy's death.'

Lenny stopped pacing, turned, his left hand grasping a fistful of hair.

'Harry, I love you like a brother,' he said sadly,

pathetically, as if he were at Harry's death bed, 'but I'm not going to lie for you.'

'Lenny, you're acting as if I've done something wrong...'

But Lenny wouldn't listen. He placed his hands over his ears and closed his eyes.

Oh, for fuck's sake, Harry thought, this is ridiculous. He tossed the unopened beer on the floor, got up, walked over to Lenny and pulled his hand away from his ear. Lenny squeezed his eyes tighter.

'Thanks a lot, *pal*,' he yelled into Lenny's ear and left.

Five

Before she even put the key in the lock, she knew something was wrong. She could sense it, feel it as palpably as if it – whatever 'it' was – was reaching through the door and grabbing her by the neck.

That there was a sixth sense, and that she had it, was something Clark took for granted. She'd known it since childhood – she'd be out in the fields, running along a path with her dogs, when all of a sudden, they'd all stop, simultaneously, alerted by a different feel to the air, a thinness, as if something had just passed through. It made perfect sense to Clark – the air, like water, was made up of molecules, and why wouldn't a solid mass, passing through those molecules, leave behind a wake, as it would in water? The dogs felt it, and humans could too, if only they'd pay more attention.

She wondered if Harry had been snooping through her journal again. She thought she'd cured him of that, after writing ten pages listing everything that was wrong with him, everything real and a lot of stuff she just made up, to infuriate him, sticking little pins in his big fat balloon of an ego. 'I don't pick my nose and eat the snot,' he whined one night when she came home from work. 'Who says you do?' she asked, serenely, inwardly giggling while he fumed and moped, and as far as she knew, he hadn't looked at it since.

She unlocked the door and pushed it open.

'Harry?' she called, sticking her head in the kitchen and looking around, 'Hon?'

No Harry; no Hon. Definitely something wrong, though. She sniffed the air, but smelled nothing out of the ordinary – garlic and onions from Mrs Speransky's, a little left-over roach poison from the exterminator. She sniffed again. There was something else, something she couldn't identify, definitely pungent, a little acrid, sweat mixed with something else . . .

'Ohhh!' she gasped, racing to the bed, sniffing madly, her heart pounding, thinking, I'll kill him, I'll murder him and her both . . . but there was nothing, not even the smell Harry left from his afternoon nap.

She walked over to the kitchen table, to see if he'd written her a note, but everything was as she'd left it that morning. The *Daily News* with HAPPY BIRTHDAY scrawled across Robert McFarlane's face lay there, unopened.

That was odd. Harry always skimmed the paper after he finished work for the day: that was his ritual, and Harry, for all his blathering about freedom and spontaneity, was actually one of the most rigid people Clark had ever known. If he went out, he always left a message scrawled on whatever piece of paper was handy – 'Running. ♥ U' on the back of the phone bill, or 'DoJo's. XX' across the laundry receipt.

Something was wrong, something was definitely wrong. She knew it and she couldn't help it, her fear flew instantly to Harry's fidelity. Or infidelity. It wasn't fair; Harry swore he hadn't so much as groped another woman since they'd married, and Clark believed him. He had given her absolutely no reason to suspect him. But still, she had seduced him away from Lorna and once seduced, always seduceable.

It was her biggest flaw, this unfounded jealousy, but she couldn't help it. She walked through the apartment, looking for clues. He'd left the computer on – how many times did she have to tell him to turn it off when he finished work? – and she turned it off, too irritated to snoop. Harry kept a journal, too, and Clark read it periodically but since he never wrote about her, she wasn't all that interested. She kept hoping to find a love poem, some tribute to her, but he only wrote about ideas. Ideas for his book and ideas for the Lornes and ideas for Raptor Music – one of Harry's sillier ideas, if you asked Clark. It was all air, his journal, and most of that hot. There was no sense of the world outside his head, which was probably just as well. Harry was laboring under the impression that the whole world had stopped fifteen years ago, that he was still on the cutting edge, that there was some breathless public out there, panting for him. Clark didn't have the heart to tell him that the three publishers waiting for *Butler by Butler* no longer existed – it didn't really matter; he'd find a publisher, if he ever finished. She had utter faith in his talent, although she had doubts about the new 'mystery' element he was adding. She wasn't as convinced as Harry that the mystery Fictoir was the wave of the future.

She sniffed again, following her nose over to the

window. Harry's glasses lay on the window sill, lens down. She picked them up and peered through the scratched, foggy glass. How could he see through these things, she wondered.

Where *was* he? To calm herself, she thought facts. Ten per cent of American eighteen-year-olds think Peter Ustinov was one of the leaders of the Russian Revolution. One kilometer equals .62 miles. Momus is the god of laughter.

Clark was the Filler Queen of Spenser Publications, Inc. 'Help!' the harried editors would scream as they were putting their magazines to bed, 'I need to fill two column inches,' and Clark would rattle off just enough information to fill the hole – 'One of every three Frenchwomen say they prefer chocolate to sex,' for example, or, 'The FBI has 169 million sets of fingerprints on file.' No one ever asked for her sources – she was, after all, the Director of Research – and she would occasionally entertain herself by slipping in something she'd made up. 'One of these days, you're going to get caught,' Aggie would warn, but Clark couldn't help herself. Who cared if Galapagos guinea hens didn't even exist, much less mate only in months ending in 'r'? She could always claim it was a misprint and, in the meantime, it gave her immense pleasure to see her fibs in print.

It was a pleasure she couldn't share with Harry. He exempted her from his belief that everybody lied as much as he did; he believed everything that came out of her mouth was the truth, and that belief came in handy for her. She could lie to him whenever she wanted, without the least fear of getting caught. And it was also fun to see her misinformation when it appeared in his book. 'Beanie, wake up,' he'd say. 'What's the state bird of New York?' and she'd say, 'Pigeon.' 'Oh, yeah, of course,' he'd say, scribbling in the notebook he kept by the side of the bed, just in case something brilliant occurred to him in the middle of the night, and Clark would bury her face in the pillow to stifle her giggles. She'd correct it, of course, she wouldn't let him go to print with howlers like 'the thirteenth President, Franklin Pierce,' but at the rate Harry was going on *Butler by Butler*, she still had years of private merriment ahead of her.

She walked over to the alcove and stripped off her skirt. Clark hated wearing skirts – they reminded her of grade school in Michigan, of housewives and co-eds and home ec. A skirt was something one *had* to wear to go someplace one didn't want to go – to church, to school, to some smelly relative's house.

She glanced at her watch. He'd better hurry, she thought, if they were going to make their dinner reservation.

There was a loud thumping on the door, followed by a muffled, incomprehensible name. Clark wondered if one of the bums had gotten in again, or if Mr Petrikas was wandering the halls in his Alzheimer's haze, calling for his dead wife, his dead son, his dead dog.

She pulled her skirt back on and went to the door. Through the peep-hole she could see a cop, a cop with a clipboard. A very young cop; he looked about fourteen, still pimply. REIDY, his name tag read.

She sighed. Clark detested cops. As far as she was concerned, they were still the pigs they'd been in 1968, in Chicago, but they were getting younger by the minute and she had to admit, it was hard to hate someone so incredibly young.

She opened the door a crack. 'Yes?' she asked.

The baby cop blushed and looked at his clipboard. 'Uh, are you Beatrice Clark?' he asked.

Oh my God, she thought, oh my God, something's happened to Harry!

She threw the door open. 'What?' she yelled, fighting tears; you let someone out of your sight for five minutes and they die on you. 'Has something happened to my husband?'

The cop looked surprised. 'Not that I know of, ma'am,' he said. 'We're just going through the building to see if anyone saw the uh, accident.'

'Accident?' Clark screamed, hearing the hysteria in her voice and hating it. 'What accident? Is Harry all right?'

'Harry,' Office Reidy said, checking his clipboard, 'would that be Harold Butler?'

Clark couldn't breathe. She backed up to the sink, nodding. Reidy tiptoed respectfully after her.

'Ma'am?' he asked, 'Are you all right . . .' he glanced again at the clipboard, 'Mrs Clark?'

'Miss,' she said as she nodded, '*Miss* Clark.'

'Miss Clark,' he said, looking woefully confused – who could figure out the relationships between these East Village types, he was probably thinking – 'were either you or Mr Butler present on the premises at approximately ten a.m. this morning?'

She couldn't help herself. 'Redundant,' she said, 'a.m. and this morning. You're saying the same thing twice.'

'Yes, ma'am,' he said, 'Were either you or Mr Butler present . . .'

She heard the door slam downstairs and Harry's familiar footsteps as he jogged up the four flights.

'Oh, thank God,' Clark said, running out the door, calling him to hurry. He bounded up the stairs, red-faced and sweaty, his wet hair hanging down to his shoulders in ropy coils, like some ancient warrior, fresh from battle. Clark ran to him and buried her face in his chest. He tasted salty, as if he had just returned from the sea.

'What's the matter?' he panted.

Officer Reidy appeared in the doorway with his clipboard and Harry recoiled, not much, just a little, just enough for Clark to feel it. Something is not right here, she thought, but said nothing.

Officer Reidy wanted to know if he was Harold Butler, if he had been on the premises at approximately ten a.m. this morning, if he had seen the uh, accident. That was twice, Clark thought, twice he referred to whatever happened as the 'uh, accident'.

Yes, no, no, Harry answered. He was lying, there wasn't the slightest doubt about that, he was lying, but why? Clark stood there, watching him, wondering what was going on. She wished Reidy would take his clipboard and go.

Yes, no, what accident? Clark answered in turn.

Someone uh, fell from the roof of the building over there, Reidy said, pointing his head toward the back window.

Clark gasped. 'How awful!' she said.

Harry said 'How awful,' too, but without conviction. He wouldn't look at her, his eyes were focused resolutely on the clipboard, like an actor at an audition, waiting for his name to be called, his fate to be decided. In or out.

Reidy made some marks and looked up.

'Sorry to have bothered you,' he said, looking first at Clark, then at Harry. 'Thanks for your co-operation.'

She hoped he wouldn't tell them to have a nice day; they were doing that now, trying to improve their image, make themselves more person and less cop.

He turned at the landing, and began saying something. Clark closed the door and heard nothing.

Six

Clark would never accuse Harry of lying straight out. She would trap him, wait until he had dug himself a hole and then push him in. It was a game they played, and Clark always won, although if Harry would just stop lying for ten minutes, there would be nothing to win or lose.

He couldn't help it – lying, or, more accurately, wildly exaggerating, came naturally to Harry. 'Excess holds no dangers for those who by nature tend to exaggerate,' he'd say, quoting Flaubert, as if that made it all right, and, in all honesty, it *was* all right, as far as Clark was concerned. It wasn't that Harry intended to mislead, he just liked things to sound good, and if the facts were a little skewered, they were being sacrificed to a good cause. Most of the time, his lies were harmless, and the truth was Clark found this flaw of his quite lovable. She adored watching him squirm when he realised he was caught, again; it gave her the opportunity to crack the whip, show him who was boss, to indulge in her greatest pleasure: being right.

She leaned against the door, listening to Officer Reidy trying – uselessly – to question poor old Mr Petrikas. She turned and looked at Harry, who was stretched out on the bed, which also served as a couch, desk, and exercise mat, performing his cool-down exercises, trying to appear nonchalant, as if a visit from the neighborhood patrolboy was nothing out of the ordinary.

'Isn't it awful?' Clark asked.

'Awful,' Harry muttered into his thigh.

'So,' Clark said, 'where *were* you? At "ten a.m. this morning"?'

He muttered something incomprehensible and groaned, as if he had pulled a muscle, trying to gain her sympathy.

What's going on here? Clark wondered. Somebody falls off a roof. Harry's lying about something. The two things were obviously connected, but how? Clark's imagination – which was as active as Harry's – began conjuring up scenarios, little dramatic vignettes: Harry in bed with some floozy, some birthday present to himself, as the body fell past the window; Harry watching while the person was pushed off, being spotted by some big guy with a gun who waved the gun menacingly at Harry – keep quiet or else! Harry getting pissed off at the squatters, going up to the roof to threaten some crackhead who was tossing garbage into the courtyard, the crackhead going berserk and falling . . .

What was she thinking? This was no time to play the I'm-The-Boss Game; Harry was in trouble, he needed her, and she was, after all, his wife, his support, his comfort, his lover, his strength.

'Harry,' she said, walking over to the bed and sitting down on the edge, 'Hon. What happened?'

Harry groaned again and Clark lifted up his head, brushing his hair off his face.

'I know you're hiding something,' she said, 'and I promise I won't be mad.'

Unless, she thought, it involved another woman. In which case she would kill him.

'Tell me,' she said gently, seductively, filling her voice with the promise of understanding, safety, boundless love no matter what stupid thing he'd done, 'Harry, you'll feel better if you tell me.'

No he wouldn't, but he might as well get it over with: the jig was up. She knew, as he knew she would know the minute he opened his mouth and let out the lie. He'd spent the entire day at the gym, running round and round the track, trying to come up with a plausible lie, one she might, if not believe, at least let pass. But everything he came up with had the potential to turn out worse than the truth. There was no use lying here any longer, like a kid hoping everything bad would just go away if he kept his eyes closed long enough. And besides, it was his birthday, they had reservations at Chanterelle, tickets for *Richard III*, his favorite, and then they'd come back here, screw, and Clark would give him his present. She wouldn't budge an inch until he told her the truth.

He sat up, sighed, and confessed.

Clark listened, her face a chalky blank giving no clue as to how hard she was going to hit when she came after him. Perhaps she would be lenient, Harry thought. After all, what he had done was only human. Cowardly human, but human none the less.

When he had finished, she stood up and walked, or

rather stormed, into the kitchen. He hadn't looked at her face; he didn't want to see the disgust that would be written there. It was a calculated risk – he had missed his opportunity to look into her eyes pleadingly, to win her over with his trust in her forgiveness.

'You'd better start getting ready,' she said, so coldly Harry shivered. 'We've got reservations for six fifteen.' She paused. 'That is, if you've got the stomach to eat after what you've done.'

Harry hung his head. She was going to do disgust and contempt. It could be worse. She could have gotten angry, grabbed her purse, including the tickets and her credit card, and gone off to spend the evening complaining to one of her girlfriends. Instead, she was going to sneer and snort and try to blast him with her scorn. Harry didn't care. He hadn't done anything wrong; he had just wanted to protect himself first and that was just common sense. He had convinced himself, while running the track at the gym, that he'd done the right thing. He needed to protect not only himself, but his space. If he had said who he was, he would have been bombarded, there would be endless questions – from the cops, the coroner, the media – if the dead person was anyone worth knowing. Clark would never understand that – she didn't understand his need for peace and quiet, for long chunks of undisturbed time, thinking time, time alone with himself. Harry couldn't work if there was even the possibility of an interruption – he'd focus on that, build it into something monumental, a huge tank heading his way, intent on crushing him and his ideas into nothingness.

Nothing distracted Clark. As soon as she walked into the apartment, she'd switch on the radio, worried that 'something' might have happened in the forty-five minutes it took her to walk home from work, terrified she might have 'missed' something. Like what, Harry always wanted to know. It was impossible to miss anything in this world, and he should know, he tried very hard to miss as much as possible. But still, it crept in, whether he wanted it to or not, even though he didn't own a TV, didn't read the gossip columns and barely skimmed the daily paper. Johnny Carson's son has a love child. David Bowie used to think he was the reincarnation of King Arthur. A South African granny was carrying triplets for her daughter. Someone would mention some movie, in which Danny DeVito was starring, and Harry would find himself saying, 'Danny DeVito is five feet tall,' as if he were some kind of robot, responding to a command. Annette Funicello was making a come-back in another 'Beach' movie, but she wasn't going to wear a bikini. 'Thank God for small favors,' Lenny said. He had a theory. 'They're poisoning our drinking water,' he claimed. 'If they fill our heads with useless junk, it will push out all the important stuff. It's just like *1984*, except it's 1987.' Lenny was nuts, of course, but somehow or other, the information was seeping in.

Clark thought that was nonsense. 'Attention Deficit Disorder,' she said and suggested ritalin.

'It's not fair,' he said aloud.

'What's not fair?'

Clark's tone was sharp, pugilistic, dying to back him into the ropes and pummel him with his own stupidity.

'That I understand you and you don't understand me.'

'Oh, please,' Clark said, 'I understand you perfectly well, Harold Earl Butler Junior: I understand that you're a coward, and you've been sitting there, trying to come up with excuses for your cowardice and now you're going to tell me it had nothing to do with being a wimp, it's because you had to protect your "space" and I can't possibly understand that because I don't need any.'

It was amazing, the way she could read his mind like that.

She glared at him through the opening between the living room and the kitchen, her face framed by the little plastic snowball bubbles. She looked so adorably silly, silly and indignant, that kind of summed Clark up, and Harry was overwhelmed with tenderness for her, despite her scorn, despite her holier-than-thou pugnacity.

'Well, Mr Butler,' she continued, tossing her head, 'maybe I need more space than you think. Maybe I feel a little crowded around here, too, you know.'

She turned away and began loudly removing the dishes from the lid of the bathtub, huffing and puffing and grumbling. Harry got up, peeled off his shorts and tank-top, and went into the kitchen. He stood behind her, naked, watching her as she stomped about, her butt quivering indignantly.

'Clark,' he said, 'Bea. Beanie. I was a jerk. I was an idiot. I'm sorry. Forgive me.'

She pulled the metal lid off the tub and dropped it on the floor with a furious clang.

'I was stupid,' he continued, wondering how many names he was going to have to call himself before she would give in. This was getting tedious and it was his birthday, he shouldn't have to grovel this much on his own birthday, for God's sake. If this went on much longer, he'd have to get mad, too, and what Clark always forgot was that the only reason she got to push him around was because he let her, because she cared more about winning than he did, because winning made her tremendously happy while Harry didn't give a shit whether he won or not. Most of the time. But don't push me, he thought.

'I was a jerk.'

'You already said that,' Clark said. 'It doesn't count.'

She turned on the water and squirted in a green drizzle of environmentally correct bubble bath. The stuff reeked, and Harry couldn't figure out why she bothered, when everyone else in Manhattan was flushing toxic sludge, drugs, and alligators down their toilets, but Clark insisted they use the ecological stuff, with its pathetic gray bubble-ettes. You have to start saving the planet somewhere, she always said, and we might as well begin with our own bathtub.

'I was a moron,' he said wearily.

Clark began to strip off her clothes, still with her back to him. He couldn't see her face, couldn't read her.

'A dolt,' he said.

'Coward,' she said, climbing into the tub. 'Admit you were a coward.'

She sank down into the gray bubbles and looked at him, not with the disgust he feared, or even anger, but with grief, and he realised she hadn't just been putting him through some stupid obstacle course of self-denigration; she was truly heartsick. Clark took death hard – it reminded her of her parents, dying so young, so stupidly, leaving her alone, and with every new death she became that orphan again.

Poor baby, he thought.

'I was a coward,' he said, and climbed into the tub. 'I'm sorry,' and Clark fell into his arms and sobbed.

Seven

'"Was ever woman in this humor wooed?"' Harry cooed during the intermission, '"Was ever woman in this humor won?"'

'No,' Clark growled and stomped towards the steps.

'"I'll have her!"' Harry cried and ran down the steps after her.

What a jerk, she thought, as she hurried out the front door, Harry shuffling behind her, aping it up no doubt, judging from the expressions on the faces of the people she passed. She stifled a smile, as well as the tenderness that was creeping up to her heart, beginning to soften it, knead it into something pliable and mushy, something Harry could burrow into, stretch out in, get comfy.

He'd spent dinner trying to cajole her with his cuteness, to take her mind off death with his own joy in life, acting like a three-year-old, asking 'What's this?', sticking out his tongue and jabbing it with his fork, weeping with laughter at his own jokes, but she wasn't ready to give in yet. She had already forgiven him – why not? After all, he'd just been Harry being Harry and how long could she hold that against him? – but she didn't want to let him off the hook so easily. His ability to charm her with his jerkiness infuriated her: it seemed so unfair, so effortless on his part, so facile. She wanted him to suffer – not a lot, she wasn't a sadist – just enough to know what it felt like. 'You'd be a much better person if you'd learn to suffer,' she always told him and he would pout: 'I *do* suffer,' he'd always say, 'I just don't show it,' and Clark supposed he believed himself, believed that whatever twinge of momentary discomfort he was feeling was actual suffering, but it was so short-lived it hardly counted.

She was walking toward the bodega, to get something to drink, and could hear him following, scraping one foot on the sidewalk, trying to look like a club-footed hunchback, probably succeeding but she wasn't going to turn round and find out.

'Beanie!' he called. 'Wait up!'

She ignored him and went into the store. It smelled of spices and over-ripe fruit – tropical, sultry, and just a little bit rotten. It made her long to go home, pack a suitcase, and fly away – to Mexico, perhaps, or Costa Rica, to the pyramids, to the jungle, someplace hot and ancient and mysterious, someplace with hammocks swaying under palm trees, someplace where she couldn't understand a word anyone said.

She bought a can of papaya juice and went outside. Harry was standing beside the door, talking to a youngish woman dressed in nothing but leggings and a leather vest, black of course, her long hair pulled back in a dancer's bun. Clark stifled the jealousy that automatically bubbled up and walked back to the theater, careful not to stomp, not to betray her irritation. It occurred to her that she was doing a lot of stifling for someone who was, as she considered herself to be, the injured party, and that irritated her even more.

She took deep breaths, sat down on the bottom step leading to the theater, drank her juice. It was beginning to worry her, this constant fury she seemed to be in. This was something new, something in addition to her jealousy – an irksome flaw she would just have to live with – and the rather constant ebb and flow of her irritation with her beloved but vexatious Harry; it was something else entirely: a big, shapeless, nameless rage that engulfed her, swept her helplessly along in the wake of its wrath. She would find herself stomping down the sidewalk, suddenly overwhelmed with the desire to slam her fist through a plate-glass window, to knock over litter bins, to hurl her shoulder bag at passing busses. She would stand still, horrified at the violence bubbling up within her, wondering where it was coming from. Not from her, of that she was relatively certain. She loved her life. She had everything exactly the way she wanted it, with the possible exception of not having enough time to do her own work, but even that didn't bother her. She knew that when she was ready to work, she'd find the time. She had asked her sister Dee Dee if she had shown signs of incipient rage as a child, but Dee Dee had confirmed her own notion of herself as a remarkably good-natured child. She had pulled out all her old report cards, scanning the teachers' comments for hidden warnings, but try as she might, she couldn't find anything sinister in 'A delightful child!' or 'Loves to help others'. Her subversive streak hadn't manifested itself until junior high, but even that was good-natured: she didn't want to hurt anyone, she just loved to burst bubbles and she did it with such high spirits even her victims didn't take offense.

It was a struggle. She sometimes felt as if something were somehow burrowing into her, infesting her like some kind of parasite, and the only way she could get rid of it would be to rip her skin off and hide away for seven years, until she grew a new epidermis. 'What are you so pissed off about?' Harry would occasionally ask and she didn't know so she'd say, 'The world! I'm pissed off about the whole damn *world*!' because that at least made a certain kind of sense, and Harry would take her in his arms and nuzzle her head and say, 'Beanie, Beanie, you can't take it to heart,' and she would feel better. But only temporarily, for the truth was, she couldn't *not* take it to heart. She took everything to heart. Everything that got in – and that was a lot – make its first stop there, checking in, wounding her or filling her with joy, infuriating her or making her laugh with its absurdity. That was the way she was made and there was nothing she could do about it.

She sighed and glanced across the street, at the crowd gathering outside CBGB. It was a new crowd, New Wave Punk or PostPunk or whatever they called themselves. The only difference, as far as she could tell, was that they were a whole lot younger than the first batch, which had come in the seventies and then kind of faded away. Or, perhaps they were still around and she just didn't recognise them as they aged, let their hair grow out, removed the safety pins from their nostrils. That first batch would be in their mid-thirties now, closing in on forty, and there comes a time when a bright blue Mohawk becomes a bit much. Clark should know.

She'd had one herself, if only for half a day. She'd felt so daring, at the time, sitting in the barber's chair at Freida's, high on that remarkable hash Jana had brought back from Greece, laughing hysterically while Freida buzzed her scalp with the trimmer, watching in amazement as fuzzy tufts of her hair scattered across the floor like little catnip toys. The old ladies sat under their hairdryers, gaping and rolling their eyes – 'You'll be sorry,' one old woman kept muttering and she was right, Clark *was* sorry as soon as the hash wore off and she caught a glimpse of herself in a plate-glass window and she ran back and had Freida shave it all off.

Clark laughed, remembering how she had wanted Freida to dig her old hair out of the trash and glue it back on. Instead, she wore turbans and threw phrenology parties. She'd been temping then, and she told the people at the agency she was undergoing chemo and for a few months they sent her out on the best-paying jobs.

God, life was great back then. It was so much fun. She wasn't having enough *fun* any more; maybe that was why she was pissed off all the time. 'White people are always talking about having fun,' she remembered Miles Davis saying, 'What the fuck is *fun*?' She thought it was hilarious, at the time, but now she was beginning to wonder. What the fuck *was* 'fun'? Shaving her head and having a bunch of people over to feel her bumps didn't seem very amusing any more.

She stared at the crowd across the street, trying to recognise someone she knew. Could it be that she didn't know any of them? Was that possible? She'd been here when CBGB *opened*, for God's sake, and now it had been taken over by a bunch of spike-haired brats.

It suddenly occurred to her that somehow or other, without her even noticing it, a whole new generation had moved into the East Village. Generation, she thought with a surge of panic, now there's a word with some weight. And instead of wanting to be a part of *her* world, which was completely acceptable and understandable, they wanted to make one of their own.

How could she not have noticed? She saw them moving in – who could miss them? – but she hadn't paid much attention. They had seemed harmless enough, just kids doing the rebellion thing. It wasn't as if they were yuppies, trying to turn the East Village into the kind of place in which *they'd* want to live. But maybe they *were* like yuppies, after all: interlopers, a mutant species marching in to take over *her* restaurants, *her* clubs, *her* hang-outs, changing them into *theirs*. They were taking a part of her youth, wiping it out, usurping it.

The Where?House, Phoenix Rising, Ground Zero, Da Nang, *Bad Ass Girls* – all gone. She felt another jolt of panic course through her. How could she slip back into her world whenever she wanted if her world no longer existed? Even if she came up with a new piece, where would she perform? She hadn't kept up with the scene; she'd been swept away by other things – love, politics, her job, her volunteer work. Wonderful things. Fulfilling things. Important things. Things that kept her heart from cracking every time she passed a young kid pasting up a flyer for some new performance space, filled with names she didn't recognise.

It was so *American*, she thought angrily, nobody wanted to preserve anything, to honor what went before, they wanted only to tear it down and make something comfortable for *them* . . .

Ah, what the hell? They were just kids. She never liked CBGB anyway, they could have it.

She sat there, wavering between the resentment she

did feel and the generosity she should feel – it's their turn now, she told herself. She was willing to hand over the baton, so to speak, to give over the haunts of her youth to these whipper-snappers, but if she was going to step aside, she wanted to be thanked for it. And *that* was what pissed her off – their complete and utter ignorance of her existence, their indifference to her trail-blazing, their lack of gratitude for making the Lower East Side the kind of place they'd want to appropriate. To them, she was just some old cow, trying to take credit for forging a path for them, although that was exactly what she had done.

Oh well. One good thing about being married to someone ten years your senior, she thought as she watched the kids dancing around, play-fighting, flirting, jumping up and down on the parked cars, was that you always felt relatively young. Fifty didn't seem quite so ancient, so end-of-the-lineish, now that Harry was closing in on it. Of course, Harry's forty-seven years only counted numerically. As far as behavior was concerned, she might as well be his grandmother. Harry was such a child, really, and while that could be exceedingly annoying at times, it also provided Clark with a sense of superiority. Benign superiority, of course, nothing she would lord over him or anything like that. Just something she kept to herself, to savor in private.

She sipped at her papaya juice, feeling old and fat and grumpy. I'm not old, she told herself. I'm not fat, despite Harry's assertion that I'm getting flabby. I'm *womanly*. Statuesque, without the stature. The grumpiness she would admit to, but that wasn't her fault. And she wasn't *always* grumpy, just sometimes, just when the free-floating rage grabbed her by the throat and began choking her. It wasn't just her; everybody seemed pissed off all the time, the whole country seemed to be stomping about in a snit. Except Harry. It infuriated her, his obliviousness, although she sometimes secretly envied him. Perhaps it infuriated her *because* she envied it, envied his ability to skip right past a photo of a starving Ethiopian without a second glance, without feeling as if he had to *do* something about it.

She glanced over to where he was standing, still talking to the dancer chick – modern, no doubt, too busty to be a ballerina – trying to see whether he was hiding his left hand, tucking his wedding ring safely in his pocket. No, he was gesticulating wildly, raising his arm up over his head and then bringing it down in an arc, like someone falling.

Ugh. He was telling her about the dead person. How like him. He would take it and put it in his life, in his book, make it his own, not something that happened to someone else, but something that happened to *him*.

Clark didn't want to think about it, didn't want to think about death at all. Her throat tightened – just thinking about not thinking about it made her want to lie down on the sidewalk and start screaming. She was sick of people dying – Harry was always saying she knew more dead people than most people knew live ones and he was right. And it was getting worse every year, a third of her friends were HIV positive, people were dying all over the place so what business did that dead person have, jumping into *her* courtyard, dirtying it up with his death, intruding himself on her life? She hated him, whoever he was, how dare he. How dare he add one more loss to her life?

Harry was approaching, swaggering now, after his little tête-à-tête with the dancer. He had obviously forgotten he was supposed to be trying to weasel his way back into her good graces. She sighed. She supposed she should have given in at the very first, when she actually had forgiven him. Then they would have gone to the store together, shared a drink, talked about the play, and she wouldn't have been sitting here, alone and furious, getting dirty and growing more morbid by the second. Now it was too late. She'd been thinking too much, rolling around in her own mud, and there was no help for it – Harry would have to pay.

"'Vouchsafe, divine perfection of a woman,'" he bellowed, getting down on his knees and mincing his way to Clark, "'Of these supposed crimes to give me leave, By circumstance but to acquit myself.'"

The people milling about, smoking and drinking, gaped and clapped. 'Bravo!' called one wag, and Harry beamed.

Clark sighed again, shook her head, gave in. How could she not love this man? How could she not adore him, despite his too-numerous-to-mention flaws? How could she stay mad at someone willing to get down on his knees on a New York City sidewalk, where God only knew what foul things were lurking, and publicly apologise? And to apologise by reciting Shakespeare? And by calling attention to her, Clark's, divine perfection? Who else? Who else would ever do this?

She stood up, grabbed his hand, pulled him up.

'You are such a jerk,' she said and Harry grinned triumphantly.

She'd make him pay later.

Eight

It was like a nightmare.

Harry couldn't believe this was happening: couldn't believe there were two detectives, one fat and slovenly, one young and hip, sitting at his kitchen table; couldn't believe that this, this body thing, this death thing, was still going on. The body was gone. Clark – after much tedious apologising and cajoling – had forgiven him. Why were these people still coming round to screw up his life?

Harry had a hangover. He only got drunk three times a year: his birthday, New Year's, and Bastille Day, not because he had any French blood or any particular fondness for Robespierre, but simply because he loved to spend the evening going from yuppie bar to yuppie bar, shouting 'Bring back the guillotine!'

He pulled down three mugs for coffee, hesitating, for a moment, at the pig mug, deciding against it, pulling down the Chinesy one instead. Clark wouldn't have hesitated at all: she would have plopped the pig in front of the fat cop, glaring at him, daring him to make something of it. Of course that was if she offered them coffee at all, which was doubtful.

They were sitting at a corner of the table, hunched over, talking in a low murmur. Harry was still half asleep, half asleep and half drunk; not in any shape to deal with cops.

What could they want? They had asked for Clark, not him, why would they want to talk to Clark?

Not that he wanted to know the answer – he didn't want to know why they were there, didn't want them there, didn't want to lose another day to that damn dead guy. He'd be able to use this, of course – it was raw material and say what you will about cops, Harry thought, the fact is, whenever they're around there's an excitement, a tension, a heightened consciousness. You look through your peephole and see a cop, it's an instant amphetamine rush. And there was also the fear they dragged along with them, the fear of being caught. It didn't matter whether or not you'd done anything, cops just made you feel guilty. They carried guilt around with them, in their holsters along with their guns and their night sticks, ready to pummel you with it, and the fact was, they were just hitting you with something you already had, something that had just been sitting around, waiting for a chance to get you.

He carried the two mugs over to the table. 'Milk?' he asked, the perfect hostess, 'Sugar?' He looked at the fat one. 'Sweet 'n Low?'

They shook their heads and Harry retrieved his own mug, pulled out a stool from under the table, and sat down.

'So,' the fat one said, 'you're married to Beatrice Clark, right?'

Harry nodded.

'Harry Butler, right?'

He nodded again and the detectives looked at each other and smirked.

'Ever think about changing that?' the young one asked.

A comedian, Harry thought. He didn't answer, just shrugged. He loved his name, it was his, it was him. They had no idea how hard he'd had to fight, as a kid, for that name; how many black eyes and bruises he'd come home with, and how many he'd given in return. It takes a strong man to carry that name, and he was proud of it. He had earned respect for it, but how was this idiot cop to know that? To him, Harry was just a schmoe like any other schmoe, a non-cop and a non-criminal, so therefore what good was he?

'And where's your wife?'

'Work,' Harry said.

'And where would that be?'

Did he have to answer that? What was this about? Did he need a lawyer, for God's sake? Who did Clark know who was a lawyer? Or in law school? Jesus, Harry thought, had it gotten to the point where you had to have a lawyer move in with you, just in case someone decided to take the final plunge in front of your window?

'Uh, what's this about, if I might ask?' Harry said, trying to sound both respectful enough so they wouldn't get pissed off, but firm enough so they wouldn't think they could push him around. Shit, he thought, life is getting too damn complicated.

The fat one gave him the eye, sizing him up, probably wondering what the hell he was doing, still in bed and hung over at eleven o'clock in the morning, wondering why he wasn't out working, wondering if he was some sort of junkie or drunk, freeloading off his wife. Who cares, Harry thought, let him think what he wants. I'm Harry Butler, I know who I am and that's all that matters.

The young cop reached into the briefcase by his feet and pulled out a photograph.

'Is this your wife?' he asked, waving it at Harry.

Harry took the photo and dug through the clutter on the table for his glasses. Jesus, Mary and Joseph. It was Clark, all right, Clark in her buzz-cut phase, standing on a stage somewhere, wearing tight jeans and a leotard. It was an enlargement of a snapshot, and not a good one. The photographer had a lot of half-heads in the foreground; he must have been standing too far away. Must have been back in 1979, 1980 maybe, when Clark was doing her *West Side Story* bit. She looked good. Harry had forgotten she had been so trim – maybe he could get her to join the Y or something.

'Yeah,' he said proudly, handing the photo back to the young cop, 'that's my wife.'

The cop nodded and nonchalantly returned the photograph to his briefcase.

'Do you have any idea,' he said without looking up, 'why her picture would be in the apartment of the deceased?'

Jesus, Harry thought, what is going on here? The fat cop was still eyeing him, watching to see how he'd react. His shock was genuine, not an act, but how would the cop know that? Harry knew his face had registered something, but he didn't know what that something was, and how could the cop, who had never seen Harry before in his life, even for an instant, presume to know what that something meant?

'What kind of detectives did you say you were?' he

asked, hoping his voice sounded more normal to them than it did to him.

'Homicide,' the fat one said.

Homicide. Shit. But he had called the dead person 'the deceased', not 'the victim'. That was a good sign, wasn't it?

'Look,' Harry said, 'I don't know what's going on here, but I don't think I want to talk to you guys any more, not until I've talked to my wife.'

'Hey,' the fat cop said, 'OK by us. We can understand you wouldn't want to say anything that could get her into trouble. But you don't have to worry, you know – a husband can't testify against his wife in court . . .'

'Testify!?' Harry yelled. 'Testify about what?'

The fat cop shrugged. 'I guess you didn't know your wife was seeing this guy?'

'What guy?' Harry asked. 'What do you mean, *seeing* him?'

The young detective reached into the briefcase again and pulled out a handful of photographs and shoved them at Harry. They were all of Clark – Clark standing in front of the Kitchen, Clark as King Lear, Clark in Tompkins Square Park with a bullhorn. Clark sitting in front of the computer. *His* computer. Well, *their* computer.

Harry looked up, bewildered. 'What is this?' he asked.

'They were all in the apartment of the deceased,' the young one said. 'Tacked up all over the wall.'

Harry turned around and glanced out the window. 'You mean he was up on the roof taking pictures of us?'

'There aren't any of you,' the fat one noted, 'just your wife.'

Shit, Harry thought. What was she up to? Clark had

been a bit of a groupie in her younger days. She'd slept with a couple of famous people, passing through. Harry knew, but he couldn't work himself into a frenzy over it – he knew it didn't 'mean' anything and in a way it was as if he, too, had touched greatness. Jealousy, at least of a sexual nature, was not Harry's thing – getting all bent out of shape because your wife had a one-night stand with some Mick Jagger or other was a waste of precious passion. It never occurred to Harry that she might have some groupies of her own, and that idea he didn't think he liked very much. In fact, he liked it very little.

'Look,' he said, 'my wife is an actress, or at least she used to be. These pictures don't mean anything. Maybe "the deceased" was just a fan.' A deranged fan, he thought, some sicko, some psycho. Some groupie. Some love slave. Some sex toy. Could she? Could she have had some toy boy locked away in some steamy grotto, someone she met between Disaster Relief lessons and Act Up meetings? Some little Lothario she disguised as Mina or Jana or Aggie or any of her thousand and one friends?

The young cop shoved another photograph at Harry, a grainy, enlarged xerox from a high-school yearbook.

'You know this guy?'

'Is this the . . . deceased?' Harry asked.

The young cop nodded.

Harry looked. A nerd. Longish hair, must have been in high school in the late seventies. Too young for Clark. Harry recognised the type – Midwestern, rural, the kind of kid bussed in from a farm, whose clothes smelled vaguely of manure. He looked like a nice kid, the kind of kid Clark would take under her wing . . .

He shook his head, pushed the picture back across the table.

'No way,' he said, 'Clark wouldn't have been *seeing* this guy.'

'How can you be so sure?'

'I know my wife,' Harry said, feeling as if he'd never known her less. 'He's not her type.'

'Well, what were her pictures doing in his apartment?'

Harry shook his head. How should he know? Clark was a public figure, at least locally, maybe the guy had a crush on her. If she had known about it, Harry would have known, too – she would have flung him in Harry's face during one of their fights.

Wouldn't she have?

'You're sure she was at work yesterday morning?' the fat one asked.

'You guys are barking up the wrong tree,' Harry said, 'Clark wasn't here when that guy fell . . .'

The young cop jumped on him instantly, like a Rottweiler let off the leash.

'How do you know, if you weren't here?'

Harry felt as if he were sitting on the outer edge of a whirlpool, whirling round and round the hole that was eventually going to suck him down, spiraling in with every word he uttered. He had sensed, from the start, that the body was going to get him into trouble, and he had been right. The longer he sat there, watching himself circling around his own doom, the worse he was making it for himself. The cops were staring at him, waiting, maybe even watching their own internal film clips, if they had that much imagination; maybe watching him flounder about, thinking, Hoist by his own petard, if they knew what that meant.

'I was here,' he said.

The cops looked at each other, obviously surprised,

and Harry felt a moment of delicious superiority as a schoolboy 'nyah, nyah' thrilled through his mind, 'I fooled you!' But it only lasted an instant. Long enough, however, to give Harry something to hold on to when the rest of his life came falling apart, as it showed every sign of doing.

'You were here?' the young cop repeated.

'Yeah,' Harry said, shrugging.

'Let me get this straight. According to the report, you said you *weren't* here. Are you telling us you lied to the officer? Why would you want to lie to the officer? Did you lie?'

Harry sighed. One ring closer to the mouth of the hole. Was it the lie to the officer, or the truth to these guys, that was dragging him in? He closed his eyes, kneaded his achy, throbbing head. Guilty, guilty, guilty, he thought, I am the picture of guilt, sitting here silent, hanging on to my head as if I were afraid it might get chopped off. Guilty, the fat one must be thinking; guilty, the young one must be agreeing.

'So,' the young one said, 'you were here.'

Harry nodded hopelessly.

'And?' the fat one goaded.

They weren't going to help him out at all. They weren't leading him anywhere; they were just sitting back, letting him fumble his way right down the path to Doom. They were a lot like Clark, in that respect.

'And I was just sitting down to work.' He'd skip the part about Ophelia and the pansies; these guys wouldn't appreciate it. He paused, putting his memory in fast-forward, trying to catch the next cut.

'Oh, yeah,' he said, 'then I started work.'

'Work?' the fat one repeated.

'Yeah, work. I'm a writer.'

The fat one smirked at the young one. 'I thought you delivered those singing telegrams or something.'

How did they know that? He hadn't given his profession to the patrol guy; how did these guys know what he did for a living? He felt a little jolt of paranoia shoot through him – just how much did the cops know about him, about Clark, about everybody? Did he have some kind of file? Back in the sixties and seventies everybody had just assumed the FBI was spying on them, but the local cops? Why would they spy on Harry? He suddenly remembered those odd little clicks he'd been hearing on the new portable phone, something he had attributed to the fact that he'd bought it from some guy on the street for five bucks. Had it been a plant? Was someone spying on him? On Clark? What was she up to? Had she started going to that Marxist discussion group at the Brecht Forum again?

He looked at the detectives, trying to place their faces, to determine if he'd ever seen them before. Fat one: round face, small gray pig-eyes, tiny little doll-like ears – very clean, by the way – losing hair, trying to make up for it with the half-head comb-over. Why did guys *do* that? Uneven, yellow teeth, mid-range suit, probably drove over to New Jersey with his wife (thick gold wedding band) to shop at the discount stores. Incongruously neat fingernails, possibly manicured. A freebie from one of the Korean nail salons? Young one: tall, thin, lean – a cowboy with class. Was that whiff of prep school real or assumed? Either seemed unlikely, perhaps fear had knocked Harry's nose off-track. Drooping eyes with those sappy long lashes women loved. Straight, skinny nose with fleshy nostrils, made for quivering. Almost as much hair as Harry but not quite. Dressed in earth-tones. What they used to call, back in high school, 'sharp'.

'I do that for a few bucks,' Harry told them, 'but I'm a writer.'

'OK,' the fat one said, 'you were sitting down to *work*. Then what?'

'Then I worked,' Harry said.

'What time was this? When you "worked"?'

Harry caught the tone of sarcasm but chose to ignore it. They were cops; they couldn't be expected to understand the life of the artiste.

Harry shrugged. 'Ten, eleven. Somewhere in there. I don't wear a watch.'

'Of course not,' the fat one said.

'Then the phone rang.'

'The phone rang,' repeated the fat cop.

'Yeah. The phone rang. I figured it was for Clark, and was going to let the machine pick it up, but then I thought it might be someone calling to wish me Happy Birthday . . .'

'It was your birthday?' the young one said. 'Hey, Happy Birthday.'

'Thanks,' Harry said.

'So who was it?' the fat one wanted to know.

'I don't know. I got up to get the phone and that's when I saw this *thing* out of the corner of my eye, and I went over to the window because I thought it might be those squatters throwing garbage out into the courtyard again and if it was, I was going to kill them . . .'

'Kill them?' the young one said.

'You know what I mean,' Harry said, watching himself fall helplessly into a spinning black and white cone, round and round, arms flailing, mouth silently shouting for help, growing smaller as he approached the abyss, 'I was going to yell at them.'

'There's a big difference between yelling and killing,'

the young one said. 'You ought to know that. You're a writer. You ought to choose your words more carefully.'

Your honor, he said he was going to kill them. Right in front of Detective Fat and myself. The judge glared at Butler from under his *periwig*. Periwig! He'd finally get a chance to use it; he loved that word . . . *'Guilty!' he shouted, 'Off with his head!'*

He told them the rest. How he thought it was a bag of laundry until he put on his glasses. How he ran through the building, looking for someone to help. How nobody was home. How he called from the street, at the very first phone he found that worked.

The fat one wanted to know whether he'd seen anything, up on the roof, anything suspicious. A person or persons.

No, Harry told him, the only thing he saw was the flash of white. He didn't even look at the roof of the building.

'And you claim you didn't know this guy was seeing your wife?' the fat one asked nonchalantly.

'He wasn't seeing my wife!' Harry cried.

'How do you know?' the fat one asked, 'I thought you didn't know him.'

'I *didn't* know him. I never saw him before in my life.'

'But obviously he knew your wife.'

There was nothing obvious about anything. The more the detectives questioned him, the murkier things seemed.

Shit, Harry thought, what a mess.

'I think I'd better call my wife,' he said.

Nine

'Oh, God,' Clark sobbed, 'oh my God.'

She'd been crying for eight hours straight. Nothing Harry said or did could console her; she wept rivers.

The body that had lain in the courtyard had belonged to a guy named Gordie Sheppard, a kid, really. A kid, like Clark, from the same farm town in Michigan, who had come to New York, like Clark, to be Somebody. Who had come, apparently, *because* of Clark.

Harry was sitting on the floor, backed up to the bookcase, trying to piece it all together while Clark shook the apartment with her sobs.

Yeah, it was sad – wasted life, all that – but this was a bit much. This was the kind of grieving she should do if *he*, Harry, died, not some kid she claimed she didn't even know. And yeah, Clark took death hard, any death, she'd get teary-eyed when Harry clobbered a mouse with the broom, but *eight hours*?

Could *she* be lying? Clark was actually quite adept at

lying – the lies flowed from her mouth with such aplomb, such authority, that no matter how outrageous they were they sounded true. She thought he believed her, and he let her, because it gave her so much pleasure to think she had secretly fooled him. And it gave him great pleasure to secretly fool her. But all of Clark's lies were of the little white type – little bits of misinformation she'd slip him when he'd wake her up in the middle of the night, wanting to know what annuit coeptis meant. She never lied about the important things, although there were times he wished she would.

So why would she lie about this? He leaned back into the bookcase, ran through it all again.

As soon as she walked through the door, Mason, the fat cop, with whom Harry was by that time on a last-name basis, had thrust the picture of the kid at Clark.

'You know this guy?'

She stared at the picture, shook her head.

'Imagine him with glasses,' O'Donnell, the young one, said. 'Black glasses.'

Clark shook her head again. She'd been uncharacteristically passive in the presence of the cops, it occurred to Harry now, almost sheepish. He'd been too busy watching himself spin helplessly in his little cone of doom to pay much attention to Clark's behavior. An oversight he might end up regretting, he thought now as he tried to remember the look on her face when O'Donnell began coaxing her.

'Black glasses with tape on the bridge,' he had said. He was standing behind her, leaning over her shoulder, pointing at the photo, his face almost touching Clark's. She must have been able to feel O'Donnell's breath on her ear, something Harry couldn't imagine her liking.

'Mod,' she said and her eyes filled with tears. 'It was

Mod?' she asked O'Donnell and burst into gasping sobs.

O'Donnell stood up and looked at Harry, but he shrugged, he hadn't a clue as to who Mod was. Some guy with a fixation on his wife, apparently. Some guy who had a damn love shrine dedicated to her in his apartment. Who had bunches of bad photographs of her taped to the walls. Who had a diary full of love poems dedicated to her. Who had ten copies of every issue of *BAG*, neatly wrapped in cellophane. Harry didn't mind Clark's having admirers – she had plenty of those and frankly, it made Harry proud, made him think, Yeah, lucky me, as he left some event with Clark on his arm. But this was different. This had nothing to do with him. This made him feel shut out, as if Clark had thrown a party and left him off the guest list.

Clark nodded. 'We never knew his name, we just called him Mod because he always dressed in bell-bottoms and stuff. You know, like some sixties' Carnaby Street character.'

'You *knew* this guy?' Harry had asked her.

'I didn't *know* him,' she said, 'he was just some kid who hung out over on Avenue A. He used to stare through the window at us, but every time we waved at him, he ran away. We figured he was in love with us all.'

Mason wanted to know if she had ever spoken to him. 'Exchanged words,' was the term he had used.

'No,' she snapped, 'I just *told* you he ran away every time we waved at him.' She turned her back on Mason and looked up at O'Donnell.

'He seemed harmless enough,' she told him. 'Just lovesick.'

Harmless, Harry thought. Harmless to *whom*? 'Yeah, well, he didn't have a love shrine dedicated to Polly or Jana. He had a love shrine dedicated to *you*.'

Harry felt unaccountably angry, as if it had all been Clark's fault, which in a way, it was. None of this would have happened if it hadn't been for Clark.

Harry had glanced over at Mason, who was watching him.

Butler was Suspect Number One.

Shit, Harry thought, they probably think I killed the kid in a jealous rage or something, something sordid like that, they just weren't saying anything. Yet. But they were thinking it. You should have seen the look on O'Donnell's face, he had wanted to tell Clark, when I told them you guys posed nude in every issue.

Clark had looked up at him, surprised, and began to cry again. Blubber, really. Clark hated it when she cried – 'It doesn't suit me,' she always said and became enraged when the tears began to tumble down the ridge between her cheek and her nose. She saw it as some sort of physiological betrayal, her tear ducts revealing a weakness she refused to admit she had. Once the tears started, it was as if her entire body gave up the ruse of strength, solidity, and she turned as red and mushy as a mannikin made of Jell-o. It wasn't a pretty sight, she knew it, and it infuriated her to the point of hysteria.

Harry quite liked it. There was always something erotic about seeing the forbidden, no matter how ugly it was, and whenever Clark started to cry, Harry got a hard on. An inappropriate reaction, like laughing in church, something his poor mother had been prone to, before they quit going altogether.

And now, eight hours later, she was still crying. O'Donnell and Mason had left, taking down all of Clark's various telephone and fax numbers, 'In case we need to reach you.' 'Do you think they suspect me?' Harry had asked her.

'Suspect you?' she had sniffled. 'Why should they suspect you?'

'They're cops,' Harry had said. 'It's their job to suspect people.'

Suspect him of what, Clark had wanted to know.

'I don't know,' he had said, 'Cops don't like coincidences. They're cause-and-effect kind of people. And maybe they think the cause was *me*.'

'That's ridiculous,' she had said.

'Since when does something being ridiculous stop it from being true?' Harry had asked her. 'To *us*, it's ridiculous. To *them*, it's suspicious. It would be one thing if it had just been some crackhead . . .'

It was the wrong thing to say.

'How can you be so *callous*?' she had screamed and ran to the bed and collapsed. She'd been there ever since.

Every forty-five minutes or so, one of the neighbors would pound on the door and Harry would go out in the hall, to discuss the 'uh, accident'. 'Suicide,' Martin declared; 'Murder,' Mrs Speransky insisted. Most of the neighbors were leaning towards murder, and what the hell, murder was much more interesting than suicide. There was danger attached to it, the thrill of being frightened, of thinking there was something lurking Out There, something scary and evil, something looking for fresh victims and you might be next. Suicide, on the other hand, was just depressing. Nobody wanted to believe a person was capable of killing himself, but they were more than willing to believe a person was capable of killing a whole building full of people. Go figure.

No one, besides the cops, had connected Clark to the body and Harry wanted to keep it that way. He especially wanted to keep her away from Martin and his suicide theories. All hell would break lose if Clark started thinking she was responsible for the kid's death – she'd fall apart, get lost in the mire of all that childhood guilt she was carrying around from her parents' deaths, end up back on the shrink's couch, which meant months – maybe even years! – of psyche-mining for *both* of them, dusting off every little chunk of the past to see if it was just a boring old coal or the secret diamond of Insight. And there was the added danger of Clark starting to think she was the kind of woman men killed themselves over, something that could make Harry's life pretty damn miserable.

Harry got up, walked over to the bed and crawled in, snuggling up from behind. Clark sniffled, turned over and buried her head in his chest. He stroked her hair, staring at the slightly uneven line of her part. Her scalp was so pink, like bubble gum, and he leaned down to taste it. Could she be lying? But why would she? There was no point; she would have been thrilled to have her own groupie, she would have flaunted him, dangled him in front of Harry when she thought he was being negligent, would have pinned him to her chest like some French ribbon of honor.

She shuddered so hard the bed shook. You wouldn't think the tear ducts could produce that much water, Harry kept thinking, and he wondered how many calories one expended in crying. Not an insubstantial amount, he thought, with all the sobbing, the deep breathing and the gasps, the shuddering and shaking. You probably got a moderate upper-torso workout with a good cry.

'Clark,' he said, gently patting her head, 'babe. It's OK.'

She pushed herself away from him, rubbed her nose

with a soggy wad of Kleenex and said, 'No. It's not OK. Jesus Christ, Harry, someone is *dead*.'

Lots of people are dead, he thought but knew better than to say. Yeah, it was sad. And a waste. And possibly even a loss, as Clark was now insisting. She was convinced the kid would have been a great poet, even though she had never read a word of his stuff, or if she had, it was only to reject it. But it was the potential that got to her, the fact that he hadn't had a chance.

Harry wondered how long the kid had been hanging out on the roof, spying on them. On him. *Bad Ass Girls* had been defunct for years; Clark hadn't performed since . . . when? Five, six years, at least. Had the kid been watching them all that time? He raised his head and squinted at the blackness outside the window. It was creepy. An invasion of privacy, that's what it was, and it was the invasion aspect he didn't like. Harry had nothing against making his life public: *au contraire*, he had every intention of making his life immensely public with *Butler by Butler*. But that was different. He was in control of *B by B*; he got to pick and choose which details of his life to display. What would someone make of his life, without Harry to interpret it?

'We should put up some curtains,' he said and Clark groaned.

It was ironic, Harry thought, if Clark had met the kid, she probably would have liked him, pulled him into one of the outer circles of her life. She had a soft spot for nerds, for the awkward and the uncouth, and she especially liked admirers, of any sort. She was always saying she wanted a love slave, and the kid might have been it. That really was wasted potential, Harry thought, the kid had bitten it before Clark had even known she was his Goddess, his Beloved Tormentress.

Harry shook his head sadly and Clark curled back up in his arms, probably thinking she had shamed him into a proper respect for the dead. Women. They always wanted to know what you were thinking but if they had the vaguest idea of what you were *really* thinking, they'd never ask.

Actually, Harry did feel a little ashamed – he sometimes wondered if maybe there was something a little bit wrong with him, nothing major, of course, nothing sick or anything. It was just that he couldn't get himself all worked up about the death of someone he didn't know. Even celebrities, who most people feel they 'know' but who, to Harry, didn't seem the least bit real in any case – even their deaths couldn't seduce a tear from Harry's eye. Was that wrong? Was he supposed to scratch out his eyes and rend his T-shirt every time some public figure died? They weren't *real*, at least to him, they were figures, symbols, human beings representing something else, an idea or a hope or an emotion too huge for people to feel themselves. It was the *idea* people were mourning, it was the murder or death of that thing the celebrity represented that made people so hysterical, and Harry just couldn't go there. And he was not a guy who eschewed crying – let anybody who said he was heartless or cold take a look at him when he was reading *White Fang*, for example, or when old Patrick upstairs died, or when they found out Ollie had AIDS. He cried like a sensible person – when there was a reason.

But this guy, this guy hadn't even existed, as far as Harry was concerned, until he became a corpse.

Harry shuddered.

'What's the matter?' Clark asked.

'I was just thinking,' he said.

'About Gordie?'

'Kind of,' he said. 'I was just thinking how weird the whole thing is. You look out your window, see a bunch of people walking on the sidewalk, and as far as you're concerned, they don't exist, not as *people*, not as individuals who like Chinese food or John Wayne movies or ballroom dancing. Not as mothers or sons or cousins or fathers-in-law. They have no relation to you or anyone else, as far as you're concerned. And *you* don't exist, either, as far as they're concerned.'

Clark wanted to know if there was a point to all this.

'I'm getting to that,' Harry said. 'I'm thinking it out as I go. Patience, my darling.'

Clark smiled for the first time that day and Harry felt elated: he felt the power of ideas, of thought.

'I mean, think about it,' Harry said, jumping up from the bed and running over to the window. 'There are ten million people in New York and for nine million nine hundred thousand of them, *you don't exist!*'

Clark laughed. 'Speak for yourself, Butler,' she said. 'I'm famous.'

She meant it as a joke, but as soon as she'd said it, she collapsed face down on the bed and began weeping again.

'Stop crying!' Harry shouted. 'I'm trying to tell you something!'

She muttered something and waved her arm at him dismissively, as if anything he had to say paled in relation to the kid's death, but that was what he was trying to tell her, that was what he was trying to get to – the fact that it was only because he had *ceased* to exist that he existed at *all*, for them.

It was mind-boggling. Think about it, he wanted to say to her, if you jumped out of a window on to a crowded sidewalk, you would, in ceasing to exist yourself, suddenly and irrevocably exist – *for ever* – for those people who saw you. It was a form of immortality, Harry wanted to shout, because although Gordie Sheppard might be dead, he was more alive than he had been before, as far as Harry and Clark were concerned, and while the cops and his neighbors and his friends back home would eventually forget him, they, Harry and Clark, never would. It was as if, in jumping past their window, he had moved right in, settled himself comfortably between them, like some kind of foster child, and he would stay with them for the rest of their lives.

'Oh God!' he wailed, and collapsed on the bed with Clark.

Ten

Clark was trapped; shoved half out of the bed and dangling by the clump of her hair caught under Harry's snoring bulk.

'Owww!' she cried, trying to pull herself out from under him, 'Harry, wake up! You're killing me!'

He snorted, reached for his notebook and rolled over, smacking Clark on the head with it. She tumbled out of bed on to the floor.

'Harry, wake up!' she shouted, but he was dead to the world, sleeping the sleep of the just despite the fact that he'd spent half the night obsessing about the cops suspecting him. 'I don't have an alibi!' he kept wailing, 'I can't prove my innocence!'

She sat on the floor, watching his body heave under the covers, and suddenly remembered an image from the dream she'd been having, before Harry knocked her out of bed. Harry had been up on the roof of the squatters' building in his Monster-Gram get up, lumbering towards the edge with his arms outstretched . . .

'Ugh!' Clark moaned, 'Ugh, ugh, ugh!' She closed her eyes, hoping the image would go away, but there it was: Harry in his platform shoes, with his face painted green and a bolt through his neck, lurching forward to . . .

Oh my God! Clark thought. Lurching forward to push Gordie off!

She pulled herself into a ball and began to rock. Oh God, oh God, oh God, how could she have a dream like that? It was terrible, evil, unthinkable.

She glanced toward the bed, wondering just who it was she was married to. 'This is insane,' she told herself, 'get a grip.' But insane or not, she felt afraid.

'It's just a dream,' she told herself. 'Grow up.'

She unrolled herself and began quietly crawling over to the desk. She reached up to Harry's drawer and began silently fingering the objects inside it. Pencils. An eraser. His writing rabbit foot . . .

Suddenly, the light went on and Harry was sitting up in bed.

'What are you *doing*?' he demanded.

'Bagels,' Clark said, 'I need bagels!'

Harry jumped out of bed and stood over her. 'You're looking for bagels in my personal drawer?' he asked. 'That's *my* drawer. It's private. And I don't keep bagels in it.'

Clark rolled back up in a ball. 'I must have been sleep-walking,' she said, beginning to cry. 'I need bagels. Right now.'

She looked up at him. He seemed huge, menacing, malevolent in the gray morning shadows, as if he had just stepped out of her nightmare. He reached down for her but she scooted away; she didn't want him to touch her, not now, not until she shook the dream off . . .

'What's the matter with you?' he asked. 'It's practically the middle of the night.' He reached over to the end table by the bed and groped for his glasses and the alarm clock. 'It's five thirty!'

Clark began to sob. 'I want a bagel,' she wept. 'A fresh one! From Bagel Heaven!'

'Bagel Heaven!' Harry moaned. 'That's practically in the Bronx!'

'It's only on 55th Street,' she sniffed, 'I want a bagel with vegetable cream cheese. The kind they make at Bagel Heaven.'

Harry wondered if she was pregnant. She used an IUD, but nothing was foolproof in this world, everything could be going along just swell and then suddenly life comes along and gives you a big boot in the buttocks – it sends a kid flying past your window one second and impregnates your wife the next. He looked at her, curled up like Charlotte Corday in a bad production of *Marat/Sade*. With the exception of occasional bouts of hysteria, Clark would make a great mother.

'All right,' he muttered, pulling on his sweatpants.

'Bagel Heaven cream cheese,' she insisted. 'Don't try to fake me out with that stuff from Bagelrama.'

'Yeah, yeah,' he said and left.

She listened to his footsteps retreating down the stairs and then jumped up and pulled out his drawer again. A pad of Garfield Post-Its, a roll of duct tape, push pins, rubber bands, a photograph of the two of them, standing in front of Grant's Tomb.

'Ugh, ugh, ugh,' Clark moaned. This was terrible, awful, insane. What was she *thinking*? How could she be afraid of Harry, her own husband, her dear, sweet husband who kept a photo of her in his own personal private drawer?

Index cards scribbled with 'ideas'. A butane lighter. Why would he need a lighter? He'd better not be smoking again . . . a pack of cards, a colorful mass of two-for theater tickets. She pulled out one of the index cards and scrutinised his handwriting. Sloppy, but benign.

'What am I *doing*?' she wailed.

It was all Harry's fault. If he hadn't gone on and on last night about the cops suspecting him, she would never have had such a hideous dream, never would have imagined him lurching across the roof to push the kid off. He had planted that, and now it wouldn't go away.

She closed the drawer and went to the bathroom. 'This is nonsense,' she told herself as she sat on the toilet, and she wasn't going to let herself give in to it. To think, for even one second, that Harry was capable of hurting someone was ludicrous.

But what if he could?

'Stop that,' she told herself.

She thought about the time they'd run over the fox. She had been beside herself – 'Stop! Stop the car!' she had demanded and Harry had grumbled and pulled over and they'd walked back to the fox, which wasn't quite dead, and Harry went and got a tree limb and beat it to death. To put it out of its misery, he said and she had been furious because he was smiling when he did it, and even though he convinced her that he wasn't smiling, he was grimacing, she never forgot that look and that was the look he had on his Frankenstein face when he was hulking across the roof in her dream . . .

'Stop it!' she told herself again, 'Stop it, stop it, stop it!'

Oh God, what was she going to do when he came back? She didn't want to see him right now, didn't want to look at him and see that leering grin. Even if it wasn't there, she'd see it, she was caught in the grip of some macabre fantasy and she didn't want him to come close to her until she was out of it.

She felt closed in, claustrophobic. There was no place to hide in their apartment, no place to get away from one another. She suddenly wished she had listened to Harry when he tried to convince her to move to a bigger apartment. The thought of a room with a door that closed had been enticing, but so was rent control.

Think facts: hair spray will remove ink stains from a shirt. The spin-dryer was developed by Savage Arms Corporation in 1924. Richard Nixon lives three blocks away from the Russian Consulate . . .

She took deep breaths. 'I am a rational human being,' she chanted, 'I am a rational human being.'

What was this *really* about? Grief? The need to blame someone and Harry was the only blamable one around? Or was it simply that suspicion, itself, was contagious – the detectives came in here, reeking of it, spreading it around like the plague, contaminating her life, and now it was gnawing away at her, even though she knew it was crazy.

She remembered how sycophantic Harry had been with the cops, sashaying around the table with the coffee pot, filling their mugs, trying to charm them with his helpfulness. She had felt disgusted, itching with shame for him and of him. Was that was this was about?

'I want to go home!' she found herself wailing, even though she *was* home. She pushed open the plywood door and looked out. *Her* apartment. *Her* home. *Her* safe spot, but it didn't *feel* safe any more.

She got up and walked into the living room. A peachy vapor was crawling down the side of the squatters' building. The rosy-fingered dawn, she thought, but

Clark was afraid it was more like a big, balled up fist ready to pound her life to bits.

She opened the window gates and crawled out on to the fire escape. There were bright yellow police ribbons fluttering on the squatters' roof and she thought about the kid, sitting up there with his notebook, staring at her window, hoping for a glimpse of her but getting only Harry.

Gordie Sheppard. A person of no importance, except to his parents. Maybe not even to them. The East Village was full of them, little invisibilities, unremarkable in any way other than the fact that they were indistinguishable from one another. She felt a sudden urge to get dressed, run out, find a few and befriend them, stamp them with some sort of individuality, the uniqueness they had come to the East Village to finally express. 'See *me*!' they all silently cried and the tragedy was, no one did.

Why hadn't he introduced himself to her? She was furious with him, she wanted him to be alive so she could take him by the shoulders, shake him, slap him if necessary. She didn't think she would have wanted him as a lover, but she would have befriended him, taken him under her wing. She would have been his mentor, in the old-fashioned sense: she could make him take out the garbage and do her laundry while she lectured him on the four aspects of character. He could have been the little brother she never had.

She thought about Billy, the make-believe brother she and Dee Dee created after their parents died. A little tow-headed, freckled-faced Hucky kind of kid. They had made him up with the intention of loving him, but mostly they tormented him, pushing him off the hay loft, locking him in the root cellar, tying him to the willow tree and forcing him to eat concoctions of mashed weeds, rotten eggs and chicken poop. Thank God he hadn't been real.

Dee Dee would understand. Why did she have to be off at some conference in Glasgow, for God's sake, why couldn't she be available when Clark needed her?

Some pigeons settled on the roof of the squatters' building and Clark wondered how someone could sit up there without Harry noticing. It was true Harry was not the most observant person on earth, and that when he was working his concentration was centered entirely upon himself, despite his endless complaints about his distractability. But even now, just the pigeons waddling around was distracting, little gray and white blips on the periphery of her field of vision, enough to make her turn her head and look, to see what the blip was, automatically, even if it wasn't important enough to remember having looked. But a person, that would be an oddity, out of the ordinary, and it was the odd things that grabbed our attention, that insisted we notice, not the unextraordinary, not the pigeons. And a person, a person staring into your window with a pen and an open notebook, that was extraordinary. That was odd. That was worth registering.

She wondered if the cops *did* suspect Harry. It didn't look good for him. Innocent until proven guilty, Clark thought. What a crock. Maybe that was true once, but she doubted it. There is no more innocence in the world; we have all been tainted. Guilty by association. Guilty by insinuation. Guilty, guilty, guilty – even the tiniest hint of suspicion led to a free-fall of speculation, all of it dealing with guilt. Nobody speculated about anybody's innocence. Innocence wasn't, Clark had to admit, interesting. Whereas guilt – guilt was not only endlessly interesting, it provided hours, weeks, months of joyful conjecturing. Innocence just sat there, doing nothing, a boring little lamb grazing in the meadow while guilt leapt over fences, soared over mountains, mischievously skipped across oceans. Guilt was just a lot more fun.

It was ludicrous, of course, there was nothing to suspect Harry *of*, but he was acting suspiciously nonetheless. That stupid lie about not being here didn't look good at all. And the fact that Gordie had been in love with her. She had to admit, if she were a cop, she'd have to suspect him. Who would believe he was so utterly unobservant that he wouldn't notice someone staring at him? That he wouldn't notice some guy taking photographs of his wife? That he wouldn't be insanely jealous? Jealousy, after all, was the default drive of humanity – who would believe it was the one flaw Harry didn't have?

But what if he *had* known? What if he *had* noticed Gordie up there watching him? What if he *had* gone over there to confront him, not because he knew Gordie was in love with her, but simply because he didn't like being stared at? Because it was running his 'concentration'?

Impossible, she told herself. Nonsense. She would know. He would have told her. Wouldn't he?

It suddenly occurred to her how little she knew about Harry, knew about her own husband. She thought she knew everything there was to know about him, but what if she didn't? What if there was another side to him, a Mr Hyde he kept hidden so well even his wife didn't know he existed?

Things like that happened. Polly's father had been a bigamist – he'd had two completely separate families and no one knew until he died, without a will, and they all met in Probate. Surprise!

Clark shuddered. What did she know about Harry, really, other than what he had told her himself? Harry's entire *life* was based on making up stories about himself, how was she supposed to separate the fact from the fiction? It had never occurred to her to bother – the fiction seemed so benign, so ludicrous, so egotistically silly, so intentionally false. But how true was the real Harry? How much of what he had presented her with was real?

What, for example, did he *do* all day? He wrote, of course, his book was over fifteen hundred pages, so far, but if you averaged that out, it came to about a hundred pages a year. Less than a third of a page a day. Obviously, he didn't sit in front of the computer all day, so what *did* he do? The only person who knew – Gordie Sheppard – was dead.

She thought about all the things Harry didn't know about her. The fact that she'd joined the Teen-Age Republicans in 1964, for example. Only for a month! Only long enough to get her picture taken for the yearbook, sitting next to the club president, Fergus O'Sullivan. All the girls had crushes on him – who wouldn't have a crush on someone with a name like that? And he was so cute! She was young. She was silly. She didn't have a clue about Goldwater's politics, although she liked *his* name, too.

When she considered it, there was a lot Harry didn't know about her, but then again, he didn't look too hard. He didn't know about Jake Springer, with whom she'd had her final fling before marriage. 'It's not too late,' Jake had said, a week before Harry and Clark were due to take off for Atlantic City to see if they could find an Elvis impersonator to marry them, but yes it was, at least as far as Jake was concerned. 'This is your last hurrah,' she told him and, God love him, he went out in style. A room at the Plaza. Facing the Park, no less. Room service. The little antique locket with . . . she blushed. *That* was something she would never tell anyone. And when she had stumbled home, at five in the morning, groaning and saying, 'Rough night at the Hotline, Hon,' Harry just grunted and rolled over.

Harry. What *did* she know about him?

She'd known him seven years. Stole him away from that awful Lorna in 1980. He moved in right away. They got married in 1982. Their fifth anniversary was coming up – he'd no doubt forget.

During that time, she thought she'd explored every bit of him. She'd gone after him like a dentist with a hook, digging out even the most microscopic morsel of his being. But what did all those morsels add up to? Did she know what he *meant*?

Who was there to verify him? Who had known young Harry? Adolescent Harry? Harry the Boy Scout? What proof was there that he was who he said he was?

She'd met his family, once, on a disastrous trip to the Midwest, before they were married. His father was kind of weird, constantly asking her if she had a 'scent', but otherwise OK – one of those ghost fathers of the suburbs: present in form but somehow less than corporeal. His mother was definitely *not* OK – she hated Clark from the minute she met her. From before that, really; she'd hated the notion of her from the moment Harry was born. Clark had a fuzzy idea that it was nothing personal, that it was her duty, as the mother of an only son, to protect him from any and all predatory females, but that didn't make her any more tolerable. She had followed Clark around, dragging that ghastly oxygen canister after her, hissing like a leaky balloon, wheezing out her nasty little comments: about Clark's hair (which was green at the time, and yes, she probably should have dyed it red or something, something more acceptable in *Ohio*), about her clothes, about her manners, about her 'mysterious background', which wasn't 'mysterious' at all – her parents had died in a car wreck when she was six, which was tragic, not 'mysterious'.

Three days of Ma Butler and Clark was ready to call the wedding off – she didn't want Ma and her big old metal canister hanging around Harry's neck, around *her* neck. 'Get me *outta* here,' she told Harry and they left, before she had a chance to meet any of his old friends, any of his other relatives, any of the people who could tell her who he had been.

That he had been someone else was beyond question. People didn't come to New York to keep on being who they'd been, they came to be either who they truly were but hadn't had a chance to be in Dublin, Ohio or Avoca, Michigan or whatever Smalltown they were fleeing, or they came to be who they weren't but wanted to be.

Why couldn't he go home, she wondered, why couldn't he go visit his parents. He hadn't been back to Ohio in over six years, he should go do the filial thing. If *she* had parents, she wouldn't neglect them like he did his. Of course, if she had parents, they wouldn't be the kind who would engender neglect. There was nothing good about losing your parents young, but the consolation was that you got to make them perfect, as they surely would not have been if they had lived into your adolescence.

She started to cry again, when she thought about how alone she was in the world. She forgot about her friends, her sister, her colleagues – what were they in the face of her orphanhood? And now, she was losing her husband as well.

Well, not losing him, just getting rid of him for a while. She would never be able to cure herself of this stupid suspicion while he was still around, making it worse every time he opened his mouth. And she knew herself – she'd egg him on, handing him the shovel so he could dig himself another hole to fall into, not because she wanted him to fall but because she couldn't help herself. She'd work herself up into a state of ungovernable perversity and go after him, just because a stupid, ugly, evil idea had crawled into her brain like some disgusting roach, befouling everything it touched.

'I want to go home!' she wailed again and she realised what she really wanted was for her home to feel safe again, to feel like it was *hers*. Ever since Harry had moved in, she hadn't had a minute to herself; he was always here, always hogging the apartment, hogging the bed, hogging the bathtub, hogging the computer, hogging her every thought. Everything was about him. He usurped everything. Even this, even the kid's death – the only thing he was concerned about was whether or not the cops suspected him; he hadn't shown the least concern for *her*, for how this might be affecting *her*.

And how was it affecting her? She didn't know; she couldn't think. Harry would be back any second and what would she say to him? She didn't want to see him; didn't want him – her own husband! – to touch her. Why couldn't he go away somewhere, why did he have to be here all the time, taking up every inch of space, except when he occasionally went out to deliver some gram or other . . .

Paul! That was it! She could send him up to Paul's place up north. He was always saying he needed time alone, without interruptions – the interruptions being *her*, in her own apartment! – and Paul was always offering his house.

It was perfect. Of course getting Harry out of Manhattan was no easy task; it took her a month to talk him into taking the ferry to Staten Island for the day. Somehow she had to make him *want* to go. How? She didn't know; she could figure that out when he came back with the bagels. But go he would, one way or another, and while he was gone she could find out what really happened on that roof.

She glanced at her watch. Six fifteen. Paul probably wasn't up yet, but she would call him anyway. This was an emergency.

She climbed back through the window and went to call Paul.

Eleven

Harry thought about taking the car, since he'd have to move it later in any case, but decided to run up to 55th Street instead. He hadn't been out before dawn in years, not since the good old days when they'd stay up all night, drinking bad wine and arguing about Flannery O'Connor and Catholicism, something neither of them knew anything about, but back then, it didn't matter if they didn't know anything about what they were talking about. Their passion, their joy at being in the same room, talking about books and words and writers and ideas, made it seem as if they *did* know everything and they would argue so convincingly, so eloquently, that they had to believe what they said because it sounded so true. Every once in a while, they'd stop, mid-sentence, look at each other as if realising for the first time how unspeakably alluring the other was, and they'd race across the room, leap into bed, and make love while bellowing John Donne at each other.

'Mark but this flea!' Harry would pant and Clark would purr, catlike, 'I am two fools . . .'

The street people were all tucked away in their cardboard beds, snoring and dreaming of whatever it was the truly indigent dreamed of. Food, Harry supposed, a roof over their heads. He shuddered, feeling lucky again for the first time in two days – he'd heard or read somewhere that most people in America are only two paychecks away from the street. Two of Clark's paychecks.

The last time he had run up First Avenue, he'd been trying to run out the sound of that kid falling into the courtyard. One minute you're alive; the next you're a sack of laundry. One minute you're living the life of Riley, the next you're sleeping in the container for some yuppie's Sub-Zero. McFate. Chasing Humbert H across America; chasing Harry B up First Avenue in the dawn.

'I'm *alive*!' Harry shouted, pounding his chest and sprinting across 14th Street, 'I'm Harry Butler and I'm *alive*!'

He began da-daing the theme song from *Rocky* as the sun began emerging from somewhere in Queens and the garbage trucks gorged themselves with last night's droppings. His vision had never been so sharp, the Con Edison building had never seemed so beautiful, so palatially umber. And up ahead, he could see the UN, that multinational monolith of hope, where people of every color, race, religion, ethnicity mingled together without blowing each other to bits!

'I'm *alive*!' he shouted as he courteously crossed over to the east side of the street to avoid the homeless encampment, 'I love New York!'

Butler felt as if something new was happening to him, but he didn't know what. He wasn't going to end up like some

Ivan Illich, lying on his death bed full of regrets, getting stuffed into a sack, over and over; he lived every moment of his life, followed every dream, every whim, every desire and while it was true they got him into trouble more often than not, well, that too was living, although not as much fun.

And, best of all, he'd done it without ever leaving Manhattan.

New York! Harry loved everything about it; living here was like being a citizen of the world – he could play Mah Jong down in Chinatown, then eat pastrami at Cohen's, then watch the fat old Italian men play boccie ball on Houston Street. He could run uptown to the old Irish tenements, stop in a bar for a Harp or a Guinness, keep on going, through the Hungarian neighborhood with shopfronts full of spices, into the German, get a schnitzel to eat while he crossed over into Spanish Harlem to watch the young girls dancing on their stoops while the buildings throbbed with salsa and merengue. Then west, to Harlem, up to City College where he'd sat in crumbling stone nuns' quarters, listening to his professor quoting French medieval poetry with a Bronx accent. Then up a bit, to Sugar Hill where the rich Harlemites lived, where Alexander Hamilton shot Aaron Burr, or vice versa – Clark would know! – then down St Nicholas Terrace, happy as Santa Claus, soul food at Sylvia's, collard greens and barbecue, the real thing, not that ketchup-coated backyard crap; across 125th – Hi, Apollo! – down Broadway, past Columbia, another alma mater, and all he had to do was close his eyes to bring back the ghosts of the CORE boycott, marching in front of John Jay Hall with his DON'T BUY JIM CROW FOOD sign, picketing Queen Freddie of Greece when she came to get her honorary degree, and best of all, those early meetings of the Sexual Freedom Forum –

Daphne the Wild Woman, oh God, how could he have forgotten about her? Through another little pocket of salsa and dreamy, dancing girls; into and out of Shrinkville; Lincoln Center – the Met! Chekov at the Vivian Beaumont! Jazz all summer at Damrosch Park! And it was free! Cut across Central Park – avoid Midtown and all those Suits at all costs, except to go to the Library. Delacorte – free Shakespeare! Bandshell – free Opera! Great Lawn – free Philharmonic and whatever rock star was on tour. Free! Free! Free! A city made for the plebs, and pleb he was, down to his hand-torn toenails. Back down the East Side, to 8th Street to steam himself off and get beaten with a branch at the Russian Baths. Around the world in four hours! Why go anywhere else?

He cut west and headed up Second Avenue. A few insomniac cabbies, the newspaper trucks, the voracious garbagemobiles. Here and there, a bleary-eyed shopkeeper, unleashing his metal accordion gates, sending them grumbling up into their daytime hiding place, revealing all the goodies they'd protected all night – flowers, cigarettes, the usual deli display of wrapped bread and dangling sausage.

Mine, mine, mine! Harry gloated; this world is mine, New York is mine, I live here! He stopped, as if struck for the first time by the enormity of it. 'I *live* here!' he shouted, 'I live *here*!'

He wanted to get down on his knees and kiss the sidewalk, but though it was cleaner than it would be later, it wasn't clean enough for that. He had Butler do it, in his mind: *Butler collapsed on his knees, and weepingly kissed the cracked . . .*, no. Cracked was too common. The sidewalk was more than cracked, it was . . . he looked down, tried to decide what it was. It wasn't, in fact, even cracked, it was just plain old cement, with no hardy little treelets struggling to break through, but who cared? *His* sidewalk would be cracked, and cracked by a hardy little treelet, and he would bend down and kiss that little shoot, the spirit of New York, struggling through no matter what they tried to pour over it.

He wanted to go home and work, but Clark was there. Clark, his darling damsel, who had sent him out on a quest for the perfect vegetable cream cheese. Perversity or pregnancy?

Maybe it wouldn't be so bad, having a kid. Another little Harry. Harold Earl Butler the Third. Harry cubed. Little Prince Hal. And he could play Falstaff to his own kid, Falstaff of the *Merry Wives*, that is, not the bloated old corpuscle of *Henry IV, Part 2*. But what if he *did* turn out to be a bloated old corpuscle? Would his Hal desert him? Usurp him? Unthrone him in his own bathtub-in-kitchen castle?

He thought about his own father, probably waking up right now, turning his face and looking at his wheezing wife, with plastic tubes stuck up her nostrils and her lips quivering fishlike, grasping at air bubbles. There was no bawdy, rowdy old age in store for his poor old dad, no throwing off of the covers and shouting, '"For God's sake hold your tongue, and let me love!"'

And Clark, would *she* desert him, turn her love and attention on Halsey-Walsey to the detriment of his father-wather? Would she, in an attempt to make up for her own parentless childhood, quit her job and devote herself to making every second of her babykin's existence pleasurable? Would she, dangling his little progeny on her hip, demand that Harry abandon his life's work and go out and get a *job*? And what kind of a job could he get? Past work experience: telegram singer. Costumes included.

He looked behind him, to see if perhaps McFate had sneaked up on him unawares with his own unsavory agenda in his many-stickered suitcase. The only person on the street was an early-rising bum, hobbling up Second Avenue for the first of his hand-outs.

Harry shivered, and bolted the last two blocks to Bagel Heaven.

Twelve

'I don't know anything about you,' Clark said before he even got through the door.

She was sitting at the table, wrapped in her bathrobe, fingering a piece of notepaper.

'What?' he asked.

'I don't know anything about you,' she said again.

Harry stood in the doorway, clutching the bag of bagels, wondering whether he should just turn around, close the door, and try again. He sighed, came in, tossed the bag on the table and sat down.

'What do you mean?' he asked. 'You know everything about me.'

'No I don't. What about your history? I don't know anything about your history.'

'There's nothing to know.'

'That's ridiculous. Of course there's something to know. You *have* a history, don't you?'

'Not in the exciting sense.'

'I'm not giving you a score, Harry. I just want to know who you are.'

He sighed. This must have to do with the kid again. He was right, the damn kid had moved in, kicked him out of his bed, whispered 'bagels' in Clark's ear and she had sent him off into the night.

'You know who I am,' he said, pulling a poppy-seed bagel from the bag, 'I'm *me*. Want one?'

'But who *is* that?' she asked, waving the bagel away. 'Who is Harry Butler? What do I know about you, really?'

'You know everything about me!' he said, 'You've mined me down to the core, what do you want?' He pushed the bagel at her again. 'I thought you wanted bagels. And cream cheese. I ran all the way up to 55th Street for these. By the way, did Burr kill Hamilton or Hamilton kill Burr up in Sugar Hill?'

She shook her head. 'Burr killed Hamilton. In New Jersey.'

'Not Sugar Hill?' Harry asked.

'I just told you,' Clark said. A little more testily than was necessary, Harry thought.

'Are you sure?' he asked. In the mood she was in, it was too much to hope she was merely playing with him, tossing him a bit of misinformation to cheer herself up. He felt vaguely disappointed in his memory, which so surely had placed the hot-headed Founding Fathers up in Harlem. He had been so certain of the venue of the shooting, if not the outcome. It was almost as if his memory had betrayed him and he wondered if this was what it felt like to get old, to suddenly find one's senses, one's functions, abandoning ship, deserting, running off and leaving one helpless and befuddled. He had been so *sure*. He could practically see the two of them, dressed in their tights and frock coats, standing atop the hill, back to back, waiting to begin counting off paces.

Unlike Clark, Harry didn't always need to be right, but he hated to be wrong. Not knowing was fine, but being wrong was humiliating; it was like being in grade school and blurting out a stupid answer, when his entire body would be engulfed in a wildfire blush as the whole room stared at him and giggled.

'Are you sure you're sure?' he demanded.

'Of course I'm sure I'm sure. I wouldn't have said it if I wasn't sure.'

'Why New Jersey?' he asked and Clark glared at him.

'Maybe that's where the Duelling Grounds were.'

The Duelling Grounds! Butler had a date at the Duelling Grounds . . .

'Well, then who shot whom in Sugar Hill?'

Clark wanted to know why he was so interested in murders, all of a sudden.

'I'm not interested in murders,' he said. He didn't like the way she was looking at him, with her eyebrows drawn together in an angry V. Since her eyes were gray, she could do 'steely' to perfection and she was doing it now. She was up to something. The little copy boys were running amok in her brain and Harry could see that the news they were relaying wasn't going to be good for him.

She grabbed a bagel and began playing with it, tearing pieces off and rolling them into little pellets, the kind they used to make after lunch in Mrs Martin's class; Fartin' Martin they called her, because she did, constantly. She'd be standing at the board writing down the original thirteen states or the dates of the Constitutional Conventions or something equally boring to pre-adolescent boys, and she'd let out the loudest, longest, unstoppable farts; wet, juicy ones, the kind boys delighted in, and she'd keep right on writing, as if her rear end wasn't backfiring like an old jalopy, as if she couldn't care less, as if she couldn't hear the boys tittering and scraping in their desks for their straws, as if she was surprised when the volley of bread bullets descended upon her. It never occurred to them that she couldn't help it, that she was probably standing up there, dying of shame, shaking a little and wondering how much longer before she fell apart altogether, that she was merely getting old, losing control of her functions, and that someday it would happen to them. But of course it wouldn't occur to them to have any sympathy for the old scarecrow; they were kids, it was their job to revel in anything scatological, to make cruel jokes, to torment the afflicted. Youth is wasted on the young, George Bernard says, but the truth is, the middle-aged would never have the heart for it.

Clark had a little pile of bagel pellets piled up in front of her like a stack of minuscule white cannonballs. 'I don't know who you were as a kid,' she said as she added one last ball neatly to the top. 'What kind of trouble did you get into? Did you torture animals? Did you paint water towers? Did you torment fat kids with glasses?'

'I *was* a fat kid with glasses,' Harry said.

'You see!?' Clark crowed, 'I never knew that!'

Harry pulled the container of cream cheese from the bag and thrust it at Clark. 'Are you pregnant?' he demanded.

'Pregnant!' she cried, 'Of course I'm not pregnant. What on earth gave you that idea?'

Harry shrugged. 'Well, it isn't every day you send me out on a pre-dawn quest for cream cheese and greet me at the door with the accusation that I'm some sort of psycho stranger.'

Clark said she wasn't accusing him of being some kind of psycho stranger.

'You are too.'

'I am not.'

'You are too.'

Why else would she be trying to dig around in his childhood, looking for relics of deviance?

'You know me as well as anyone is ever going to know me in this world,' he said, 'so shut up and eat your bagel. I ran all the way up to fucking Bagel Heaven to get you your fucking cream cheese and your fucking bagels and you're not even *eating* them.'

Clark told him not to be so vulgar. It wasn't that she objected to the word, after all, she heard it a thousand times a day. But she hated the way it sounded in Harry's mouth; simultaneously sibilant and guttural, wet and rough, like something erupting from the depths of some swamp. Coming from Harry, it wasn't an obscenity, it was a nightmare.

'Well, then,' Harry asked. 'Why *do* you want to know about my childhood all of a sudden?'

Clark dipped a bagel ball into the cream cheese and popped it into her mouth. 'I just want to know everything about you, that's all. You're my husband. I *should* know everything about you.'

'What is this, some kind of quiz? Are you making up one of those stupid tests for one of your magazines or something? "*Did You Marry Mr Wrong?* Take our test and find out!"'

'Ha ha,' Clark said mirthlessly.

Something was up. Definitely. This was all a ruse, but with Clark there was no telling where her ruses would lead. The connective thread between what she *seemed* to be doing and what she actually *was* doing was often based on a special kind of logic that was Clark's very own. If you really thought about it, it made some bizarre kind of sense, but the thing was, it was never anything you would ever think about thinking about, if Clark hadn't foisted it on you. He would fight ruse with ruse. A battle he never won, but what the hell?

'Not everything,' he said. 'Aren't you supposed to want to keep the mystery alive, the allure or whatever they call it?'

'I want to know who I'm married to!' she cried.

'You're married to me, and if that's not good enough, then maybe you should be married to someone else.'

'Well, maybe I should.'

They glared at each other.

'Like who?' Harry asked.

'I don't know. Someone I know something about.'

'And just who do you know better than me?'

Clark had to think about that. She *didn't* know anyone better than she knew Harry. That was the problem with people, you could know only so much and then there was that black hole that was the human heart, completely inaccessible, unless perhaps with the help of truth serum. She decided to change tactics.

'What are you trying to hide?'

'I'm not trying to hide anything!' Harry cried. 'I had a normal boring childhood in a normal boring subdivision of a normal boring town!'

'What's "normal"?'

'Oh, Christ.' Was she going to some kind of support group? What kind of support group would she need to be in? Harry hoped she wasn't on pills again – she'd be furious with him for not noticing the difference. And the truth was, he *hadn't* noticed the difference – he'd been floored when she came home one night, back before they were married, red-eyed and soggy-nosed, wanting to make amends. 'Amends for what?' he had asked and needless to say, she didn't make any.

Clark crossed her arms over her chest, like a child about to throw a tantrum, and turned her back on him. Good, Harry thought, she'll give me the silent treatment for a while.

Actually, there *were* things Clark didn't know about him. But they were so small, so petty, that they weren't worth knowing or so awful he wished he didn't know them himself. There was something to be said for everything, Harry thought, including repression.

What was she after? Harry leaned back in his chair, teetering dangerously. 'You'll break the chair and your back, too,' his mother used to say when he'd do that, always thinking about the chair first, his welfare second. Was that the kind of thing Clark wanted to hear? My mother cared more about the furniture than me? And what would she *do* with that little piece of Harriabilia? Would she think of him as some self-pitying moron, bewailing his mother's cold materialism? Or would she see it as a sign of his urge to destroy things, 'proof' of his destructive tendencies? That she wouldn't see it as what it was – something every self-respecting suburban Mom bleated at children teetering in chairs, and something every child so bleated at remembered when they leaned their chairs back – was unquestionable.

She turned around, looked at him, and it hit him so hard it took his breath away.

He felt himself falling, not from the chair, which he let down with a thud, but as if from a great height, a mountain or a tower.

Or a roof.

Thirteen

It was insane, but insane or not, she suspected him.

It was one thing to be suspected by the cops; they were just doing their job. But Clark? She was his wife; it was her job to believe in him, to trust him, to defend him.

It was almost as if he could see the suspicions forming in her head. He imagined the copy boys setting up the screen and the projector to play a bunch of fluttering film clips of things he'd said, things he'd done – benign, silly, meaningless things on their own, but strung together in Clark's hypercritical mind, they became Evidence.

'Could you?' Clark was asking in one film clip, a relatively recent one, from last month. 'Could you kill someone? Just for kicks?'

They were coming out of Theatre 80. Hitchcock double feature. *Strangers on a Train* and *Rope*.

'Could you?' she demanded, as if it were even conceivable.

'Sure,' he said.

Just to shock her, just to watch her jump up and down, just to watch her eyebrows bounce. Harry loved Clark's eyebrows. Wide, fuzzy, deep blue-black man's eyebrows, wriggling all over her forehead like trained caterpillars, animating her, giving her away.

'You're just saying that to shock me,' she had said, pulling her jacket tight and zipping it up to her neck. Hard to believe that just a few weeks ago they had needed jackets.

Harry imagined her rolling the film clip forward, watching as they squeezed their way through the line of people waiting for the next show, standing there surprisingly patient and orderly in their black leather jackets, smelling slightly of damp, even though it hadn't been raining.

'Could *you*?' he had asked her, when they got outside.

'Of course not!' she had snapped. 'What a stupid question!'

I love you, he had thought, but she wouldn't know that. There was no voice-over from Harry in her internal news-reel; she couldn't know he was thinking, I love you. I love your indignation. It was so Clark, so female, so adorably unreasonable.

'I just can't believe it,' she had said, 'I just can't believe you'd do something like that.'

It was too cold to be standing on the sidewalk arguing about whether or not Harry could kill someone for kicks. It was as stupid a question for him as it was for her, but of course that wasn't the point. He hadn't been sure what the point was, what she was trying to get at, what she wanted to know. Whatever it was, he would give it to her, but he liked her to work for it.

It gave her the creeps, Clark had said as Harry had

placed his arm around her shoulder and turned her towards DoJo's, it gave her the creeps to think about people like that. What was to prevent one from killing *her*?

Ah, Harry thought, that was it. Fear. She's afraid. Afraid of some Leopold or Loeb lurking around the corner, looking for someone to stab, just to prove he's superior to a corpse. She's afraid of the randomness of it, the out-of-nowhereness of it, and how that makes her eternally vulnerable.

'Don't worry, I'll protect you,' he had told her, pulling her in closer, fitting her tightly into his side, rubbing her arm reassuringly, but she was having none of that. She didn't want to be protected, she said, she wanted to be safe.

'Samey-same,' Harry had said but Clark insisted it wasn't the same at all. 'If you're safe, you don't *need* to be protected,' she had said, wriggling out of his grasp. 'He was their *friend*,' she had said. 'He was their *friend* and they killed him. Of course, in real life he was their cousin. They killed him "in the interest of science", whatever that was supposed to mean. Clarence Darrow was their lawyer. I lost a lot of respect for him after I read that.'

And now, staring at him narrow-eyed over the rim of her coffee mug, dipping bagel pellets in the cream cheese and popping them in her mouth absent-mindedly, she was running all that through her head. Losing respect for him, Harry. If he looked hard enough, he could probably see himself reflected in her pupils, standing in the lobby of Theatre 80, grinning malevolently and saying, 'Sure.' She might even be editing it. Putting words into his mouth, having him say something like, 'Sure. I could do that', or 'Sure, sounds like fun to me.' Something evil, something she could convert into proof, and even though he didn't say it, even though it was just a figment of her imagination, she would believe it.

She kept staring at him, unblinking, and he searched her eyes for clues as to what she was seeing. He leaned forward, nearly nose to nose, and looked into her dark black pupils, ringed with gray, almost silver. Her 'windows to the soul'. Indeed, there he was, Harry Butler, his face stretched out like silly putty, but still himself. He blinked, then looked again, and imagined he saw himself changing, sprouting rough thick hair from his cheeks. The tips of his ears became pointed and hairy; his nose receded into a little wet black snout, his mouth opened, revealing long, sharp, glittering teeth.

Werewolf, he thought miserably, my wife looks at me and sees Lon Chaney on a bad night.

'Grrr,' he said.

Clark shook her head and put down her mug.

'What?' she asked.

'Grrr.'

'Grrr?' she asked. 'Grrr what?'

'Grrr,' he said, 'you know, a growl. The sound werewolves make.'

Clark wanted to know if she'd missed something.

'You think I'm a monster,' Harry said.

Clark sighed and try to hide behind the mug again.

'You do,' he insisted. 'You think I had something to do with that kid's . . .'

He trailed off, unable to say 'death'.

'That kid's . . . demise,' he finally said.

'As a matter of fact, I *was* thinking about that kid's *demise*,' she said. 'I was thinking that he was only twenty-two years old. He was barely old enough to *drink*, Harry! He was such a nerdy-looking guy, he probably hadn't even had sex yet! He was just a baby, a little hick kid who came to the City because he wanted to be Somebody and where else can a kid who wants to be Somebody go? He thought this was the place to be. He was just like me, Harry. He came here because he wanted to live and what happens? He dies. He dies a stupid, ugly, senseless death and all because he wanted to get a glimpse of me. *Me*, Harry, not you.'

She started to cry. Oh shit, Harry thought, not again.

'You think I—' he began and Clark jumped up.

'You, you, you,' she sobbed. 'You think everything is about *you*.' But so what? As far as Harry was concerned, everything *was* about him and that didn't make him much different from anybody else, except he was honest about it. Who *didn't* think everything was about himself? Or herself? No doubt even Mother Teresa thought everything was about her work with lepers in India and as far as Harry was concerned, that was the way it should be.

Clark was stomping around the kitchen, banging crockery about. Harry was overwhelmed with desire for her. The time wasn't right, but that made the idea of standing up, dragging her over to the bed, ripping open her bathrobe, ravishing her, in fact, all the more enticing.

It was out of the question, of course. He knew he'd have to wait until she stopped crying, until she'd made herself solid again, but the thought of enveloping himself in all that warm, mushy softness was too much to bear.

She glared at his lap and Harry blushed.

'Ugh,' she said, 'you are just too disgusting.'

'I can't help it,' he said.

'Christ Almighty, you *are* a monster. Here I am, talking about death, for God's sake, and you want to screw.'

Harry thought that was perfectly reasonable. A purely cellular response to the idea of death. It wasn't him; it was Instinct, calling on him to preserve the race.

There was no point in arguing with her. Usually, he would fight back and they would circle around one another like boxers, watching for an opportunity to lay the other flat, waiting for the instant of the lowered guard, just for a second and WHAM! 'You didn't show up when I played Macbeth!' she'd shriek. 'Yeah, and you took the opportunity to go to bed with that Panamanian has-been!' and on and on, dancing around each other, beating each other with their failings, their slights, their inadequacies, until they'd collapse, exhausted but free, if only briefly, of all the resentment, jealousy and spite that poisoned them. Clean, pure, they'd abandon themselves to wildly sweet lovemaking – glorious, magnificent, rollicking, off the Richter Scale screwing.

He'd never admit it to Clark – he'd never admit it to anyone, if he did, he'd have Clark and her colleagues at the Domestic Abuse Hotline over here, beating him to death with their telephone cords – but it made him think he understood the appeal of wife-beating. Not that he wanted to *do* it; he didn't, he wasn't a violent kind of guy, but if Clark and his lovemaking was so fantastic after just jabbing each other with words, what would it be like after beating each other bloody? 'I will never understand it,' Clark would say every week when she came home from her shift. 'How can they go back?' but Harry thought he knew. It was the sex.

Harry was afraid sex was off his own menu. Gone. Dead, like the kid in the courtyard. Clark hadn't let him touch her since the cops left. Damn stupid kid. Moved right in; sleeping in the middle of their bed like some Oedipal brat.

'You suspect me,' Harry said.

Clark blushed, but said that was ridiculous, of course she didn't suspect him.

'You do,' he said, 'I can see it in your eyes.'

'Well, it's *your* fault. You're the one who brought it up in the first place. If you hadn't brought it up, it never would have occurred to me that you were suspectable.'

'What kind of a word is "suspectable"?'

Clark ignored him, grabbed a handful of clothes from the floor near the bed and stomped into the loo. She tried to slam the door, but it was just a piece of flimsy plywood. It made a little whooshy noise, pathetically undramatic.

What if she did suspect him? It didn't matter if it was insane – suspecting him gave her something to do, something to mull over in her mind to avoid the guilt she might have to feel if she didn't have him to blame. After all, it was *her* fault the kid was up there in the first place. If it hadn't been for Clark, he probably would have been hanging out at Yaffa or someplace, someplace street level or below.

But how could she suspect him if Harry hadn't even known the kid existed until he splattered on to the courtyard? Maybe she *was* lying. Maybe she *did* know the kid all along, maybe he *was* her love slave and she'd given him the boot and he couldn't take it and jumped.

No, he told himself, suspecting Clark was just as ridiculous as suspecting himself. Things were getting a little on the paranoid side. It didn't help that the cops were still nosing around, still asking questions. 'Don't leave town,' O'Donnell said when he left the other day, and while Harry wanted to believe it was meant as a joke, still, it made him nervous.

The fact was, if they did suspect Harry, which was

insane, but if they did, he was in deep shit. He had no way of proving his innocence, absolutely none. He had been alone in the building. After he left, he went first to the health food store, where the girl with the nose ring might remember him, but only because he had talked – rather callously, he thought in retrospect – about watching the body fall. *Yes, Your Honor, Miss Nose-Ring said, I guess you could describe his affect as sociopathic. No feeling whatsoever. He raised his hand and said 'Whoosh.' Then he lowered it and said 'Plop.' Like he was talking about a piece of garbage or something, not a human being.*

Then he went to Lenny's, and what could be more sinister and suspicious than asking your best pal for an alibi? *I told him no, Your Honor, I mean what else could I do, I couldn't lie for him, and he got all huffy and yelled at me and left.*

He had passed hundreds – maybe thousands – of people on the street but who would remember having seen him? He'd had no contact with anyone, other than a wave at the guy at the corner news-stand and a grumbled threat to the purple-haired Punk kid who lived in front of the library. Who were they to him? Just figures, making up the background of his life. They had no name, no identity, just as he had none for them.

He had never felt so alone in his life. And now even Clark, even his dearly beloved wife, was pulling away from him, leaning back and eyeing him with suspicion.

Fourteen

Clark emerged from the loo, wrinkled but dressed.

'Are you wearing that?' Harry asked. 'You look like you slept on the subway or something.'

Clark tossed her head. 'So what?' she asked, tugging her black tube skirt down to her knees. She was wearing that and a rumpled black and white striped tunic-top. She had her hair pulled back in a matching black and white garter belt thing – 'scrunchie,' he remembered with a little wave of shame – and he could see the wisps of downy silver at the nape of her neck. It made him want to weep, that gray, it gave her a frailty, a vulnerability she would never acknowledge, and that made him love her all the more. Harry had never really thought about the two of them growing old together, mainly because he couldn't imagine *himself* growing old, but now the image seemed rather appealing, kind of cozy and warm-bready. It gave him a weird nostalgic kind of feeling, nostalgia for a future that might not happen, and it made him want to weep. He felt a sudden yearning for rocking chairs, a front porch, little neighborhood brats to terrify with his Bela Lugosi imitations. He wanted a little white-haired Clark there, beside him, slapping his arm playfully and saying, 'Now, Harry, don't torment the poor things.'

Instead, she was snarling at him. 'It will give them something to talk about at work,' she was saying. 'They can spend the whole week wondering why I've been sleeping in my clothes.'

'They'll think you're having an affair.'

'Let them,' Clark said, 'what do you care what they think?'

'I don't,' Harry said, but he did, he cared very much. If the women at work thought Clark was having an affair, they would think Harry was losing his touch. They'd look at him with pity and scorn when he stopped in, as he did periodically, to pick up Clark's keys when he locked himself out, to drop off an important piece of mail, to take Clark to lunch. Worse yet, their thinking it might make it so. Clark was not a person of moderate appetites, of any sort, and if she wasn't letting Harry touch her, it wouldn't be long before someone else would be. Cuckold was a great word, but not one Harry ever wanted to be used in reference to himself.

As if she were reading his mind, she sat back down and reached across the table for his hand.

'Look,' she said, 'I'm sorry. Well, kind of sorry. I'm sorry I yelled at you. But I'm not sorry about what I said. It's true. You *do* only think about yourself.'

'It's not true!' Harry insisted, 'I think about you sometimes.'

Clark threw back her head and laughed. Harry didn't see what was so funny, but he grinned anyway, happy to have made her laugh.

'I've been thinking . . .' she began.

'Oh no! Not that!' Harry teased, trying to keep her laughing. That was the key – make her remember how much she adored him. He pulled on her arm, pulled her out of the chair, over to his lap.

'I've been thinking,' she said again and stopped.

'OK, OK,' Harry said, 'out with it.'

She took a deep breath.

'I think we should take a break from each other.'

She said it fast and then buried her head in his armpit. The words whistled past his ear, like a train shrieking in the distance. He heard them, but he didn't want to take them in; he wanted them to keep going, zooming across the bed, past the bookcases, over the computer and out the window into oblivion. How could he not love this woman, this woman burrowing her head in his armpit, she was so ridiculous. He didn't want to take a break from her, ever, he wanted to sprinkle her with a magic potion, shrink her into a little portable Clark he could carry around in his pocket, wear round his neck on a chain.

It frightened him, his need for her. This was something new, something he'd have to think about, something he wasn't quite sure he liked. His love for her, well, that was familiar, that he understood, that he accepted. But part of the deal, as far as he was concerned, was that *he* was the one who was needed. Clark needed him and, out of his beneficent love for her, he gave her himself.

There was nothing else to do. He'd have to scare her.

'Funny,' he said, 'I was thinking the same thing.'

Clark raised her head. She wasn't smiling; she looked appropriately surprised. A little chagrined. Good, Harry thought, chagrined is good. Put the fear of God into her.

Clark had always been terrified of his leaving her, and with good reason. She had stolen him away from another woman. Good old Lorna. She'd put up a fight, Lorna had, in fact she'd been damn well demented. She'd call up Clark at the *BAG* office, making progressively wilder threats: 'I'll have you know I'm Vito Genovese's niece,' she told Clark one time. 'Get lost, if you value your knees.' Clark had been furious, but she liked the knee line so much she used it as the title for a performance piece. Lorna too was a thief – she'd stolen Harry from Kate, and so on down the line, an endless series of thefts with himself as the prize. It made him feel like Helen of Troy, although, naturally, he kept that to himself.

'I'm glad you're taking it so well,' Clark said, getting up off Harry's lap and walking over to the counter to pour herself another cup of coffee. 'And, actually, it would be good. It would give you some time to be alone and finish your book.'

Harry asked where she would be going.

'I'm not going anywhere,' she said, '*you* are.'

'Me?' Harry said, 'Why me? You're the one who wants the "break."'

Clark shrugged. 'I've got a job, Harry. And besides, this is *my* apartment.'

'*Your* apartment? Excuse me, I thought we were married. I thought this was *our* apartment.'

'I was here first,' Clark said. 'I'm the one on the lease.'

'And I'm not?' Harry cried. 'You mean to tell me you never put my name on the *lease*?'

Clark shook her head. 'I never thought it was an issue,' she said. 'And besides, I pay the rent.'

'And I do all the work!'

Clark swept her arm around the apartment, like a

game show hostess, from the warped loo door to the sagging bookcases to the rickety clothes alcove.

'And thank you very much, Mr Fix-it.'

Well, what did she expect? His imagination was his treasure, not his hands. He wasn't a Handy Guy – you learned that kind of thing from your father and Harry's father had been a perfume manufacturer's rep. He spent his weekends down in the basement, like all the Handy Dads, but instead of building dog houses or gazeboes, he mixed scents, trying to come up with the smell that would make him a million.

'I've got a job, too,' Harry said feebly.

'I've already talked to Paul and he said you could use his house —'

'You already talked to Paul?'

Clark shrugged again. It was her all-purpose gesture, signifying everything from disdain to surprise to disclaiming responsibility.

'Since when are you my social secretary?' Harry asked.

'Excuse me,' Clark mimicked, 'I thought we were married.'

Maybe we both thought wrong, Harry didn't say. It would be too tempting a thought for Clark to grab and run with, out the door, out of his life, not just for now but perhaps for ever.

'Thank you for arranging my life for me,' Harry said, 'But it's out of the question. I can't leave town.'

Clark wanted to know why not.

'I'm a witness,' Harry reminded her, 'I'm not supposed to go anywhere.'

'That's nonsense,' Clark said, 'you can go anywhere you want. You just have to tell Detective What's-His-Name.'

'O'Donnell,' Harry said.

'Right,' Clark said vaguely, 'O'Donnell.'

That was odd. Clark never forgot a name, never. She remembered every person she ever met and that was part of her charm, part of her power. She'd run into someone she'd met briefly, years before, hold out her hand and say, 'Oh! Susie Jones!' giving her the gift of her own name, the gift of feeling memorable. Harry himself could never remember anyone, although O'Donnell was certainly burned into his memory. Young. Natty. In pretty good shape. Handsome, Harry supposed. He didn't like this one bit.

'You just call him up,' Clark was saying, 'tell him you're going to Paul's and that's that.'

'No. That's not that. Maybe they need me for something,' he said. Like a turn on the grill, he thought. Like a line-up. Like torture to force a confession. Maybe Paul's place wasn't such a bad idea after all. It might be just the right spot, to hide away for a while. And Clark was right, maybe he could finish *Butler by Butler*. Maybe it would be good to get away from the city for a while, give himself perspective, the clarity of memory without the clamoring insistence of reality mucking things up. And, although he would never admit this to Clark, it might not be so bad to get away from the apartment, which, quite frankly, was giving him the creeps, now that the kid's ghost had moved in.

But Paul's place was in the middle of nowhere. Surrounded by woods and forests and wild animals.

Harry hated Nature. Clark had once dragged him on a camping trip and he had complained the whole time – he hated the idea of all those slimy blind creatures of the lower orders crawling around a few inches under his sleeping bag. He preferred cement under his feet and although God only knew what was crawling around under *that*, it was unlikely it could get through.

'Harry,' Clark was saying, 'they're not going to need you for anything.'

'How do you know? Maybe they're uncovering a piece of evidence as we speak and they'll need me to tell them I don't know anything about it.'

'Right,' Clark said.

'And besides, there's no phone up there. If they needed me for anything, they couldn't get hold of me.' He gave Clark his best little-boy-lost look. '*You* couldn't get hold of me.'

'If they need you, they'll call the Sheriff or the State Police or the Mounties, whatever they have up there, and they'll come get you.'

'And what about you?' Harry asked, winsomely he hoped. 'What if *you* need me?'

'I'll come up on weekends,' Clark said. 'You can read me what you've written during the week. We can correspond. It will be romantic, Harry, just like the old days. We can lie outside, under the stars, and you can read to me by candlelight.'

'But I hate the country,' Harry said. 'You're so unprotected up there. What if I get attacked by bears?'

'You're not going to get attacked by bears,' Clark said.

'What about bugs?' he asked. 'They've got those killer mosquitoes up there. What if I get malaria? Or that other thing they get up there, that thing Bettina had, what's it called?'

'Beaver Fever,' Clark said.

'Yeah. What if I get Beaver Fever and I can't call anyone – you'll come up on the weekend and I'll be dead on the floor, half eaten by rabid squirrels.'

Clark told him to stop being such a baby.

'And what about aliens? Paul's place is up there in UFO land. Even *he* doesn't go up there any more, not since he got abducted.'

Clark was becoming exasperated. 'That's ridiculous,' she said. 'He just got drunk one night, fell in the woodpile, and doesn't remember how he got there.'

'Yeah? Well, how do you explain the tic tac toe game drawn on his back?'

'For Christ's sake, there wasn't a tic tac toe game on his back, he just made that up. There are no aliens, and even if there were, I'm sure they have better things to do than play tic tac toe on Paul Striker's back.'

Like abduct me, Harry thought. After all, it wasn't likely they could find a more perfect specimen, at least not up there. Paul was flabby and asthmatic and, frankly, a little on the stupid side, even if he had made a fortune. Good for doodling, not much else. But Harry was, well, Harry.

Harry didn't doubt that there was somebody out there, somewhere. How could there not be? We're just a speck of dust, one tiny mote among billions; it only made sense that there would be some kind of life on other motes. Why not? And why was it so implausible that they'd pass by here on their travels through the galaxy? They probably saw Earth as one big shopping mall, a gigantic pet store or something, and somewhere out there some Andromedan was probably walking around with Jimmy Hoffa on a leash.

'I'm going to be late,' Clark said. 'There's really nothing to discuss. We both need some time alone and since I can't go, you have to. I'll come up on weekends. You can take the computer.'

'I'm not going,' Harry said.

'You are,' Clark insisted.

'I am not,' he said.

'You are.'

'Not,' he said, but yes he was. This was a battle he was going to lose, but pride demanded he put up a fight. He didn't want to go, but the truth was, he didn't want to stay, either. He wanted his life to be exactly as it had been two days before and he had the unhappy feeling that was an impossibility.

'What about the juicer? I can't live without the juicer.'

'Take the damn juicer,' she said. 'Take whatever you want. Just go.'

She handed him a crumpled piece of paper.

'Here are the directions,' she said. 'The key is on a hook under the third step of the back porch.'

'My, you're efficient,' Harry said. Icily, he hoped, although he was afraid she could hear the little give-away squeak hiding in his voice.

She shrugged her Well-I-gotta-be-me shrug.

'I had the oil changed when I went to that conference. You're all set.'

'Thanks,' he said mournfully.

'Harry,' she said. She was trying to make her voice soft but she wasn't succeeding. She sounded like a school marm, pissed off at her favorite pupil who has turned out to be just as rotten as all the other brats. 'I need some time alone. I need to think. And so do you.'

She walked to the door. 'I'll see you on Saturday,' she said and left, without kissing him goodbye.

PART II

Fifteen

Standing on a cliff, peeing into the rocks below, it occurred to Harry that he could be standing in one of the few spots in America where one didn't have to wonder what it was 'before'. He thought, with a little shudder of excitement, that he might be standing exactly where Chingachgook, Hawkeye and Uncas ran happily through the forest, hot on the trail of a bear or an Iroquois, their hair flying behind them, shimmering in the mottled forest sunlight, their spears decorated with enemies' scalps . . .

Harry was glad he was alone; glad he didn't have to speak. He couldn't have; what he felt like doing was crying, but he didn't know why. It could have been anything: Clark booting him out, the kid's death, having to spend God only knew how long up in the wilderness by himself, the end of the Mohicans, anything. It could have been the beauty of the place: a sheer drop of gray-blue rock on one side of the ravine; monumental pines climbing the other; little budlets of pink and rose covering the shrubs along the path; a waterfall tumbling into the rocks below. He was so out of touch with Nature he had no vocabulary for it and he felt something he hadn't felt in years: a yearning, a voluptuous longing he vaguely remembered from childhood, when he'd go on trips with his parents in the car, traveling from the boring flat nothingness of Ohio into the wilderness of West Virginia where everything, from the road itself to the unruly rivers and stark raw mountains, seemed contemptuous, lawless, beyond the reach of man and his silly rules and Harry would sit in the back seat, crying, because he wanted to get out, get out of the car and out of his family and out of himself; he wanted to run up to the side of the mountain and embrace it, melt right into it, *be* it, and he was so filled with grief all he could do was weep.

It was his Boy Scout leader who explained it to him. 'It's nothing, kid,' he said. 'You're just experiencing your own insignificance,' and that was that, Harry walked out of the woods and never looked back. Why should he spend time with something that made him feel worthless? He quit Boy Scouts and as soon as he could, he packed up and moved to the City, to New York, where everything he saw, including the trees, had the mark of man.

He got back in the car and pulled out on the road. He hadn't seen another car in ages. It was kind of eerie: even though he was in the middle of nowhere, there should still be traffic passing through, people on their way to somewhere. Of course, it was still early in the season, barely the beginning of spring up here. He'd had to turn on the heat hours ago, turn on the heat and put on his sweats. What was Clark thinking, sending him up to the Arctic Circle by himself, to an unheated house right in the middle of the UFO Highway? What was he supposed to do for heat? For food? For sex?

He was sure of it. By the time he turned off the Thruway on to the Northway, he was convinced Clark had sent him away so she could go after O'Donnell. It didn't make much sense – Clark hated cops; she hated cops and O'Donnell wasn't her type, in any case. She disliked lean, hungry-looking men, or so she always said, she thought they weren't getting enough of something.

If there were things Clark didn't know about him – and God knew she had tried hard enough to winnow out every detail of his life – then it just stood to reason that he, who hadn't much bothered to look, wouldn't know everything about her.

What did he know about her, really? He had met Clark's sister Dee Dee – her only surviving relative – and her husband, a pair of epidemiologists at the University of Michigan. The husband – Bill or Bob, Harry could never remember – was studying the development of something called the Underclass, which as far as Harry could tell, was made up of well-armed poor people with short fuses. Dee Dee was tracking the evolution of destructive fads among teenage girls. They'd spent most of the weekend talking about unemployable boys with automatic weapons and girls who cut themselves, depressing stuff, but Harry admired their determination to make a difference in the world.

Harry wasn't political, at least not any more. He let Clark handle all that. He'd occasionally go to some rally or benefit, if Clark was performing, and she had even roped him into a three-day sit-in at Gracie Mansion to protest against the closing of a hospital, but he did it for the experience, not because he believed.

He would never admit it to Clark, but quite frankly, he didn't think any of it mattered. There was an old high-school football cheer that he thought summed up politics: 'Swing to the left/ Swing to the right/ Stand up/ Sit down/ Fight, fight, fight!' Personally, he preferred it when the swing was to the left – there was more grant money available and fewer people sleeping on the street – but in the long run, he didn't think it mattered. What mattered was life. What mattered was how people muddled through it, and no matter who was in power, the rich were rich and the poor were poor and they were the only ones who really felt the difference.

Clark would have a fit, if she knew that.

Could she, right now, be chasing after that lean and hungry detective? Harry remembered him hovering over Clark's shoulder, breathing his hot cop breath – stale coffee and cardboard cups – in her ear. She hadn't flinched, which was completely out of character for her, she should have been snapping her head away, wrinkling her nose in disgust and scraping her chair away from him.

Clark's ears were her Achilles' heel, Harry thought, and laughed aloud. Harry loved to mix his metaphors. He'd pile them on, five or six deep, just to watch Clark explode when she read them.

But it was true. Her ears *were* her Achilles' heel; no matter how mad she was, if Harry could get close enough to take a little nip of her ear, she was a goner – instant mush.

And was she letting O'Donnell take a bite of her? Was he nibbling away as Harry was driving back in seasons, going in reverse, the trees growing bare, the little pockets of gravelly snow along the side of the road expanding, creeping over the landscape like a glacier on speed, gobbling up everything in its path and leaving behind only the white nothingness of winter?

It wasn't fair. He'd already been through winter once this year, why should he have to go through it again just because some kid fell off a roof and Clark had developed a crush on the detective who wanted to fry her own husband? There was something sick about that, something really perverse.

If she was going to suspect him, it was only fair that he suspect her. And infidelity was as good as anything else to suspect her of. Could she have been screwing that kid? No, Harry thought. He didn't see how she could possibly have have had time. Unless she was lying about going to see Polly in the hospital or doing an extra shift on the Hotline or having to go to some conference on Information Retrieval. Or the energy. Harry kept her pretty busy in the sex department. So if she *did* manage to find the time and the energy to keep a love slave on the side, then Harry could do nothing but admire her stamina.

Butler's wife had a love slave, a horny kid she kept locked in the basement, chained to the boiler. He had been amusing, at first, but now she was sick of him – after all, how interesting can a guy who lets himself be chained to a furnace be? She had to get rid of him.

'I guess you didn't know your wife was seeing him,' Mason had sneered. Could she? Could she have been sneaking around, behind Harry's handsome back, giving that stripling a piece of Harry's pie?

Impossible, Harry thought.

But it was true that she had been growing more and more testy recently, waspish even. He hadn't really thought much about it; he just blamed it on her menses and shrugged it off.

What if she was sick of him, Harry? 'It's *my* apartment,' she had said; what if she was sick of supporting him; what if she had looked at his life and decided she'd like to be the supportee for a change?

Could she really suspect him? No. It was impossible. How could anyone suspect him of killing someone? That was madness – but the cops didn't know him, didn't know how peaceable he was. They probably thought everyone was capable of murder, given the right circumstances, and the circumstances, in this case, pointed directly at Harry Butler, jealous husband.

Could he? Could he kill someone? Harry's one physical flaw, his eyesight, had kept him out of the army, otherwise he would have had to go to Vietnam and he would have found out soon enough whether or not he could kill anyone.

He thought about a conversation he'd once had with the Lornes about Vietnam, the revisionist version. They'd been sitting around, drinking beer and talking about the Good Old Days, performing at anti-war demonstrations up at Columbia and Lenny had started tugging at his hair and saying how sometimes he wished he'd been there, wished he'd gone, and Paul said yeah, he knew what he meant.

'Are you nuts?' Harry had asked.

'It's like we missed the definitive event,' Paul said, 'the event that molded the men of our generation.'

'Molded them into bums,' Harry said. 'Two-thirds of the men in homeless shelters are Vietnam vets.' It was true. Clark had found it out when she was doing a sidebar for a piece on poverty in America that got cut in favor of Michael Jackson's marriage to Elvis's daughter.

Lenny and Paul ignored him.

'And being part of the anti-war movement,' Harry

continued, 'that was a definitive event, not going was as definitive as going.'

'You just don't get it,' Lenny said with a sigh, but yes he did. Anything can look good from a distance and they weren't thinking about Vietnam, the slaughterhouse; they were thinking about the movie version – brutal and gory, sure, but with an undertone of courage, heroism, adventure and male-bonding. Slaughter with a message; where one could be a hero *and* a hippie.

'Aren't you curious?' Lenny had wanted to know and he had said yes, because he *was* curious, curious to know if he would have come through whole. He would go to his death bed never knowing whether or not he could kill someone, whether or not he was strong enough to live in a bamboo cage full of rats and water snakes, never knowing what it was like to be in the thick of a battle, to be eaten alive with fear and hatred, to suffer unspeakably . . .

Jesus! he thought, it was a good thing he hadn't told the cops he'd been at Lenny's – they'd go up there to question him and he'd tell them Harry had always wanted to know what it felt like to kill someone, and then Clark would pipe in with her 'evidence' from Theatre 80 and before he knew it, he'd be carving marks in his cell on Death Row.

'I could just *kill* you,' Farley Granger tells his wife in *Strangers on a Train*, and when the cops start looking for her murderer, they look for him, because after all, he *said* he wanted to kill her, in front of a whole store full of witnesses, no less. But he was innocent! It was just a figure of speech! Who cares? He said it, they hated each other, she was a low-class bitch getting in the way of his romance with the Senator's daughter (a real priss, if you asked Harry), and sure enough, even *she* begins to suspect Farley, although she fights it in her prissy backboneless way. Everyone suspects poor old Farley, except the priss's younger sister, played by Alfred Hitchcock's daughter, who, as far as Harry was concerned, was the much better woman but not much to look at.

Harry imagined himself in chains, shuffling down a dark corridor, jeers greeting him from the other side of the peep-holed doors. 'I'm innocent!' he'd cry as they strapped him on to the gurney and he'd look out through the picture window and see Clark, with O'Donnell next to her, his earth-toned arm around her shoulder. And Lenny, pulling out hair by the fistful, and Paul, dressed up as Godzilla, singing,

> *I'm sorry about the pardon*
> *The guv'nor's heart has hardened*
> *There's no one else to blame at alllll*
> *So Harry has to take the faaaalllll*

and his mother with her oxygen canister on her lap, wringing her hands and wondering what people would think of a forty-seven-year-old son who dresses up like Tarzan and gets executed, and his father wandering around the room, sniffing the women . . .

Harry's eyes filled with tears as his imaginary room filled up with a procession of all the people he'd ever harmed or hurt: Miss Speedwell, the spinster they used to torment by leaving flowers and candy and love notes on her porch at night; Jimmy, the newspaper guy with cerebral palsy, who they'd follow down the street, calling 'Gumby!'; Ricky Lopez's little sister, who they used to strip and leave in the woods; Wanda Armstrong, who he stood up for the Prom because he got a better date; and in the back, hovering in the air above Wanda, was Gordie Sheppard, waving and laughing . . .

He pulled over, wiped his eyes, got out and leaned against the car.

Butler had been a shit in his youth. But on a Shit Scale of one to ten, he was only about a five. He had some things to be ashamed of, sure, who didn't, but as far as atoning for one's sins went, wasn't this a bit much?

He suddenly understood the comfort of believing in a bunch of bored gods hanging around Mount Olympus, having nothing better to do than screw up mortals' lives for their own entertainment. And, in a sense, hadn't he brought it upon himself? Hadn't he been too exuberantly happy with his own life, with his own self, hadn't his joy been irritating to the gods in their ennui, hadn't he been mucking about in their territory, taking everyday life and making it into something grand? And so the gods, those jealous, spiteful, all-too-human gods, had tossed him this.

Well, he, Harry Butler was up for it. He was no weak-greaved flutterer, no hare-hearted arrow-dodger, no milk-livered knee-knocker! He was Butler. Butler of the flowing hair! Bright-helmeted Harry!

He wiped his nose on the sleeve of his sweatshirt and looked around him. Wilderness. He was in middle of the Adirondacks, the most treacherous mountain range known to man, full of bears and wolverines and rednecks. He had no weapons, no shield, nothing but his wits to protect him but he would fulfill the challenge, he would take on the wilderness and win!

He got back in the car, whooped a jungle war cry and floored the accelerator.

Sixteen

'It's MAY!' he kept shouting the last hundred miles or so, across the Adirondacks still nestled deep in snow, passing cars laden with skiers and their snow paraphernalia. 'This is supposed to be SPRING!'

Everyone seemed so happy and bright, in their neon parkas and goofy stocking caps, their faces tanned but for all the wrong reasons. How can they be so cheery, Harry wondered, don't they know it's spring in New York? That the trees have *leaves*? That it's renewal and all that? How can they cling to that grim old geezer, winter?

He turned the heat up a notch and kept going. He hadn't been able to get anything on the radio except the Christian station, but he didn't mind: Harry liked passion of any sort and he especially liked the fire and brimstone types. He liked the deep, bullyish booming of their voices, threatening Harry with hell and worse if he didn't repent.

'Repent, repent, repent!' Harry sang, and the car

responded with appropriate fear and trembling, shuddering and sputtering its way up an incline as it approached the thin air of Heaven; sighing with relief on the way back down.

On the other side of the mountain, he lost even the Christian station: nothing but static up and down the dial; nothing but pine trees and snow outside the car.

He'd been putting if off the entire trip, but now he couldn't. He was stuck, alone with himself. For the past fifteen years, he had been saying that was exactly what he wanted, what he must have in order to finish *Butler by Butler*. But the truth was, he wanted to be alone with himself only between the hours of ten in the morning and four in the afternoon. Writers were supposed to be solitary types and Harry was quite happy to play the part and complain endlessly about not having solitude, but solitude, for him, meant being left alone while he was working and waited upon when he wasn't.

'I don't need to be *waited upon*,' he told himself, 'I just want a little human contact. I don't want to turn into one of those nutcases who drive around talking to themselves.'

He laughed at his own joke, and told himself he was easily amused. So? It was true, what of it?

'Have you ever noticed,' he asked himself, 'that people talking to themselves rarely seem to be having a pleasant conversation?'

He slammed on the brakes and pulled over to the side of the road. What a great idea, he thought, he could do the next chapter as a series of dialectics, have an argument with himself and – and wouldn't this be brilliant? Wouldn't Clark be dazzled? – and he would win *both*! Incredible! Where was his notebook? Shit.

He dug through the pile of stuff on the passenger

seat: balled up paper bags, maps, squished paper cups. Couldn't find the notebook. Shit. He flattened out a paper bag and began scribbling: 'Dialectic. Butler vs. Butler. Butler wins. Proof that truth is relative.'

He pulled back on to the road, ecstatic. Maybe his lies about wanting solitude were true after all, maybe he really *did* need to be alone with himself, maybe this wasn't going to be as bad as he had feared, maybe he wouldn't get up to Paul's place and discover he was a wimp without those apron strings to puff him up.

There. He'd admitted it. He had been trying to push it down, ignore it, keep it hanging out in the alleys of his consciousness. But now, now that he had nothing to fear, he could admit it, laugh at it – ha ha, he would say to Clark when she came up, ha ha, he would tell Lenny and Paul, and I was afraid what would happen because I'd never been alone before. But of course that wasn't *my* fault, he would say to Lenny and Paul but not to Clark, I can't help it if I'm pulled from the arms of one woman straight into those of another.

And here he was, not even there yet, not even *living* alone with himself yet, and already he'd been walloped with an amazing idea.

Up ahead, on the left, he saw what could only be the Famous Fifty-Foot Pheasant, the landmark for the turn that would take him the final thirty miles to Paul's. He thought about stopping, not to take a closer look at the Famous Fifty-Foot Pheasant, the World's Largest, which Paul had told him was made out of real feathers, but to take a closer look at the person who would think such a thing was worth making. He would make a great character, Harry thought – Butler and the Pheasant Man. No, Butler and the Bird Man. But Harry was in a hurry, he wanted to get to Paul's and get settled in, so the Pheasant

Man would have to wait. It didn't matter. Kooks, Harry had discovered, were much more interesting as an idea than a reality.

But he would come back. He felt it was his duty, as an American, to visit at least one tourist trap per trip, to make up for what he perceived to have been one of the great deprivations of his childhood. His parents had packed him up and loaded him into the back seat and dragged him off on countless 'outings', but they had never stopped for tourist traps. His father was always in a hurry and his mother 'wouldn't be caught dead' in a place like that. Like what? Like what? Young Harry wanted to know; he wanted to discover the mysteries, he wanted to see the World's Largest Watermelon and the Incredible Amazon Woman and the Authentic Replica of a Pygmy Village. He wanted to see dancing bears and wild boars, he wanted to see the genuine footprint of Bigfoot. Torture Chambers! Halls of Horrors! The Secrets of King Tut's Tomb! All right here, within his grasp, and his parents drove right on past, with nary a glance from his father and a loud dismissive snort from his mother. Harry would climb into the way-back of the station wagon, watching the mysteries of life disappearing. Oh please, oh please, oh please, he'd beg as new signs would begin to appear, large and bright and enticing, big yellow billboards with a huge black '?': '?', only 115 miles. QUESTION MARK? What was QUESTION MARK? Oh please oh please oh please. Instead, they took him to Gettysburg. Which was cool, in its own right, with its authentic Civil War cannons and a gift shop where you could buy tin soldiers. Or to Monticello. Or the White House. And yeah, Harry supposed Gettysburg and Monticello and the White House were 'America', too, but they were more like history, in the past, while tourist traps were filled not only with facts but with mystery and adventure and wonders. And fireworks. Tin soldiers were nice, something to play with in the privacy of his own room, but cherry bombs were better, the kind of thing he could sneak into school and show off in the bathroom. Tourist traps were *now*, not then, and at the end of every trip Harry would feel bereft, no matter how much he'd seen or done, no matter how much fun he'd had or how many soldiers he had stuffed in his pockets, because he felt he was missing the most important part, the Question Marks of life.

He made the turn and it was as if he had driven not only backwards in seasons, but backwards in time as well. There was nothing physically different from the road he had just been on, but there was a feeling – he couldn't put his finger on it, just a kind of thump, a jolt of some sense that had been snoozing peacefully, as if he'd crossed into the Twilight Zone or something, gone back a few decades. Not good. Harry didn't need to be thinking of the Twilight Zone and that kind of shit – it was bad enough, having the kid's ghost tagging along, hogging the back seat as if he were real and not just a figment of Harry's imagination.

He'd first noticed him around Albany, when he glanced into the rear-view mirror to see if it was OK to move back in the right-hand lane, and instead of the big red nose of the semi, he saw Gordie Sheppard, perched on the computer like a nerdy little gnome. Harry had been ignoring him, pretending he didn't see him when he'd flutter around the back seat – after all, it was just his imagination, priming itself, getting ready to let itself loose once he plugged himself in at Paul's.

Harry didn't believe in ghosts, but he didn't disbelieve in them, either. '"There are more things in heaven and earth, Harraitio, than are dreamt of in your philosophy.'"

Harraitio. That was good.

Ghosts, aliens, spirits, evil demons, angels – why not? Devils especially: what else could explain the fact that after several thousand years of so-called civilisation, people were still butchering each other like cave-men? And over what? Religion? An accident of birth. Race? Another accident. Harry couldn't see the point in killing some poor guy over something he couldn't help, but apparently he was out of the mainstream on that one. Power? Now that was understandable. The lust for power. And greed. Two concepts one could sink one's teeth into although he, thank God, wasn't afflicted with either.

He checked the rear-view mirror, but the kid was gone. He wondered if he was trying to haunt him. Harry supposed it was rather foolish to believe in ghosts, kind of skittish and unmanly, as if that belief came with a bit of the hysteric attached to it, like a too-large tag sewn in a T-shirt, sticking out for everyone to see and laugh at behind one's back. But this ghost didn't seem malicious, there was nothing the least bit scary about him, nothing to get hysterical about. He hadn't been accompanied by a blast of frigid air or the rattling of chains; he'd just been sitting there, waving in what seemed like a perfectly friendly way. Like Casper.

Harry liked the idea of having a ghostly pal. As long as he was good company, Harry didn't mind if he wasn't real. Most of the people in his life weren't.

It was the kid's business, no doubt, to clear up the mystery surrounding his death, if there even *was* a mystery, something that was itself questionable. Instead of trying to avoid him, brush him away like a dead fly, perhaps he should try to engage him.

'C'mon back, kid,' Harry said. 'How's death treating you?'

A bad joke, he knew, but he laughed none the less. Harry loved all his jokes, he couldn't help it. Even the smelliest of the stinkers amused him. The kid would like it, probably; it was a young person's joke, a young person's or a dead person's and since the kid was both, it couldn't miss.

Most people didn't appreciate jokes about death, Harry thought, they thought death was no laughing matter but as far as Harry was concerned, it was the biggest joke of all. The joke of life itself. It was the point, and if you didn't get that, you didn't get life, and you couldn't enjoy it.

Like Lenny. The guy was obsessed with death. He was afraid of everything: afraid of taking the subway because even if he made it through the ride without getting mugged or pushed in front of an incoming train, what was to prevent the tunnel from caving in? So he was always late for rehearsals because he took the bus and the other Lornes would torment him with all the ways he could die on a bus and he'd end up having to walk the sixty blocks home.

The Lornes. God, those were the days, Harry thought. Harry believed that most people got stuck at what they perceived to be the high point of their lives and if he judged people at all it was according to how pathetic their high point was. Of course, most people didn't realise they were stuck. They were completely unaware that they'd tell the same story over and over again, branding themselves with it. They were always the hero, of course – leading the take-over of the Science

Building at Podunk U; making the critical touch-down at some Bowl or other; screwing some famous person; driving cross-country in an acid daze in search of something they obviously didn't find. It got to be sad, after a while, listening to their tales of shopworn glory, although Harry always liked it when they added a new twist, some new little lie to make themselves look a little less dusty in their own mirror.

Harry hoped he never got stuck. If his life went according to plan, things would just get better and better until he went out in his blue blaze: still healthy, still in love with life, still with all his marbles. But if he did, getting stuck being one of Four Lornes was nothing to sneeze at. He didn't need the panache of an era to puff himself up; he didn't need the dull light of reflected fame to illuminate him – he was Harry Butler, leader of the Four Lornes. He'd actually been a love object, for a few glorious years. He'd received photographs from all sorts of ridiculous girls, most of them in their bathing suits and a couple in less than that, which was pretty damn daring for back then – all of them vowing eternal love and devotion and a whole lot more, if only he'd send for them.

Harry wondered what happened to all those girls. They'd all seemed slightly hysterical, trapped in some sort of medieval castle, locked in a tower only Harry could climb. It was 1959; who knew the Sexual Revolution was just around the corner, that in a decade or so they'd be zipping up and down those walls without the help of anyone?

Harry had liked what was then called the New Woman, who now isn't called anything at all, except perhaps 'bitch' by some guy she's screwed in one way or another.

It was starting to snow again and Harry turned on the windshield wipers. It couldn't get more gloomy and maybe that was what made it feel as if he'd tumbled back into the fifties, the black and whiteness of it: bare black tree trunks, white snow, fuzzy gray background. In any case, it was weird. 'If you could get in a time machine,' Clark once asked him, 'would you go forward or back? To the future or the past?' It was a trick question; every question of Clark's was a trick. But he wasn't fast enough to figure it out so he gave her a trick answer: 'It depends on whether or not I could come back.' She rolled her eyes. 'If you could come back, you'd go to the future, but if you couldn't, you'd go to the past. You're so predictable.'

Those were fighting words for Clark. She thought being predictable was a fate worse than death, it meant being boring, rigid, firmly ensconced in the dreaded Middle Class. It meant one lacked curiosity, a sense of adventure. Guilty, Harry thought, at least as far as the latter was concerned. He thought 'adventure', as a concept, was silly – why run around all over the world, climbing mountains and trekking across deserts and canoeing down piranha-infested waters to get an adrenalin rush when all you had to do was take a stroll down Avenue D after dark?

Harry didn't have a problem with predictability. It just meant he preferred order to chaos and what was so bad about that? But Clark was ten years younger than he, still in the first half of her life, still convinced that when people spoke of the youth culture they meant her.

Not that Harry felt old – he didn't, he identified with the young, with things youthful: wild abandon, self-indulgence, good stuff like that, but at the same time he had to admit that he was occasionally troubled by a kind of creeping conservatism. To his own surprise he would find himself sneering at the Punks hanging out on St Mark's, with their fake toughness and their hideous mutilated bodies, thinking, When I was your age, rebelling *meant* something, or Whatever happened to respect? The trouble with the world today is nobody's got any *respect*, or, worst of all, Why don't you get up off your lazy ass and get a job? Stuff like that, stuff that should be said in a querulous voice, punctuated by the shaking of a cane and the rattling of dentures.

It was one of the reasons he had wanted to die young. To prevent himself from becoming Them. Of course, everybody is a Them, depending on who the Us is.

Butler was a Them to the cops; to the yuppies and the rod-up-the-butt right-wingers; to the Punks and the Suits. To the rednecks in their pick-ups plastered with I'M THE NRA bumper stickers, Butler was a Them.

It was scary, when you thought about it, all those Thems out there and Harry all alone, with only his imagination for the Us. How could Clark do this to him? 'I don't know anything about you,' she had said. Did that mean she was Themifying him, turning him into someone she could disclaim when they hauled him off in chains for the murder of Gordie Sheppard? Someone she could dump so she could run off with her Detective What's-his-Name? What's-his-Name Harry's ass.

She wanted to get rid of him, but why?

Seventeen

Clark sat at her desk, feeling stupid.

'Oh my God!' Polly had said when Clark told her about the kid; 'Oh my God!' Jana had said when Clark told her about the detectives; 'Oh my God!' Aggie had screeched when Clark told her she'd sent Harry away. She left out the part about the love shrine, although she did tell Polly the kid had had a crush on her. Polly considered herself a femme fatale, she thought every man, including Harry, was in love with her, and Clark couldn't resist. You're not the only femme fatale in Mudville, she thought.

She also skipped the part about *why* she had sent him away.

'Don't you think that's kind of mean?' Aggie had wanted to know, 'Harry's not exactly Natty Bumpo.' But what did she know? She thought she was an expert on human nature because she wrote the 'Marriage Saver' column for *Young Frau*, despite the fact that she hadn't even had a date in over five years.

She wondered if he was gone yet. Probably not. He was probably puttering around the apartment, putting off his departure, gathering together all the things he couldn't possibly live without – his dog-eared collection of Jack London; his free weights; the boom box and all the Johnny Cash tapes. Bartlett, Roget, Webster and the rest of his pals. Harry liked to litter his work with quotations: 'A tip of the hat to my predecessors,' he'd say, but as far as Clark was concerned, a quotation was just a cliché with class. 'With a pedigree,' Harry would counter, tossing them about with abandon, completely out of context. 'Who cares?' he would bellow, 'this is 1987; there *is* no context any more!' and how could she argue with that? It hadn't occurred to her, when she left in the morning, that she would be returning to an apartment rifled of his presence and that thought made her heartsick – she had wanted to be rid of *him*, not his essence. She hadn't spent a night alone, in her apartment, since he had moved in, and the thought of sleeping by herself in their bed – something that she sometimes wished for, when Harry was smushing her up into the wall – without even the comfort of filling in his space with a few of his favorite things, overwhelmed her with loneliness. She remembered something Polly had said, after her second divorce. 'I don't miss him. And I don't even miss the sex. The only thing I miss is having him next to me in bed.' Clark now understood what Polly had meant.

All she had to do was pick up the phone, call him, say, 'Don't go,' and he wouldn't. Although he would no doubt recognise his advantage and make her sweat a while, say something like, 'Naw, you were right, it *is* a good idea, some time apart would be good for us,' not meaning a word of it and Clark, today, this minute, this time, would let him win.

But she wouldn't call. She couldn't. In another hour or so, while she was verifying the details of some celebrity's nose job, the image of Harry lumbering across the roof would return to her head, filling it with all sorts of evil notions.

What was she doing here, sitting at her desk, staring at her in-box when she should be out doing some detective work? She didn't trust Mason and O'Donnell – they were probably looking for the easy way out, the simplest way to solve their case and what could be more convenient than to pin it on Harry? It was one thing for *her* to suspect him – he was her husband and what woman hasn't woken in the middle of the night wondering if her husband was an axe-murderer? It was a perfectly common – if irrational – phenomenon. She remembered the time Jana was out in California, auditioning for a role she didn't get, and had called in the middle of night, in a frenzy because she was convinced her husband was the Hillside Strangler. 'Every time we come here, there's another victim!' she had whispered into the phone. 'It's Larry! I know it!' Clark had, of course, talked her out of her hysteria, but she hadn't been the least bit shocked by it. Almost every woman she knew had had a similar experience. It no doubt dated back to cave-man days, when a woman could serve not only as a breeder, but as breakfast, if necessary. Her suspicions didn't *mean* anything; they didn't mean she loved Harry any less, they just meant she was temporarily in thrall to some kind of atavistic fear.

Of course knowing her fear was irrational didn't do a damn thing to dispel it. The only thing that could turn her back into her rational, practical, common-sensical self was to find out what really happened on the roof. Maybe one of the crackheads had pushed Gordie off. Maybe he had leaned over too far, trying to get a good look at her apartment. Or maybe, and this was the worst to think, the thing she'd been trying to avoid thinking, the thing she really didn't want to consider because it would place the blame squarely upon herself – he had jumped.

Clark's biggest secrets were the ones she tried to keep from herself. The notion of suicide had been there all along, but she had been stuffing it down into that area of her unconscious marked 'Off-Limits'. If she didn't think about it, it wouldn't exist. Thoughts without words never to Heaven go. Or to Hell, as the case may be.

She shook her head in an attempt to toss the notion out. It couldn't possibly be true. It just didn't *fit*. It didn't fit in her life; it didn't fit in her way of looking at the world – people didn't go around jumping off roofs in her world and they certainly didn't jump off roofs because of *her*.

Clark was as vain as anyone else, but she was also a realist. That she was worth struggling for was understood. But people didn't kill themselves for love any more; they killed themselves because they embezzled or ran over some kid when they were drunk or because they had incurable cancer or because they were so utterly baffled and depressed by life they didn't know how to do anything else. But love – not since Werther.

She shuffled some papers, called in her assistant Peggy, delegated. She was useless herself and Peggy was one of those overly-competent star-struck Journalism majors from some Midwestern cow college and even the most tedious, mind-numbing task – searching through hundreds of rolls of microfilm, for example – thrilled her; she would find something magical about it and return to the office beaming because she sat next to Jimmy Breslin at the Newspaper Annex.

She reminded Clark of herself when she first came to New York, a cheerful little ball of hope and wonder and dreams, bouncing all over the city in search of the places where her heroes had been: Edgar Allen Poe lived *here*! Walt Whitman spoke *here*! Kerouac got drunk *here*! Working as a Tempo Girl – oh, how those other girls at the agency had intimidated her, their hair perfectly coiffed in a Jackie flip, complete with clip-on bows, their beautifully manicured nails, their accessories. Clark had never learned to accessorise – a scarf was for tying around your neck in winter, a belt was to hold up your pants – and she felt terrified of those girls, they seemed so sophisticated, so powerful, doling out the plum jobs to the other Jackie clones and tossing the refuse at Clark. She hadn't cared; the refuse was good enough for her. As long as the job was in Manhattan, it didn't matter what she did for the day because the point was simply *being* there: getting from the Tempo agency to whatever backroom full of dusty files she was sentenced to was exciting enough for her. And the nights!

She thought about her first apartment, on 7th Street between Second and First. A walk-up, of course, top floor, with a view of the brick wall next door, living across the hall from a pair of Brazilian whores, freelancers, who brought their johns up at all times of the day and night and humped endlessly and loudly. She had come to New York a virgin in every sense of the word, but she would never have admitted that; she wanted to seem as worldly as the rest of the Tempo Girls, sitting around the plastic coffee table in the reception area with their little lipstick tubes of cover-up, dabbing it on the circles under their eyes and sighing happily, saying, 'I'm *exhausted!* He was an *animal*!' She'd stay up all night, cultivating her own dark circles, going from St Mark's to the Village Gate to Slug's, listening to poetry, dancing, drinking, ending up at the Electric Circus, trying to find someone to take her virginity. It didn't take long. She found a lumpy, sweating, leering Big Ten Frat Boy – Tim! That was his name, Tim Smith, although she had questioned the 'Smith' part – to stumble home with her. 'Awk!' she said the next morning at the coffee table, 'I'm *exhausted*! He was an *animal*!' The truth was he had passed out halfway through, but Clark didn't care, she just lay in bed, slightly baffled by all the furor, but happy that the deed was done. Or at least she thought it was. No matter. She was initiated, she was a New York Woman and every minute of every day was an adventure; just being alive, being here, in New York!, was like a dream come true and she was the happiest she'd ever been in her life.

Peggy opened Clark's door, stuck her face in, called 'I'll be back!' and closed the door. Clark sighed. Peggy would go far, she thought, once the City sculpted her a bit, wore down that happy-faceness, gave her a few sharp edges.

Clark suddenly felt not exactly old, but older than she had a few minutes before. Thinking about Peggy made her realise she was no longer *that* young, and that was depressing.

She grabbed her bag, marched through the cubicles, told the receptionist she'd be out for the rest of the day, and left.

It still amazed her that she could do this, walk out whenever she wanted, that she was head of a department. The boss. How had that happened? How had she gone from being a Peggy to being a *Ms* Clark? It wasn't anything she had wanted; she had never had a burning ambition to climb to the top of a masthead, and yet there she was. Director of Research. Beatrice Clark. She had her own office, with a door that closed and a big brass nameplate she used primarily as a back scratcher. She had responsibility, authority, things she didn't particularly want but enjoyed none the less. But at heart, she still felt like a Peggy, still, she thought proudly, looked like a Peggy. Still lived like a Peggy, in her tiny walk-up. Her life still felt like play. Or had, up until yesterday.

As she stood in the elevator, watching the floor numbers descend, it occurred to her that a life of play was the same thing as playing at life. Not that that was a bad thing, on the contrary, it was quite pleasurable, but still, it indicated a lack of seriousness she suddenly found troublesome.

But she *was* serious. She was a person with a nameplate. A spot on the masthead of eight different magazines. Every month she arrived in thousands of homes, sat neatly cradled in wire racks at the supermarket counter, behind the photo of whatever celebrity had just lost weight or given birth or endured some trauma – there she was, under only the publisher and the editor: BEATRICE CLARK, with her own department and her own assistant. A person of substance, someone who could prove her existence, who could point to herself in print.

She got out of the elevator and waved to Herman in the news-stand. If anyone had told her she would reach a point where she would think that being someone with a nameplate meant anything at all, she thought as she stepped out into the glaring sun, much less took on the importance of propping up her whole being, she would have laughed, howled, mocked, rolled on the floor like an antic cartoon character.

She walked south and east, hurrying to get away from Midtown. It was warm outside, and crowds of office workers, not just the huddling smokers, were outside, leaning against the warm stone walls, sitting on the edge of fountains laughing, as if removing their jackets and baring their arms to the sun was cause for unbearable joy. Which, she thought sadly, it was.

She paused in front of a deli window, looking at her disheveled self. Disheveled and tense, she captioned. She had the look of someone who had just been 'through' something, something tragic and unpleasant. Which was true enough.

She turned down Second Avenue, free at last from the crowds, and slowed her pace. As she walked, she watched the faces of the people approaching her, wondering what they thought of her tragic air. She thought about the time she fell off her bike, breaking her nose and scraping her face badly, and how she would walk down the street, bandaged and bruised, and certain men would leer at her, eyeing her up and down as if she were naked, as if they knew her dirty little secret, as if they'd like to take her home and give her some more of where that came from.

The looks they gave her had filled her with shame, and she wouldn't go anywhere with Harry in public until she got the bandages off. Poor Harry. He always paid for her shame, and that made her feel even worse, which made her even more angry with him.

It was a flaw. Clark prided herself on not taking pride in her flaws, as so many people do. They talked about them with remorse in their voices, but a twinkle in their eyes, as if it made them somehow cuter to be perpetually late or a cheapskate or to never return borrowed books. Clark genuinely regretted her flaws, and would periodically embark on a self-improvement program, like a housewife finally getting round to cleaning out the attic, but she would get so overwhelmed by the immensity of the task that she'd just push everything back where it was, with the faint promise of 'next year'.

No one seemed to be noticing her. If she'd catch someone's eye, they'd look down and do a little side-step, as if avoiding a pile of dog-do, as if they had to pretend there was a reason they wouldn't look at her, that there was something compelling keeping them from acknowledging her.

She found it kind of endearing. People were so ridiculous, most of the time. Clark liked to think that the vast majority of people were just side-stepping through life, trying to avoid as much doo-doo as possible. The others, the leerers, were the aberrations, and as far as she was concerned the world would be a much better place if someone would remove them from the gene pool.

Up ahead, she spotted a book display in front of a second-hand shop and crossed over to take a look. It was uncanny, the ability she had to sniff out valuable books in the jumble of someone's trash – she had a whole shelf at home, filled with her finds: a signed *McTeague*, a French *Ulysses*, an illustrated Blake with all the plates intact. She didn't even have to search – it was almost as if the book wanted to be found, to be taken home and admired by someone who would appreciate it, and all Clark had to do was stand there until the book caught her eye.

She stood there, staring, but nothing happened, so she moved on, heading south, back into her own world.

South of 23rd Street, people were out in shorts and

sandals. Soon it would be summer, Clark thought, and with summer came not only the brutal heat but the newest wave of pilgrims, seekers, Peggys. Of Gordies, she thought with a heart-cramping wave of grief.

Damn kid, she thought, damn kid, damn kid, damn kid. Why hadn't he introduced himself? Why hadn't he come up to her, after a reading, and handed her a rolled up baton of his poems? She would have helped him; she liked nothing more than having protegées following her around like little adoring puppies. There was always room for one more in *her* entourage. She loved being the teacher, the guru; loved hearing her little band of Clarkettes whispering her name in awestruck tones. There had been a time when she couldn't walk more than a couple of blocks without someone coming up to her, shaking her hand, telling her how much they admired her work. Now, she could walk for days without anyone noticing her. That made her feel rather sad and Norma Desmondish, pathetic.

Gordie Sheppard, she thought, my last fan. And now even he was gone.

She suddenly felt an overwhelming desire to see Gordie's love shrine, to see how the poor kid had honored her, had worshipped before her. It's only what I deserve from everyone, she thought, wondering how she could fit that into a performance piece. The idea was right, the rhythm, wrong. It's only what I deserve.

She felt the same heart-skip of panic she had felt the other night, watching the kids outside CBGB. She had lost touch with her work, with herself. She had become someone she hadn't intended to become. Straight. A dreaded Suit. A hanger-on, standing in the footlights of Harry's life instead of her own bright spotlight, where she belonged. She was getting comfortable, with her high-five figures and her office and her underlings.

The love shrine. It was a possibility. Lots of conflict. Pride. Shame. Grief. Love, of course. Obsession, everyone's favorite. Humor? It would have to be black, but that was fine, that was the only kind she knew how to do in any case.

But was it ethical? To capitalise on a poor boy's death to reclaim her own spot in the light? Harry no doubt would use it, he was no doubt using it already, thinking it out as he drove up north, making it into something that happened to *him*. He would be peeved if she used 'his' material. 'You can't use that!' he'd always say, when she took something from their lives and put it in her work, 'that's mine!' 'First in print!' she always said in return, making him wild with panic, but the truth was, she always let it go, gave him whatever little slice of her life he wanted to gobble up.

Well, she would see.

She knew she couldn't get into the apartment, but she wondered if she could climb up the fire escape and take a little peek. O'Donnell had told them where Gordie had lived. Over in Alphabet City, in a ratty, druggy building that some yuppies wanted to renovate. 'Gentrify.' Ugh, even the word reeked. It smelled of class, privilege, aristo-trash; everything America wasn't supposed to be. Clark still – stupidly, she admitted – believed in the concept of fair play, an equal shake of the die for everyone, and it infuriated her to discover, over and over, that the dice were loaded. They didn't teach her that in Avoca, where 'class' meant minding one's manners and wearing clean underwear.

She was already at 14th Street; she turned east and headed toward Avenue A, blasted forward by the throb of a boom box, acting as sentinel, letting you know this is not the New York you just left. A *new* New York. An *other* New York. She loved it.

Gordie had lived on 4th Street, between C and D, not the kind of place you'd want to be after dark. A tenement with a stoop, complete with junkies nodding out on the steps and needles buried treacherously in the cracks of the sidewalk. There was a wrought iron fence beside the stoop, guarding six overflowing garbage cans, and then a narrow alleyway leading to the back of the building. On the brick wall, there was one of those graffitied upside-down martini glasses, marking it as a building being gentrified. 'The Party's Over', it was supposed to mean, but as far as Clark could tell, it was just beginning. For the yuppies, at least. As far as the poor were concerned, the party had never even begun. Clark opened the gate and sauntered through, hoping no one would think she was some yuppie real estate broker, come to steal their home. A person could get maimed, real bad, for that, and while she was pretty confident of her ability to fast-talk her way out of just about any bad situation, she didn't want to get caught sneaking around in dark alleys, looking like the predator rather than the predatee.

She walked round back and was delighted to see the fire escape ladder already pulled down, as if waiting for her. A sign that she was doing the right thing. Perhaps Gordie himself had arranged the convenience. Perhaps he was swimming about in spirit-land, unhappy at the thought that Clark might misunderstand him, misinterpret the benignity of his love, the purity of his adoration.

Whatever, she thought, climbing up the ladder, mincing her way across the holey steel to avoid getting her heels caught.

She wasn't sure what floor his apartment had been

on, nor, for that matter, whether it faced front or back. She wished she had considered that before, she could have saved herself the trip. But she was here now so she might as well have a look.

She felt rather elated, spy-like, as she climbed up the steps to the second floor. The blinds were drawn on one window; through the other she could see an unmade sofa bed, a small table covered with books and papers, and a large white cat sleeping in an armchair that obviously doubled as a clawing toy. She knew she shouldn't, but she felt as happy as a schoolgirl playing hooky. She *was* playing hooky! Spying on other people's lives, seeing the secrets they quickly tucked away if someone knocked at the door – the dirty laundry on the floor that they'd stuff under the sink and the porno magazine they'd slip under the mattress – I know *you*, Mr Jack Meoff, she thought. This was heady stuff, this spying, and she suddenly understood the appeal of sitting up on a roof, staring into someone's apartment, discovering a being no one else knew.

She shuddered. What if Gordie had discovered something about Harry, something Harry didn't want anyone to know, some compromising thing – 'What kind of thing?' her better self interrupted – 'I don't know, just some *thing*, some thing Harry had to hide?'

'Stop it,' she told herself, 'stop it, stop it, stop it'.

She sat down on the step, took deep breaths, chased it away.

She climbed up to the next landing. One empty apartment, being renovated. All the fixtures and appliances had been removed, to be replaced no doubt by brass, crystal and sub-zeros. And a couple of yuppies, willing to pay rent equal to the Gross National Product of a sub-Saharan country for the privilege of colonising the jungle of the East Village. The locked gate was not regulation, and Clark remembered her own fury at having to finally give in and install a gate, after her fifth robbery, after, ironically, she had nothing left to steal. 'I'm not going to live behind bars!' she kept swearing, but she did, not because she had anything worth having, but because she hated the feeling of violation she'd have when the burglars broke in. For months, she would burst into tears every time she looked out of the window – her view, her freedom, her space, blocked by those ugly steel diamonds.

She got used to them. It's amazing what a person can get used to, she thought, look at me. Who would have ever thought I'd spend fifteen years living in a roach-infested tenement?

She had a moment of panic, thinking that perhaps the empty apartment had been Gordie's, but then remembered O'Donnell saying something about its being a crime scene. Off-limits. Besides, even the most greedy speculator would have the decency to give the family time to come in and take the kid's things. Wouldn't they?

She wondered how she could get hold of Gordie's diary. She had become convinced that he would have been a great poet, and perhaps there was something in his diary to prove it. She could publish it and he could live on for ever. Besides, she wanted to see what he said about her.

Maybe, after a decent amount of time had passed, she could write to his parents and ask them if she could read it. Maybe sometime when she was in Ann Arbor, visiting Dee Dee, she could take a drive over to Avoca, drop in, sympathise, get a look at the diary.

She climbed up to the next landing. Fourth floor. By

now, she was a little the worse for wear – not that she cared, she didn't, she wasn't going anywhere and walking down the street in a crumpled skirt, with big holes in one's stockings, gave one a certain cachet in her neighborhood.

The window of the first apartment was closed, shade drawn.

She looked into the other window, kneeling down and putting her hands to the glass to get a better view into the darkness.

There, standing in the middle of the room and staring straight at her, was O'Donnell.

'Shit,' she said and burst into tears.

Eighteen

Paul's house was about a mile and a half down what Harry assumed was a dirt road, under the gray crusty snow. There wasn't quite as much of it here, now that he'd come down the last mountain. The end of the range.

It was the end of the line for Butler.

He followed along in the tracks made by some Mastadonian truck, feeling rather silly in his little Chevette, which was not a Guy car under the best of circumstances, and he wished Clark hadn't covered up the rust spots with DIE YUPPIE SCUM bumper stickers.

He passed a couple of trailers, both with dead deer hanging up outside, like clothes out to dry, and a house which was apparently made out of brick-colored Con-tac paper. Citified as he had become, Harry still knew when hunting season was and it wasn't now. His neighbors apparently didn't mind breaking the law and didn't mind flaunting it. That could be good or that could be bad.

'White farmhouse,' Clark's neat directions read. 'Large tree in front.'

Harry pulled into the driveway, wondering where the farm was. There was nothing around but woods, woods and more woods. Already, before he was even out of the car, he longed for open space, wished Paul's house was in Montana or someplace like that, someplace where you could see what was coming.

'A guy could get claustrophobia up here,' Harry muttered as he walked over to the steps and groped for the keys. A guy could go nuts, wondering what was hanging out behind all those trees.

He wondered what time it was. Noonish, he figured. The sun, which had been hiding behind the last of the foothills, was shining brightly here, and it seemed pretty straight up in the sky.

He found the keys and unlocked the door. Well, one good thing about being in the middle of the damned forest, Harry told himself as he pushed open the door and walked in, was there was no place for UFOs to land.

The house stank of mildew and rotting critters, a smell Harry instantly recognised from summers at Camp Onawanta. Camp I-Don't-Want-To, he and his miserable little campmates had called it. He leaned on the door frame, whiffing, remembering the half-rotted corpses they'd find under the cabins – raccoons, squirrels wriggling with maggots, and worst of all, those ugly old possums. He shuddered. Could anything on God's earth be more hideous than those pink-tailed, ratty-snout, baby-fingered possums?

'It would be just my luck,' Harry said aloud. 'If I *do* get abducted, it will be by a bunch of aliens who look like possums and they'll want me to mate with their women.'

His voice echoed through the empty house and he

shuddered again, but whether from the cold, the sound of his own voice, or the thought of screwing ten-foot-tall possum women, he couldn't tell.

According to Clark's instructions, there was a trap door in the pantry, leading to the basement, where the circuit breakers were. Harry hated basements. They reminded him of horror movies, places where everybody in the audience knew better than to go. And tornadoes. They reminded him of long, dark afternoons spent huddled downstairs in the reeking dark of his father's 'laboratory', listening to the staticky old transistor, waiting for the All Clear. His mother, of course, had been terrified and her terror infected young Harry, but he felt it his duty, as the male, to pretend to be fearless. When his father was gone, which seemed to be during every storm, Harry was the man of the house, which wasn't too bad when it only meant taking out the garbage, but was a heavy burden when it meant calming his hysterical, chain-smoking mother. 'Ma, ma,' he would say, 'what's the worst that can happen? The tornado will carry away the house, but we'll be safe,' and she would weep and smoke while Harry sat in the dark, watching his bedroom whirl round in the funnel, the Hardy Boys and Jack London tumbling out of the bookcase, his baseball cards flying around like big cardboard chunks of snow, the mattress slipping off the box spring and revealing his hidden copies of *For Men Only* . . .

He suddenly realised he had been thinking about his mother a lot recently. Clark always accused him of being a mama's boy, not because he was one, but because his mother *wanted* him to be one, and Clark considered that an infringement on her territory.

Did he think about his mother too much? In just two days, he'd thought about her four, maybe five times.

Was that excessive? How many times did you get to think about your mother without crossing over into the Oedipal?

Ugh, he thought as he descended the stairs, he didn't need to worry about *that*. The thought of kicking his father out of his mother's bed to make room for himself was worse than thinking about climbing into bed with alien possums.

Of course, he knew one wasn't supposed to take the Oedipus thing literally, but even metaphorically, he was pretty sure he wasn't guilty of any hanky-panky. The truth was, he thought sadly, he hadn't liked either of his parents enough to get emotionally attached. He thought about his father, dressed in his suits that always seemed one size too big for him, as if he kept hoping he was going to grow into them and never did. Walking to the car, with his briefcase full of scents. Until this moment, it had never occurred to Harry that his father had had dreams, that he had any kind of interior life at all. His quest to find the perfect perfume, the perfume that would define the New Woman, seemed silly and downright shameful to young Harry. But wasn't any quest heroic? The thought of his father, whom Harry had always considered a bit of a wuss, as someone heroic, as a kind of tragic visionary, filled Harry with a sudden desire to see him, to talk to him, man to man and father to son, to see if perhaps there had been more there than Harry had cared to see. The truth was, he hadn't looked very hard, and his father wasn't the chummy type. Not that he hadn't tried. He came to Harry's little league games and drove Harry's Cub Scout den back and forth to Pow-Wows, despite Harry's pleas not to. After all, it was embarrassing, having a father who smelled like a woman.

Harry felt bad about that, now, was ashamed of himself for being ashamed of his father. 'When are you coming to see us?' his mother always gasped on the telephone. 'We're not going to be around for ever, you know,' and he decided that if Clark hadn't relented by the weekend, he'd get back in the car and drive to Ohio.

He stepped on something mushy and looked down, hoping it wasn't a dead animal. Mushrooms. There were mushrooms all over the place, like a little forest for leprechauns.

He found the circuit breakers, snapped them on. The house came alive: humming and whirring and chugging; booting up, Harry thought happily, just like the computer.

He climbed back up the stairs, went to the fridge, an old Frigidare, shaped like a big white jukebox.

'Ugh!' he shouted as he opened the door and was blasted by the stench of shelves full of horrible mutants, green and gray *things*, the mold bubbling up like little hairy warts.

'Jesus,' he said, 'I guess Paul *did* leave in a hurry.'

'Ugh,' he said again, closing the door. He began looking through the cupboards for a can of air freshener or something, something that would take away that dreadful smell of rot.

Everywhere, there were opened packages and boxes: cereal, crackers, potato chips, cookies – no wonder Paul was so out of shape – everything chewed and nibbled by whatever had left those little black pellets of poop. He knew mice dung when he saw it, and this wasn't it. This was bigger. This belonged to a critter Harry wouldn't want to meet in the dark, poking its snout out from behind the Oreos, baring its fangs and lunging at Harry's valuable fingers.

Under the sink, he found a can of disinfectant spray and a box, also nibbled, of garbage bags. There was a pair of yellow plastic dish gloves, stuck together with grunge. He gingerly pulled them apart, curling his lip, and tried to stuff his hand in. Too small. He pulled out a garbage bag and tossed the gloves in. He went into the pantry, found a set of tongs, the long-handled ones for outdoor grilling, and began pulling all the boxes out of the cupboards with the tongs, ughing and yukking as they spilled into the bag: cereal and worms. Crackers and little crawly beetle things. Moths. There were *moths* in the food.

He opened the refrigerator door, stood back as far as he could, and sprayed.

'It'll be *romantic*,' he mimicked Clark saying, 'it'll be *fun*.'

When he finished removing the mutant food he went out to the car and brought in his things. He walked around the house, looking for a place to set up his desk. The place was filthy. Not only was everything covered with dust, but there was also a gritty kind of gray dirt as well, like dried mud or something. Harry was no neatnik, but still, he disliked dirt and wished Clark had had the courtesy to send a cleaning service ahead of him.

The house was old, with low ceilings and wobbly wooden floors. It seemed huge to Harry, palatial. After living so long cramped into two tiny rooms, all this space, just for him, seemed frightening. In his life, every inch was filled with *some*thing, and the good thing about that was there was no room for anything to get in that he didn't personally make room for. Here, there was no telling what could sneak in unawares.

The glass in the windows was so ancient it had begun to melt, or slide, or whatever it was old glass did that made it wave like that. To either side of the front door there was an open room, what had probably been the parlor on one side and the living room on the other. One had a large beveled window surrounded by handmade bookcases with a few tin-foil thrillers and true-crime mysteries lying about. The window overlooked the yard, which was small and overgrown, and then trees. The other room had a fireplace that had been sealed up with wainscotting, and windows that overlooked the driveway. Harry didn't think he would be comfortable working in either: they seemed cold and unfriendly, not the least bit welcoming.

If there was one thing Harry was obsessive about, it was his space. It had to be right. It had to have the right feel. He could never explain this to Clark – she would accuse him of being a big fat baby – but it had to feel *safe*. If he was going to let himself go, travel off to distant and possibly dangerous places, he wanted to make sure he was coming back to a place he knew, a place where he felt comfortable, familiar. And yes, safe.

He walked down the long hallway leading into the kitchen/dining area, off of which was a bathroom painted a repulsive shade of brown, a kind of chocolaty color, like loose stools. Horrible, Harry thought, how am I ever going to take a crap in here? He wondered if Paul would mind if he painted it.

The kitchen/dining area was massive: the kitchen on one side, with doors leading to the pantry and the back porch, and a wood stove separating the kitchen from the dining room, which was really just a large empty space with a long trestle table facing the picture window. That window, too, overlooked the pathetic little yard and Harry thought there must have been a view of something at some point, maybe there had been fields that had been overgrown, or orchards. Now, it was just scrub, a little mini-forest of brown and gray stick-like trees. Well, at least nobody could hide behind them, he thought and decided this was as good a place as any to set up.

He wiped off a corner of the table, got the computer, plugged it in. The last time he'd sat in front of it, waiting for it to boot up, the kid had gone flying past his window.

That's it! he thought, I *can* prove I was sitting at home, at my desk, when the kid fell! It would all be there, in the Directory: the date and time, down to the second, when he'd been working on *Butler*.

Thank God for technology, he thought, I renounce all my neo-Luddite beliefs. I love it, I love technology!

He brought up the Directory. He'd been working on the tryst chapter, when Butler goes up to Central Park to meet the Mystery Woman, who really wasn't a mystery to Harry, she was Polly, disguised. Harry had always had a thing for Polly, nothing serious, nothing worth following up, and certainly not worth riling Clark, it was just this *thing*. The Best Friend Thing. It was nothing new to him – he developed a desire for all his girlfriend's best friends. It made perfect sense to Harry. There was the proximity. And since they both loved the same person, of course they'd be attracted to each other as well. There was the idea – mistaken, no doubt – that the best friend knew all the secret places the beloved kept hidden and that by loving, and knowing, the best friend, he could fit all the pieces of his darling together. Add to that the allure of the forbidden and you came up with one very tantalising hunk of woman.

He scrolled up and down the Directory, but there was nothing there. No 'Tryst'. No 'Central Park'. No 'Horny Urban Insects'.

Could he have been so stupid as to not save it?

'Think, man, think,' he told himself, running the morning through his head, seeing himself stand up, walk over to the window, and then . . . leave. But he hadn't turned the computer off.

Clark. Clark must have come home, seen the screen-saver on, cursed him for wasting electricity, and shut it off.

How could she? How could she, with a curse and a flip of her finger, erase his alibi, not to mention his work?

Damn technology. Damn the new screensaver, which had been Clark's idea, of course, it never would have occurred to Harry to add anything new, he liked everything just the way it was, and if it hadn't been for that, she would have come home and seen that he was in the middle of writing and she would have saved it.

She could have saved him, Harry, as well.

He would have to punish her for that. If he were home, he wouldn't speak to her, and she'd follow him around, tugging on his arm, begging, 'Harry, Hon, what's wrong? What did I do?' Or he'd go out with Lenny and Paul, tie one on, come home very drunk and very late, and she would be beside herself, because he hadn't called, because he'd been drinking, something he rarely did except on his three big nights. He'd spray on a little of Bettina's perfume, that would really drive her wild.

But he wasn't home. He was here, in this dark, cold house in the middle of nowhere. He didn't even have a phone to not call her on.

He turned the computer off. What the hell, he thought, he wasn't any worse off, really, than he had been fifteen minutes ago, before he thought about the time being on the computer. And it wouldn't have mattered in any case, they estimated the time of death in hours, not seconds, they would have said he could have pushed the kid off the roof and come back home to type up his alibi.

Alone, he thought, I'm alone in the middle of nowhere, a murder suspect – if only in the eyes of my devoted, trusting wife – in a house full of fat, ugly, diseased critters used to a free lunch.

Loneliness. Harry wasn't quite sure how he felt about it. On the one hand, it was quiet, so quiet he could follow a thought through, stick with it a while, to the end. Maybe even to a conclusion. He suddenly realised one of the advantages of living in the midst of a thousand distractions was that a thousand distractions equalled a thousand excuses and excuses were a very good thing to have. Excuses kept everyone, including himself, from looking too closely at what they were doing.

Stacking wood! Now, there was a distraction worth the name, an excuse with the immediacy of need.

He went out to the woodpile, gathered an armload of logs and brought them in. He stacked the wood relatively neatly in the wrought iron wood-holder thing, the official yuppie wood-containing receptacle, from LL Bean or Williams Sonoma or wherever city folk got their regulation country gear. It irritated Harry that Paul had become so materialistic – Paul, the former Trotskyite, the former anarchist, the former contributor to the *Catholic Worker*, now the proud owner of a five-hundred-dollar wood rack.

'Sell-out,' Harry muttered as he went out for another load. Paul wasn't as bad as Jimmy Houser, of course, at least he didn't dress up in a barber's smock and run around the commodities exchange with millions of dollars worth of options in his fat fist, but still, it was a disappointment to see Paul with all this *stuff*.

Harry looked around the house again. The place was

definitely funky, but underneath the dirt it had the aura of intentional funkiness, and that disgusted Harry. The whole point of funkiness, as far as Harry was concerned, was to be a little *off*, a little smelly, a little unclean – not enough to present a health hazard or anything, just enough to make the stiffs wrinkle up their noses and flee. Funkiness was a barrier, a defense, a Maginot Line of tastelessness.

Harry didn't much care what people chose to do with their lives – live and let live, he always said and for the most part believed – but it broke his heart to see Paul becoming a detestable yuppie. It wasn't just the *stuff* – the *stuff* he could blame on Bettina – it was his attitude, a kind of fatigued reluctance to engage in anything outside his own little life and his own little business. Where was the fire? The passion?

Comfort, Harry thought. The murderer of imagination, desire, potency, lust. Paul was just too damn comfortable in his floor-through with a view, his *stuff* had quenched his fire, fizzled it into a slow, hissing death.

It was scary. Paul was younger than Harry – he hadn't even hit forty-five and yet he acted like a septuagenarian, eating dinner in front of the TV and spitting food at Bettina while he ranted about tax hikes and raising the minimum wage and the increase of crime. 'You're turning into a right-wing asshole,' Harry had warned. 'If you keep this up, we'll have to expel you from the Lornes.' Paul had rolled his eyes and shivered. 'You're *scaring* me,' he squeaked in his snappy-come-back-TV voice and Harry never mentioned it again, although he began pressuring Lenny and Paul more vehemently for a revival.

Harry had convinced himself that getting back on the circuit was the only thing that could save Paul from himself, remove him from the constant barrage of consumerism, remind him of who he *really* was. 'Maybe who he *really* is is a consumer,' Clark had pointed out. 'Maybe he hasn't lost himself at all, maybe, in fact, he's found himself. Leave him alone.' But Harry couldn't do that. He only had two pals and he wasn't about to let half his circle of friends go without a fight.

Harry shuffled out into the living room, dusted off a chair, sat down and moped. Was this depression? He thought not. Depression, from what he could tell, had some kind of horror attached to it, something that not only made the depressed person want to flee from himself, but also made everyone else who came in contact with him want to get away before they caught it. A kind of kootie vibe. Harry was still perfectly happy being himself, although he didn't like this feeling he was having of sliding downward, not into a trough, or even a ditch, but a slight indentation, enough to twist his spirit but not to break or even strain it. Ever since that kid went flashing past his window, he hadn't been the same. And he didn't like the change one damn bit.

Of course there was nothing to be ashamed of in feeling a bit down in the dumps; even Achilles had to be bribed out of his lethargy before going on to wreak havoc on Troy. It was a time-honored tradition, a mythical pattern.

If he could just get *into* it. But try as he might, he couldn't let himself enjoy it; he felt like life was dragging him off to the dentist and he didn't want to go.

'I wanna go home!' he moaned.

Nineteen

He let her in. Clark was surprised; she thought it would have been against regulations or something. As she tried, unsuccessfully, to crawl through the window gracefully, it occurred to her that O'Donnell lived in a world where breaking the rules mattered, had consequences, whereas in her own she could break them with impunity. Who cared if she infringed on copyrights by xeroxing large portions of books? Or if she bought bootleg tapes? Or if she was rude when she was expected to be polite; if she wore jeans to a wedding or a dress to play softball – breaking the rules was the point, because the rules were stupid. In O'Donnell's world, it didn't matter whether the rules were stupid or not, one followed them, or didn't and paid the consequences.

'I must look pretty ridiculous,' Clark said as she tugged on her skirt. 'I just wanted to see . . .'

Her voice trailed off; her eyes filled with tears. The apartment was filled with street furniture, odds and ends picked up from the curb before the garbage trucks could get them. She had furnished her first apartment in much the same way. Gordie might, in fact, have some of her very own cast-offs. He had the standard brick-and-plywood bookshelves, an easy chair that had once been upholstered in a blue and white flowered chintzy kind of fabric but was now uniformly gray from wear. Mattress on the floor. Jerry-rigged end tables with three spindle legs and a stack of newspapers holding up the fourth side. And on the walls – her.

O'Donnell switched on the bare overhead light and Clark gasped. It was like suddenly being in a house of mirrors and everywhere she looked she saw a reflection of herself, in various incarnations: the blonde pony-tailed Clark from the days on Avenue A; the green dye job – which wasn't, contrary to Harry's belief, an attempt to look like a popsickle; the half-and-half of her hair growing back to its original brown. And there it was: the history of her hair. *The History of Hair*, she thought guiltily. This was not the time to start thinking of new material.

But why not, she thought, why not? It was all O'Donnell's fault, his presence made her afraid, made her feel obligated to 'behave', as if she were a little girl threatened with detention. Right and Wrong, Good and Bad, seemed to carry a weight they shouldn't – they're just stupid labels. She wanted to shout, Go away, you oppress me! but she just stood there, silently gazing at herself, wondering what she had ever done to deserve *this* much adoration.

God! He even had a picture of her wearing the Mohawk. How could that be, she wondered, it only lasted a few hours. She wondered if he kept some kind of stake-out, following her around like some kind of papparazzo, hanging about outside Freida's, stuffing her in his camera and carrying her around dangling from his neck. She suddenly understood the aboriginal fear of having one's soul stolen, although of course in her case, she had managed to keep it.

In one corner of the room, there was a very badly built alcove, like something Harry would build, with a little table littered with devotional candles, the big jar-like bodega ones, on which he had pasted her face over that of the saint's. She sniffed. 'Red Dusk.' Jesus! How had he known? Had he sneaked up and *smelled* her?

This was heady stuff. She couldn't help it; she felt proud. How could she not?

She wondered what O'Donnell was thinking, looking at all these accoutrements of awe, all this worship, this rapture? Mustn't he be wondering, What has this woman got?

She knew instinctively there was nothing threatening about this love shrine – it was not the work of some maniac out to 'get' her – there were no slash marks across any of her faces, no eyes scratched out, no bandaids placed across her mouths. This was just sheer and utter enchantment.

Enchantment. She had never thought of herself as enchanting before and despite the fact that she knew she would make herself pay for it later, she felt elated. She thought about her own love shrine, the one she'd had in her bathroom on 7th Street, to Sam Shepard. She had plastered her bathroom walls with posters from his plays, photos cut from the *Voice* and the *Soho News*. She had been in love with him, but not in a carnal way – she hadn't wanted to sleep with him, although she'd heard that wasn't so hard to arrange – her love had been on another plane entirely: love of the work, love of the words, love of his *vision*. The man *got* it. American perversity. He understood it, understood *her*, she imagined, back then when she was young and impressionable and wanted so desperately to be understood. Back then, it was bold; now, it was the stuff of sit-coms, and Clark wasn't at all pleased about being *that* well understood.

Jesus! Sam *Shepard*. Gordie *Sheppard*. Oh my God, she thought, how could I have missed that? What could it *mean*? She thought about her own obsession, the innocence of it, the pleasure it had given her when she was young and alone in New York. She hadn't really wanted anything from Sam – he gave her everything she wanted in his work – and although she had gone to all his plays and readings and anywhere he was appearing with Patti Smith, she had never dreamed of introducing herself to him. In fact, she hadn't *wanted* to meet him, she didn't want the real person, full of flaws, full of weaknesses, full of bodily needs, messing up her image of him. Ugh, what could be less enchanting than thinking of your hero sitting on the toilet?

Gordie really *was* just like her.

But then again, she had never considered jumping off a roof for Sam.

There. There it was. The truth staring at her from a hundred different versions of herself. She began to weep, thinking of the thousands of ways she could have saved him. She could have noticed his existence, for one. When she saw him standing awestruck outside *BAG* she could have gone over to him, invited him in, dragged him in, if necessary, given him some task to perform. She remembered how they had taunted him, calling, 'Mod! Mod, come back!' as he ran down the sidewalk. She should have been above that.

It's all my fault, she thought as she stared at the love shrine. How could I have let this happen? She felt herself shrinking in her own estimation, shrivelling as she totted up all her sins: not noticing Gordie, suspecting Harry, avoiding taking responsibility and, worst of all, the unruly, disgusting and despicable pride that was clamoring around in some venal corner of her heart. He killed himself over me, she thought, and I'm proud of it.

It was the most shameful thought she had ever had in her life. She wanted to call it back, but it was too late, it had formed itself into words and was scurrying forth, on its way to Heaven or Hell, and there wasn't a damn thing she could do about it.

Sick, sick, sick, she thought, but she couldn't help it. As bad as she felt for the poor dead kid, and she felt truly heartsick, she couldn't quiet that contemptible part of herself that was all puffed up with pride, like some stupid simpering starlet, whispering, 'It was for *me*! He killed himself for *me*!'

'How *could* he?' she moaned.

'How could he what?' O'Donnell wanted to know.

Oh God, she had forgotten about *him*. There he was, behind her, watching her, trying to pry into her mind by watching her actions, her responses, waiting for her to betray herself – or Harry! she'd forgotten about Harry! – with some psychological clue he learned about in Detective School. Was he thinking the *he* in 'how *could* he' meant Harry, as in how could he push the poor sucker off a roof just because he was in love with his wife?

She had to protect Harry. Her own suspicions had vanished the minute she saw the love shrine and realised the truth, but O'Donnell no doubt still suspected Harry. He was standing there, staring at her with his professionally inscrutable cop look. She wondered if they taught them *that* in Detective School, too, and wondered if she could sit in on a few classes.

Ugh, she thought, growing more disgusted with herself by the minute, how could she think of a thing like that at a time like this? It was too late to save Gordie, but she could still save Harry. She would sacrifice herself if necessary. It would be the right thing to do. The stand-up thing to do. Say she'd been having an affair with the kid and had told him to buzz off.

'Jump,' she said through her tears.

O'Donnell walked up behind her and placed his hand – manicured, she noticed – on her arm. Was he arresting her? Was it a crime to be the cause of someone's suicide? Involuntary manslaughter, she thought, negligent homicide. No, homicide by neglect. It didn't matter; she deserved whatever she got.

She looked up at O'Donnell, terrified.

'Hey,' he said, kindly, softening her up for the kill, probably. She winced, preparing herself for the worst.

'He didn't kill himself,' he said. 'It was an accident.'

'What?' Clark asked.

'It was an accident. There was a witness, a bum who lives up on the roof. Saw the whole thing.'

'A witness?' Clark repeated, 'I thought *Harry* was the only witness.'

O'Donnell harrumphed a little, as if to say, 'Some witness,' and shook his head.

'Naw, this guy, this bum, saw it. The kid went to sit down on the ledge and the thing just caved in.' O'Donnell shook his head. 'Poor kid. Young, too.'

An accident! An accident! Clark wanted to grab O'Donnell, hug him, dance him around Gordie's apartment. She wanted to shout for joy, but then she remembered that Gordie was dead. She started to cry again, hating herself for thinking about herself rather than Gordie. O'Donnell was right. It was horrible, tragic. Poor Gordie. Poor little love slave. She was a terrible person. But she would atone for it, somehow. She would atone for suspecting Harry. She would atone for her pride. She'd volunteer at the Samaritans, work on the Suicide Hotline, for Gordie. And for Harry? She'd think of something . . .

But why then, it occurred to her, if they had this witness, had they kept snooping around, acting like they suspected Harry?

She asked.

O'Donnell seemed genuinely surprised, even grinned.

'We never suspected your husband, Ms Clark,' he said. 'We were just trying to find out what happened. It took a while to find this Rex guy. He's a squatter. He wasn't too eager to come to us.'

'Of course not,' Clark said dreamily. Harry was innocent. *She* was innocent, at least of being the cause.

'But why did you tell Harry not to leave town?' she asked.

'That was a joke,' he said.

Cop humor, she thought, an oxymoron if I ever heard one. But who cared?

'We're innocent!' she wanted to shout. 'We're innocent! We're free! We can go back to life as it was before!'

But someone was dead.

That was horrible, dreadful, tragic. It was wrong of her, to be so happy when she should be so sad. She felt like a balloon, stretched too tight with her conflicting emotions; how does one hold all these opposing thoughts at one time without bursting, without falling apart?

'God, life is a bitch,' she said and O'Donnell said she had that right.

She asked if she could see the diary and he said no.

'Well, could I at least have that one picture?' she asked, nodding her head at herself in the Mohawk, 'I wouldn't want that in the wrong hands.'

O'Donnell laughed, shook his head.

'I think you'd better go now, Ms Clark,' he said, walking over to the door and opening it, 'and don't tell anybody I let you in.'

'Oh, I won't,' she promised and ran down the stairs.

'We're innocent!' she thought as she ran to Rent-a-Wreck to get a car. She'd drive up, now, tonight, to tell Harry the good news. Well, good news for them, at least. Well, not even good news for them. Relieving news.

People were staring at her as she ran along, alternately laughing and weeping, and she thought about the time she and Harry had been sitting on a bench outside Central Park, after going to the Van Gogh show at the Met, and Harry for some unfathomable reason had kept asking her what it felt like to be mad, as in crazy. 'This,' she wanted to tell him now, 'this is what it feels like. To have your head so full of opposing thoughts it feels as if it will rocket right off your body.' Ambivalence, she could deal with. Paradoxes, no problem. She had, at one time or another in her life, been everything. She had been courageous; she had been a coward. She had been wise; she had been a fool. She had been spiteful; she had been generous. She had been cruel; she had been kind. But never had she been all these things at one time, and that, she would tell Harry, was what madness felt like. Being everything at the same time.

By the time she reached Rent-a-Wreck, it was already closed. She leaned against the door, panting and disappointed. She thought about poor Harry, up at Paul's all alone, thinking she suspected him of being a murderer. It suddenly occurred to her that he hadn't been terribly angry when he realised what was going on – if *he* suspected *her* of being a murderer, she'd be furious. But then again, no one would suspect her of being a murderer because she would never have let a body lie in the courtyard while she slunk away to make an anonymous tip and then later lied about it.

Since there was nothing else she could do, she decided to go home, take a bath, see if she could find a way to reach Dee Dee in Glasgow. A night alone would do Harry good. Build some character. Maybe, after this, he would learn to stop lying. And maybe, she told herself, she would learn to stop being so suspicious.

Twenty

It was the oddest thing. Harry woke up in the middle of the bed, cradled in a kind of ravine where the mattress springs had collapsed. He was still fully dressed, but he couldn't remember having climbed the stairs last night. He wondered if the alien possums had come for him, had their way with him and then after erasing his memory, dumped him on Paul's saggy bed.

He rolled out of bed and stretched. Every muscle in his body ached, but whether from the bad mattress or a night of debauchery with the possum women, he couldn't tell.

He was starving. He had emptied the house of everything edible, but he still had half a Blimpie he'd picked up on the road, stuffed in a bag somewhere in the car, and that was as good a breakfast as any, he supposed.

It was warmer today, balmy almost. Harry was astonished by how quickly the weather had changed – winter yesterday, spring today.

Nature didn't mess around, Butler thought, if it wanted to change, it did, and it didn't waste any time agonising over it.

It was starting to get green; the snow was retreating to little shade-filled havens and the spongy ground, covered with the remnants of last year's grass, squished beneath his feet. He tried not to think about what was under it.

He went back inside, munching his soggy tuna salad, wondering what he was going to do with himself. He didn't want to spend the day sitting around moping, feeling sorry for himself while he waited for his wife to stop thinking he was a murderer. Or stop chasing after the natty detective. Or doing whatever it was that made her send him away in the first place. He'd have to make her pay for that, but he couldn't make her pay until she came crawling up here, begging for forgiveness, something Harry hoped would happen very soon. In the meantime, he should begin the day by doing something useful.

Something like snooping.

He started with the pantry – he'd never been in a house with a pantry before. It was huge, almost as large as his whole apartment, with all sorts of odd little drawers and cubbyholes, hiding places, Harry thought, and he set about trying to find something interesting, some little part of Paul he hadn't known about before, a secret that would reveal Paul as someone other than the person he presented himself to be.

Harry liked to believe that everyone was really someone else. Take Clark, for example. Clark was a hundred someone elses, but what was different about Clark was that the someone elses always added up to Clark. No matter who she surprised him with, she always had the stamp of Clark upon her, the smell, the aura, the essence of Clarkness, although if pressed, he could never really define what that was. There was no such thing as being out of character with Clark – whatever she was, was Clark. It was never an act, never phoney. Clark always rang true. He couldn't imagine life without her. He'd become accustomed to a life full of guest appearances and anything else, now, would seem dull.

But Clark's someone elses were always up-front, not like most people, who kept their secret selves hidden for one reason or another. He thought about the night Lenny came out – he'd had the Lornes over for dinner and the four of them were sitting squished around Lenny's little kitchen table, eating Chinese take-out and arguing about whether or not they should go commercial, hire a manager. Lenny was just sitting there, picking at his Kung Pao, looking from one Lorne to another, when all of a sudden, he tossed his chopsticks on to his plate, stood up, grabbed a fistful of hair in each hand and shouted, 'Shut up! I have something to tell you!' They all stopped eating and looked up at him, waiting. 'I'm gay,' he said and sat back down, covering his face with his hands so he wouldn't have to look at them. It was a good thing: Harry and Paul started laughing – big surprise, they'd known for years – but Jimmy wasn't fast enough to catch the revulsion that skimmed across his face. 'Hey,' Paul said, leaning over and patting Lenny on the shoulder, 'it doesn't change a thing. To each his own, right?' 'Hear, hear,' Harry had agreed. 'Everybody's in some kind of closet.' He patted Lenny's other shoulder, but he was looking at Jimmy, who had recovered, his secret tucked firmly back into its hiding place. Bigotry? Homophobia? Homosexual tendencies of his own? A closet Fundamentalist? Harry didn't know what the secret was, he just knew it was there. They spent the rest of the evening working on a song about various kinds of closets but Jimmy never gave himself away and that was the beginning of the end of the Four Lornes, at least as a quartet.

In a large cupboard covered with about a hundred coats of paint, Harry found two stacks of old *Life*s and *Look*s from the fifties. Must have come with the house, he thought, unless Bettina had picked them up at some garage sale with the intention of papering the bathroom walls with old photos of famous people, something that had been a very popular decorating scheme a few years back and would have, Harry thought, made a vast improvement over the turd-colored paint that was in there now.

He pulled out the stacks, thinking he'd take a look at the photographs of his youth, see if they brought forth any astounding memories for *B by B*. As he reached in, he felt a small door-like square behind the magazines. Oh boy, he thought, and pushed them aside, reaching into the dark and pulling the door open. At first he saw nothing. He was afraid to stick his hand in the darkness, afraid there might be a rat trap in there, or worse yet, a rat. He ran into the kitchen, got the flashlight from under the sink, ran back into the pantry. 'Oh boy,' he sang, 'oh boy, oh boy, I'm gonna find a secret.'

He crawled into the cupboard and shone the light in the hole. Way back in the corner he saw it: small and compact, more threatening than a pair of beady eyes. A gun.

He took the butt of the flashlight and used it to scoot the gun out of the hole. Harry knew nothing about guns, except that they were dangerous. He pulled the gun out into the light and had a look – it was the old-fashioned kind, toyish almost, with a long barrel, a wooden handle, or grip, or whatever they called it, and a round cartridge for the bullets. He could see their brassy backs shining from the chambers – six of them. A six-shooter. How John Wayne!

If this were a novel, Butler thought, the gun would have to go off. He carried it into the kitchen to get a better look. Smith & Wesson, the barrel said on one side. Regulation Police it said on the other. It must be pretty old, Harry thought, from the twenties or thirties maybe and he wondered how many bootleggers it had killed.

He held it up and pretended to point at an adversary. Al Capone. Bonnie and Clyde. 'Blam!' he cried, lifting the gun and blowing at the barrel. He stood up, twirled the gun on his finger, aimed at the doorway. 'Gotcha!'

He wondered if it were possible to shoot aliens. In the movies, they were always nearly indestructible. Bullets bounced off them or passed harmlessly through their globby skin stuff, their ectoplasm or whatever it was that looked like pulsating frog guts. The humans always had to fry them or drown them or bury them, use one of the elements to kill them off. Anything man-made was useless, a point repeated ad nauseam in horror movies and the main reason why Harry hated them.

He decided it would be best not to tempt fate. Since he had found the gun he should take it outside and shoot it, just once, to ensure it wouldn't need to go off again. He looked round the pantry for something to shoot, preferably a beer can. A Budweiser would be nice, none of that namby-pamby micro-brew stuff for target practice, he wanted a *real* beer can, a Bud or a Genny. All he could find was a grocery sack full of Bettina's empty Diet Dr Pepper cans, white with a kind of pinky-red lettering, girl stuff, but it would have to do.

He went out to the woodpile, the scene of Paul's alleged abduction, and placed the can on the top. He backed up twenty paces, which he assumed were just steps, but longer, and aimed.

He felt like Gary Cooper. 'Take *that*, ya yella bellied sap sucker,' he said and fired.

The can was still there, mocking him. He aimed again, using both hands, and although he missed the can again and even the woodpile, he did manage to hit a nearby tree.

He walked over to the tree and was amazed at the damage the bullet had done. How could a person survive that, he wondered, how could even a blob of frog guts survive that?

He looked at the gun and remembered the time he'd been out in the woods, dead drunk, with a bunch of kids, Ricky Lopez and Charlie Potter and that Novack kid, what was his name? God, he was a weirdo: a farm kid, with eleven older sisters, and because he was the only boy, and the youngest, they let him run wild. He was forever getting into some kind of trouble and everyone's mother would always say, 'You stay away from that Novack kid,' which made him immensely attractive to all the boys just starting out on the road to rebellion – all they had to do was hang out with 'that Novack kid' and they were *bad*.

It had been a day much like this, and they'd piled into the Novack kid's pick-up and driven out to the wildlife sanctuary at Davis Hill and the Novack kid pulled out a shotgun from under the seat and they'd gone into the woods and taken turns shooting . . .

Harry dropped the gun and held his hands up to the sky: 'Thank you, thank you, thank you,' he muttered, to God or fate or whoever was watching over them that day, preventing some unsuspecting bird watcher or dog walker from crossing through their line of fire.

How did he get through his youth, how does anyone get through their youth? So heedless, so idiotic, so downright mean. How was it that he didn't get caught? How was it that tragedy, which was lurking around every corner, let him pass by?

How is that determined, Harry wondered, why is it that some get by and others get caught? Are they born with some little mark on them that separates them from all the hundreds of thousands of drunken, heedless, stupid teenage boys out doing something potentially disastrous, some smudge of destiny that says, 'This is the one who will get caught'?

He thought about Clark, about all her poking and prying into his past, and was glad she had never dug out that little tidbit. Not that he was hiding it – he hadn't thought about it in years, and probably would never have thought about it again, if he hadn't shot the gun. What would she have made of that? Would she have stuffed it in some filing cabinet in her brain, under 'Harry, Destructive Tendencies of'? Jesus, he thought, there were probably hundreds of things she could stick in that folder, thoughtless kid stuff on its own, the misdemeanors of youth, but when put together in a bulging catalogue, they could add up to one big felony.

Did *everything* count? Did everything add up to something? Was nothing innocent?

He felt paralysed, afraid that any move he made would be the wrong one, would lead to something irrevocable. The gun lay at his feet. He was probably the only person up here who didn't know how to use one, and he could understand why Paul would have one, although what good it could do, hidden away in that old cupboard behind the magazines, Harry couldn't figure. What was he going to do, say, 'Excuse me, Mr Burglar, I've got a gun downstairs and if you'll just give me a couple of minutes, I'll go get it and shoot you . . . ?'

Or perhaps it was just hidden because Paul didn't want anyone stealing it, breaking into the house, finding the gun, going out and murdering someone with it and then having the gun traced back to him and he'd be charged with murder. It could happen.

'Look at me,' Harry said, and he wanted to throw himself down on the soggy ground and weep: homeless, wifeless, cityless and all because some stupid kid with a crush on Clark went toppling off a roof.

He thought about Clark, looking at him and seeing a monster. Suspecting him. *Him*, Harry Butler. Peaceable Harry. Mr Nice Guy. How could she, even for a microsecond, suspect him?

He supposed that if he, Harry, believed that everyone was really someone else, Clark could conceivably believe the same thing. And was it so incredible that the someone else she thought he was, was a murderer?

Yes. It *was* incredible, as in unbelievable. No one who knew Harry would ever believe him capable of hurting someone's feelings, much less killing them. So why would she think that? It didn't make any sense, unless . . .

Unless she *was* letting that O'Donnell nibble away at her. Unless she'd been seeing him from even *before* the kid's death. Yeah. Maybe that was why she let O'Donnell breathe in her ear all afternoon – maybe they'd been having an affair and the kid found out and had threatened to tell him, Harry, about it and *O'Donnell* had pushed the kid off the roof. And Clark and O'Donnell were taking the opportunity of the kid's death to get rid of Harry.

For ever.

Harry picked up the gun and envisaged O'Donnell, impeccably earth-toned. 'Take *that*, ya dirty Homewrecker!' he snarled, 'Blam! Blam!'

'Ugh!' he cried, tossing the gun away again. If someone *did* break into Paul's house and steal the gun and murder someone with it, *his* fingerprints would be on it. Oh boy, what couldn't Clark and her detective do with *that*? They'd put two and two together and turn him into a serial killer.

He looked at the gun. 'Pick me up and put me to your head,' it told him and what could be more fitting? Butler, giving in to the bleak hopelessness of his situation, goes out in a blaze of blue light of his own making.

'Wow!' Harry cried. 'That's *great*!'

It was perfect, magnificent! The perfect ending for *B by B!* And, while Butler was descending into the sinkhole of despair, he could also come up with the tone for Raptor Music! If he was going to be depressed, he thought as he ran back in the house, he might as well make the most of it.

Twenty-one

Clark realised her mistake around Glens Falls. Up until then, she had been happily driving along in her Rent-A-Wreck, a massive 1982 Cougar that made her feel she should pull over to the side of the road, jump in the back and take a nap, just so as not to waste all that space. But she wouldn't stop; she'd save the back seat for later, when she was reunited with Harry. They could find some lovers' lane, crawl into the back, and make-out like a couple of lust-crazed teenagers hidden behind the steamy windows.

To make up for having suspected him, and having sent him away, she had decided to offer him the ultimate atonement – she would give up her rent-controlled apartment and buy them a nice little two-bedroom somewhere, two bedrooms with doors, maybe one of those cute little pre-wars with the french doors dividing the living room from the kitchen. They would have doors galore, and they would never have to part to get away from one another.

The idea of a mortgage was terrifying; it was more than just the responsibility, the taking on of massive debt, it was crossing over a line she had never thought she would cross. It was forever relinquishing her Peggyhood; becoming a Have, being encumbered with all the accoutrements of ownership. It was giving up her freedom, locking herself for thirty years into a job she couldn't quit.

And she would do it, give up her freedom, the notion that she could, whenever the whim hit her, quit her job, go back to temping, go back to her own work, reclaim her youth. She would give it all up. For Harry.

What I did for love, she thought.

Thinking about the sacrifice she had, in her own mind, already made for Harry, relieved her of any guilt or shame. She couldn't imagine what had come over her. Now that it was gone, it seemed silly, a joke almost, something she and Harry could laugh about in their new apartment. A fireplace! They'd get an apartment with a fireplace that worked. She'd curl up in his lap, and he would put his long arms around her, holding some big fat old nineteenth-century novel, Scott perhaps, and read to her of Lucy and Edgar and their impossible love.

How could it be that her love for Harry, which at this moment was the driving force of her life, hadn't overcome her ridiculous suspicions? Her love felt strong, invulnerable: an island fortress for the two of them to live in, happily ever after. Alone in the car with her love, without the reality of Harry to challenge it, she adored everything about him. She even loved the things she hated about him. Maybe she loved those things the most, in a way, because they proved how true her love for him was.

She imagined Harry's face, registering surprise, a

moment's indecision while he wondered whether he should pretend to be angry, followed by joy. She would run into Paul's house, into Harry's arms. There would be tears, of joy, much ripping off of garments, sex, sex, and more sex, and when they were finished, when they lay dreamily spent on the floor, that's when she would tell him about the apartment. The only thing he had ever wanted; the only thing – besides sex – he had ever begged for.

And that's when she realised her mistake. She should never have sent him away. She should have just dealt with her stupid suspicions. She should have called her old shrink, if necessary. She should have just gone to work and waited for them to evaporate in the bustle of fact-finding. She should have called O'Donnell, *asked* him if he suspected Harry instead of just taking Harry's word for it.

How could she have been so stupid? Harry had never spent a night alone in his life, what on earth had made her think he'd be safe at Paul's? Right now, he could be in some haystack with a milkmaid. He could have taken one look at Paul's, said, 'To hell with this,' and kept on driving, up to Canada, into Montreal where at this very moment he could be sitting at the end of some bar, trying to *parlez* with some foul cigarette-smoking R-rolling chickie-poo.

'Stupid,' she said, flooring the accelerator, 'stupid, stupid, stupid.'

She turned up the radio. Klaus Barbie was refusing to attend his own trial. Nazi pig; hanging was too good for him. The first civilian president of Guatemala was visiting the White House. The cicadas of Brood 10 – great name! – were emerging from their seventeen-year snooze. There's some tribe of people in Equador who live well into their hundreds – Harry would be interested in that. There are four thousand civilians living at Guantanamo – a good little factoid; flight line crews composed entirely of women maintain the aircraft there. Jesse Jackson was heading the polls going into the primary. Hurrah! Local news: the three Kerley Corners teenagers accused of the brutal torture and murder of two Canadian students were coming up for trial. Kerley Corners! That was where Harry was!

What had she been *thinking*? The idea of sending Harry away seemed idiotic now; absurd, nonsensical. Clark prided herself on being a take-charge kind of person, immensely practical, a problem solver. But what good was common sense if she didn't follow it herself? Why did she have to *be* like this?

Think facts, she told herself.

Glens Falls, destroyed by the British in 1788. Resettled by John Glen, no relation to the astronaut, two 'n's. Farm team for the Detroit Tigers. Lake George: site of Fort William Henry. *Last of the Mohicans*. Execrable book, but Harry loved it. Three-quarters of high school students don't know what Reconstruction was and can't identify Walt Whitman or Henry David Thoreau. Instant coffee was invented in 1901 by Satori Kato. The term 'America' was first used to denote the New World in 1507.

She was in the Adirondacks now. She passed the Scenic Turnouts with a slight sense of guilt; she should stop, she should admire, she should be duly awed by the majesty of Nature. She should allow herself to be reminded that her little insanities mattered not a jot in the greater scheme of things, that ultimately it didn't matter if Harry was lying in the arms of a milkmaid . . .

But it did! It did matter. Maybe not in the greater

scheme of things, but in *her* scheme of things it mattered more than anything else. What was a mountain range compared to her love for Harry? What was a forest, a waterfall, a canyon, compared to love? Nothing. Just scenery. Unlike Harry, Clark was fond of Nature, although by no means enraptured. Growing up on a farm had given her a respect for it, but she was too familiar with Nature's vicious side to trust it. And besides, it wasn't going anywhere – if she missed the sights today, she could always stop on the way back. With Harry. Nature was ten times more beautiful when one gazed upon it with one's lover. They could form a little convoy – Clark in front in the Cougar, Harry chugging along behind in the Chevette – and she would lead him off the highway, down a dirt lane, where they would find a mountain stream and swim, naked, making love in some pine-needled bower. That was, if she could get Harry to get out of the car.

If she could get Harry to forgive her.

How could she have sent Harry up here? Aggie was right; it was cruel. He was probably furious with her. Would he ever forgive her?

Yes, yes. Of course he would, especially when she dangled the new apartment in front of him. Harry was infinitely forgiving; he was the best-natured person she had ever met in her life. He never held a grudge, something that Clark found incomprehensible.

Clark had 'baggage'. She hated the term, hated all that psycho-shorthand, but 'baggage', she had to admit, was at least apt. Carrying one's resentments from place to place, job to job, relationship to relationship, *was* like going through life buried under a load of steamer trunks. It was a great burden, one Harry didn't know and didn't understand. Clark knew. Clark understood.

'It's not fair,' he had said, 'that I understand you and you don't understand me.' Ha! What good-natured people never understood was that most bad-natured people would much rather be good-natured, too. Who wants to go through life loaded down like some poor ox? 'Why don't you just take life easy?' Harry was forever saying and when she'd say, 'I would if I could,' he'd just shake his head and say she wasn't trying hard enough. 'That's the point! That's the point!' she'd holler, 'if you have to *try*, it's not *easy*, is it?'

It was a curse. Why did she have to be bad-natured *and* sensitive enough to care about it?

Was it possible to change one's nature? she asked herself.

Of course, she answered, hadn't her own nature been changed, from the good little girl of the report cards to the grump she was now? But it wasn't something she had wanted, something she had tried to do, it had just happened. Against her will, she might add.

How? How had that happened? 'A leopard can't change his spots,' her grandmother always used to say, but apparently, Clark had.

How could she be both good- and bad-natured? Clark had always believed that each human being came screeching out of the birth canal with her character already intact. One could make adjustments, but that was the best one could do – tinker. And that tinkering, as far as she was concerned, was what life was all about, the struggle to make oneself better than one was born.

But now she had to question her belief. Could it be that her entire character had changed?

She wondered if she was having a mid-life crisis. She had always felt herself exempt from that sink hole – she'd already had hers, when she was six, when her parents died and she was faced with the immensity of the end of existence: one day her mother was singing to her while braiding her hair, the next she was shut up in a shiny black box, unreachable, untouchable, never to be seen again.

She had convinced herself that everything bad that was ever going to happen to her had already happened; that she had, in essence, a free ride – a little bumpy, sure: a few heartaches, some disappointments, the usual up and down bars on the graph of life, but the great tragedy of her life was behind her and anything else would be just too unfair.

They were saying on the news that Rafsanjani had said Oliver North was referred to as 'Ollie the Brainless' in Iran. Robert McFarlane called Richard Secord a 'borderline moron'. They were all a bunch of idiots, if you asked Clark. Dangerous idiots, but idiots nonetheless. A Polish jetliner crashed, killing all 163 aboard. Awful! When she got home, she'd go over to the Red Cross and pack boxes for the survivors. But there *were* no survivors. Well, she'd pack boxes anyway. She had to do something; she just couldn't sit around, letting all the bad news wash over her, like Harry did, if he paid attention at all. Helping out, in whatever small way she could, made her feel better, at least temporarily. It calmed her rage, gave her back a sense of potency.

The reporter droned on: Amnesty International has cited Iran for human rights abuses. Seven thousand executions since the Revolution. Ugh, Clark thought: summary executions, torture, floggings, amputations. Good God, stonings for adultery!

Adultery! She switched off the radio.

'Think facts,' she told herself again.

The Adirondacks were named after the Algonquin

Indians, whom the Iroquois called 'Ha-De-Ron-Dah,' which means 'bark-eater'. That was a fact Harry would like.

Harry! She hoped she wasn't too late.

Twenty-two

Butler had never thought about killing himself before.

That was as far as he'd gotten. The truth of the matter was, he couldn't do it; he couldn't kill himself, even in fiction. It was out of character. Butler would never kill himself; he wasn't the suicidal type. He loved life, lived it to the hilt, gobbled it up in big, hungry gulps. Only his table manners left anything to be desired: he was voracious, insatiable, a vampire of life, sucking it out of everybody and everything he met. Yum, yum, life!

He remembered an old *Our Gang* episode, where Spanky and Alfalfa and the kids are being chased through some old house by a hairy old guy who kept saying, 'Yum, yum, eat 'em up!' And he, Butler, was like that old guy, chasing his own memories – as well as those of anybody else that suited him – through the rickety house, which was Life itself. Mysterious. Scary. Full of secret places, trap doors, basements. He shuddered. Critters.

But also full of charm, potential, possibilities. Women. Life is what you make of it and Harry wasn't ready to let Butler bite the dust. He was going to die young, but what the hell, with modern science what it was, eighty was young these days.

Thinking about life made him hungry. He'd go for a quick run and then get in the car and drive until he found a town large enough to sustain a grocery store. He'd noticed a little round dot on the map, a little north of here, with the circle around it indicating there was some kind of congregation of human beings around.

It was quite pleasant outside, with that embracing warmth of spring: moist, but not humid, full of potential. Harry did his warm-ups, then started running up the slushy road. He passed a couple of driveways, leading up into the woods; heard a few barking dogs and the soft popping of a distant gun. At least he hoped it was distant.

Harry couldn't remember ever having been anywhere so quiet – he could hear the scraping of the pebbles on the soles of his running shoes; the wind tussling the tops of the trees; the soft gurgling of an unseen stream, hidden behind the stalky shrubbery. A squirrel, running through the fallen leaves, sounded like an elephant.

As soon as he began to sweat, they attacked.

Flies. Masses of them, coming after him like a big black thought-bubble, surrounding him like a piece of rotting meat.

'Ugh, ugh, ugh,' he cried, waving his arms like a windmill, trying to disperse them, but they clung like leeches: biting, buzzing, sucking. He tried to run away from them, but they followed, locked in on the scent of his warm blood. Harry had never seen flies like this before, man-eating flies, killer kamikaze flies, triangular blood-sucking flies shaped like Stealth bombers, strafing his head, attacking him through his clothes.

He could hear the distant rumbling of a vehicle approaching – one good thing about being in the middle of nowhere, Harry thought, was that nobody could catch you by surprise. Nobody in a car, that is – he was still suspicious of the woods and what they hid. You could dump a body up here and it would never be found.

And it wasn't just his imagination, either. He'd seen a newspaper when he'd stopped to get gas: big banner headline and a story about a gruesome murder. Some local kids had met some other kids at a rock concert, taken them out in a field, and chopped them up, like some poor deer they'd just bagged. For no reason. Just to prove they could do it. Just like *Rope*. Harry had bought the paper with the intention of clipping the article and sending it to Clark, with a note attached: 'See what can happen up here?' hoping she'd relent and beg him to come home.

Home, he thought. Did he even have one any more? Was Clark scurrying around, stuffing all the evidence of him away so she could make room for O'Donnell? Were they at this very moment sitting at the kitchen table – *his* kitchen table! – eating the rest of the bagels – the bagels *he* ran all the way uptown to get – groping each other under the table while they plotted?

Harry supposed it was his duty as a husband to be outraged, to work himself into a frenzy of jealousy, to drive down to New York, catch them in the act, and . . . And what? And nothing. Harry hadn't been in a fight since junior high, back in the days when he felt it his duty to beat up anyone with the temerity to call him 'Hairy

Butt'. He had never enjoyed it, as some kids do; he had hated the feel of the other guy's cheek smushing against his fist; it was like tenderising a piece of meat and hitting the T-bone.

The vehicle – a Jeep – approached in a rivulet of muddy slush, the yellow light on the roof swirling around like a lighthouse beacon. It stopped next to Harry. A bald head popped out of the window.

'Hey,' the head said, 'new around here?'

Harry ran in place, still trying to wave the flies away.

'Yeah,' he said, 'I'm staying up the road, at Paul Striker's place.'

'E-yup,' the guy – fat, round, middle-aged, ruddy, a farmer who spent too much time on his tractor – said. 'City fella, then.'

'E-yup,' Harry repeated. And proud of it, he didn't add.

'Staying long?' the farmer wanted to know.

Not if I can help it, Harry thought, but said he didn't know and asked if there was a town of any size around, someplace he could buy groceries.

'Helena,' the guy told him, ''bout eight miles north of here on the main road.'

'What *are* these things?' Harry asked him, waving another squadron of flies away.

'May flies,' the guy told him. 'Nasty buggers.'

May flies? Did that mean they lasted the whole month?

'Naw,' the farmer told him, 'they can run well into June,' and he grinned and drove away.

Harry had had enough of the country. He wanted desperately to go home, but that was out of the question.

Well, if he was going to stay up here, he wasn't going to be miserable. He jogged back to the house and jumped into the car. 'You're history!' he shouted at the flies swarming around the windshield, like a bunch of hungry ghouls trying to get at his fresh flesh, 'This is war!'

He'd get bug spray, those bug-killing candles, insect-zappers, No-Pest Strips. Butler vs. Nature and Butler had to win.

Helena was a hell of a lot further than eight miles, but he finally found it, almost up at the Canadian border. He wanted to like the town – it was a grungy old mill town and there was something so straightforward about it, so take-it-or-leave-it. It was down on its luck and wasn't going to apologise for it, and Harry respected that. The buildings, mostly brick, looked like they had been built in the early part of the century and had been pretty untouched since, with a few exceptions, where some haberdasher or shoe merchant had decided to spruce up with one of those awful sheet metal façades so popular in the fifties. But as much as he wanted to like it, he had to admit, he found it rather depressing. That could be a good thing, he supposed, it could provide him with a physical backdrop for the feeling he needed to get for Raptor Music, but strange to say, he was beginning to lose interest in Raptor Music. Maybe it was just the place, just being away from the City, being away from the constant flow of energy, that made him feel rather tired and sluggish when he tried to think about it, or maybe, and this was truly distressing, it just wasn't that great an idea.

It had never occurred to Harry to question any of his ideas: he just assumed they were all great, and he either followed through or not, as the Muse led him. The ones that got left behind were like dormant seeds, safely sealed away in a packet, to be retrieved and sown when the urge struck. That they would all fructify was beyond question.

> *When you wake up in the morning*
> *And you wish you were dead*
> *You know you got that feeling*
> *Kierkegaard called dread*

Maybe the reason he couldn't go any further with it was because there was no place to go.

What a horrible thought! He shook it out of his head and concentrated on finding a likely place to buy insect-killing paraphernalia. Up ahead, on his left, he recognised the blue oval True Value logo dangling from a storefront. A hardware store, he thought, that's the ticket.

Well, another good thing about being up here, Harry thought as he turned into the parking lot, was parking spaces. They were plentiful and free – there was no chance some psycho with a baseball bat would come after you for taking his spot.

Harry loved hardware stores, always had, ever since his first trip to Synder's in Columbus. He loved the smell of them, the pungent odor that was probably just a combination of dust and paint fumes but which Harry associated with manliness, virility, guyness. Harry would spend entire Saturdays wandering up and down the creaking hardwood aisles, fingering the ratchets and bolts and hinges, enamored not with their function but with their names. Split flanges! Swivel swag hooks! Turnbuckles! Toggle bolts! Lap links! Clevis grab hooks! And his favorite, the Hex nut.

Harry filled a shopping basket with bug-killers and took it to the front counter.

'Won't work.'

This from JIMMY, or so his smock said, JIMMY, all caps, in bright red thread. He was about a zillion years old, puckered, bald-headed, hazy-eyed, as gray as cement.

'Beg pardon?' Harry asked.

JIMMY waved his hand toward Harry's arsenal.

'Won't work,' he said again.

Harry was offended. How did this old lawn troll know what he was trying to kill? How did he know whether this stuff would work or not?

'Why not?' Harry demanded.

JIMMY shook his head. 'May flies,' he said sorrowfully, as if he were announcing the arrival of the Black Death. 'Nothing you can do about 'em.'

'There must be *some*thing you can do,' he said. 'What do you guys do?'

'Stay inside,' JIMMY said, his mouth kind of pulsating in and out in a parody of a smile.

'Well, I'll buy this stuff anyway,' Harry said, 'it must kill *some*thing.'

'E-yup,' JIMMY said, taking Harry's money and staring at him, as if he were tying to remember distinguishing features so he could pick him out of a line-up later, 'it all depends on what you're trying to kill.'

'Bugs!' Harry cried. 'What do you think?' and JIMMY nodded, but not as if he believed him.

Twenty-three

The house was dark; the Chevette wasn't in the driveway.

Clark got out of her rental car and walked up to the back porch and groped under the third step for the keys. They weren't there; that meant Harry must have been here and left.

She walked up the steps and looked in. The wan light from the open refrigerator revealed a neat row of four black garbage bags, stuffed full. The doors of all the cupboards were open, revealing the empty shelves. She sighed with relief.

While she had been hysterically imagining various lewd scenarios, Harry had been cleaning. Tidying up. How sweet, she thought as she tried the door. He was making his space nice and clean, for him to work in. For me, when I came up. What a pussy-cat. And now he was out shopping.

The door opened. Clark found the light switch, turned it on. The kitchen smelled of rot and disinfectant.

She walked through the house, noting little bits of Harry – his duffle bag, lying open at the foot of the stairs; his bag of books, propped up against the side of a very dusty armchair; his sweatshirt, lying sprawled on the bathroom floor, as if it were trying to crawl into the bathtub. She picked it up; buried her face in Harry's smell. Sweat and Ivory soap, that's what Harry smelled like, and she loved it.

She walked into the dining room, saw the computer set up on the corner of the table. The screensaver was on; out of habit, she went over to turn the computer off.

'I wonder what he's working on?' she said, and hit the return key.

Butler had never thought about killing himself before, she read.

It took her breath away.

'Butler had never thought about killing himself before,' she read again, aloud. Her own voice sounded frightening, sepulchral in the emptiness.

She couldn't breathe. I'm dying, she thought, I'm going into shock. It felt like she was being squeezed by a boa constrictor, as if some force had come into the room, taken her in its invisible hand and was squeezing the breath, the life, out of her.

'Oh my God,' she moaned, and collapsed.

When she came to, she was splayed on the floor.

'Harry!' she cried, and slowly pulled herself up. 'I have to find him!'

'It's all my fault!' she said, dragging herself outside. She had only suspected him to avoid feeling responsible for Gordie Sheppard's death, and now that she'd been cleared of that, she might be responsible for her own *husband's* suicide! How could she have been so selfish?

From the very beginning, Harry had needed her and every step of the way, she had turned her back on him. What kind of a wife was she?

A bad one, she thought mournfully, imagining the glint of superiority in Aggie's eyes when she'd come up to Clark at the funeral, telling her how sorry she was, but really thinking, 'I told you so. You should have listened to me. Saving marriages is my *job*.' Despite the fact that she hadn't been in one herself.

As she made her way out to the car, she stumbled on something, and reached down for it.

A gun! Oh my God, a gun. She lifted it up, sniffed it to see if it had been shot. It smelled, but of what she didn't know.

'Ugh!' she said and hurled it into the woods – what could it *mean*? What on earth would Harry be doing with a *gun*? Where would he have got it? And where was his body? Had he come out here to kill himself and then changed his mind, decided to get groceries instead? Or, had someone *else* been out here, stalking him? Had that someone else killed him, stolen the car, and dumped Harry God only knew where?

'Calm down,' she told herself, but that was out of the question, so she told herself to try to be reasonable. Logical.

Harry was the least likely candidate for suicide of anyone she had ever known in her entire life. This was, after all, the guy who plowed through all nine hundred and seventy-seven pages of *The Anatomy of Melancholy* and *still* didn't 'get' depression. The guy who hadn't been to the dentist in five years because it hurt too much to get his teeth cleaned. The guy who said, 'Oh well, easy come, easy go,' when he lost a Lottery ticket worth twelve hundred dollars. Harry was not the kind of guy who would kill himself.

She got in the car and headed toward Helena, the closest town. Should she go to the police? Maybe there was some psycho loose up here. Maybe some nutcase had been squatting in Paul's house and became enraged when he came back to find Harry there . . .

She took deep breaths. 'He's shopping,' she told herself: all the evidence – empty cupboards, open fridge, stuffed garbage bags – pointed to a simple little trip to the grocery store.

But what about the gun?

'I will not speculate,' she told herself. 'I will go into town, look for Harry's car, and if I don't find it, I will go to the police.'

Think facts. Mata Hari charged her customers $7,500 a night; the coldest city in the world is Ulan-Bator, Mongolia; Calamity Jane had twelve husbands. More than sixty thousand farms were sold or foreclosed in the United States last year. The snowshoe hare is the favorite food of both the lynx and the coyote. The life span of the Saint Bernard is eight to ten years. Mount Marcy, at 5,344 feet, is the highest point in New York. She probably saw it on her way up.

She passed a sign that had read WELCOME TO HELENA. Some local delinquent had painted over the last three letters and added an 'L'. 'Oh God,' she wailed. Was that some kind of an omen?

She took the turn into Helena, a typical New England mill town, with massive brick warehouses lining the river banks, the old mansions of the mill-owners turned into funeral homes, the big faux-plantation-house inn now serving as a nursing home. She drove slowly through the town, looking for the Chevette, growing sadder by the minute. Helena seemed abandoned – although it was a beautiful spring afternoon, there wasn't a soul on the streets.

'Where is he, where is he, where is he?' she chanted, glancing into every parking lot and alleyway. 'Where *is* he?'

She swerved the Cougar as someone in a parked car heedlessly swung the door open. 'You idiot!' she screamed at the driver, some whacked-out woman wearing nothing but a tablecloth. 'Watch what you're doing!'

She took deep breaths. 'Down, girl,' she told herself.

She glanced at the odometer. She'd drive another half a mile; if she didn't find him by then, she'd turn around and drive back to the state police office she'd passed on the way in.

Twenty-four

What was it, Harry wondered, clutching the bag of bug-killers to his chest as he skulked to the car. Do I look like some kind of maniac? Why does everybody suddenly *suspect* me?

He got in and adjusted the rear-view mirror to get a look at himself. He looked fine – a little scruffy perhaps, he hadn't shaved, but the stubble look was all the rage, at least in the City. Up here, who knew what it meant? Probably that you'd been out on a bender or out in the woods poaching some out-of-season animal.

Butler felt hounded. Harassed. Harried.

Like a hapless buck, hunted down by bullies in their monster trucks, the cab roof covered with searchlights, roaring through the woods whooping and belching and running over anything in their way. Harry had nothing against hunters – Paul was a hunter and before his abduction, he'd come back from trips up here with a cooler full of venison, which Harry loved but Clark refused to touch, which didn't make much sense, seeing as how she had spent her childhood wringing chickens' necks. Truck-hunting, that was something else, that wasn't manly. There was no element of danger, it was carnage for carnage's sake and Harry couldn't approve of that, even though he was about to commit a massacre himself. But that was different. There were too many bugs in the world and they deserved to die, despite what the people at Save the Insects said.

He tossed the bag on to the back seat and walked back out to Main Street. It's amazing, he thought as he turned right, to see if he could find a diner or pizza place, the things people want to protect. The concept of insects making it on to the Endangered Species List was mind-boggling; they somehow seemed too vile to even be considered a species. On the radio, on the way up, he'd caught a Vermont public station and some young woman, one of those querulous girls whose every utterance was a question, was telling the interviewer that rattlesnakes were endangered in Vermont? And they were trying to reintroduce them?

Jesus, Harry had thought, there were certain things that *should* be extinct, and rattlesnakes definitely fitted that category. If they want to live, let them go move in with their cousins out in New Mexico, or Texas. To bring them *back*, when they'd already left, that was ridiculous. And Vermont was right next door. What did they know about state lines, they could slither across a bridge and end up in the woods along with all the other disgusting things crawling around back there.

And besides, wasn't reintroducing a species kind of anti-Darwinian in any case? They hadn't survived. Man, who somehow always got left out of the equation – we *are*, after all, a species, too, he imagined himself telling

Miss Save the Rattlesnake – man, he would say, had survived at the Vermont rattlesnake's expense and that was just too bad for the Vermont rattlesnake, but that was life. If it was man's destiny to run the earth into the ground, so to speak, there was nothing she or anyone else could do about it. Life wasn't fair – not for people and not for rattlesnakes, either.

Life isn't fair, Butler told the young woman. He gingerly removed the ten-foot rattler from the cage. No. Fearlessly. He fearlessly removed the twenty-foot rattler from the cage. The young woman ... Claudia ... Claudia shuddered with terror. Butler deftly swung the rattler around, like a rope, snapping its neck.

Cather. *My Antonia.*

They'd have to have sex, of course. He couldn't have himself waving around a twenty-foot snake without following it with a sex scene. He imagined her body: young, firm, smooth, soft. Little downy white hairs on her upper lip. He'd give her small tits, the triangular kind, and substantial hips. The opposite of Clark, just to piss her off.

Clark hated his sex scenes. 'Lurid, lurid, lurid,' she'd chant, going over them with her blue editor's pencil, 'Overwrought. Cliché. Ugh, that's dis*gust*ing,' and so on. It was so funny, watching her get jealous over someone who didn't even exist, someone who wasn't even a fantasy, for the truth was, the real thing was good enough for Harry, and Clark was definitely the real thing.

There were only a few people on the street, a couple of men wearing those insulated plaid jackets they sold at the Feed and Seed back in Dublin, and a gray-haired woman wearing a neon-pink jogging suit. Harry was used to his sidewalks being full; he was used to being surrounded by thousands of people every time he went out of his building. There was something creepy about the emptiness of Helena, as if everybody had left for a reason, a toxic train wreck or something, and he was going to be the only one left.

He was standing in front of a dime-store kind of place. He decided to go in and see what kind of animals they had trapped in the back. That was another of Harry's favorite memories from childhood: going to Newberry's to watch the fish swimming around in the tanks while the canaries chirped and the gerbils ran hysterically in their wheels. Once, he and Petey Hilyard had sneaked in a little jarful of Petey's dad's dandelion wine and fed it to the white mice, wanting to see what they'd act like when they got drunk. They acted dead.

Bad as Harry had felt at the time, watching those tiny white creatures roll over on their backs and kick their little legs like they were doing bicycle exercises, he had them to thank for his aversion to drunkenness. Three times a year was plenty. Anything more than that could kill you.

He opened the door. It was like walking into somebody's death. It was one large room and instead of aisles there were big wooden bins, like one of those Times Square Dollar-or-Less places, where all the unwanted merchandise of the City makes its way after having failed on the sales rack, in the bargain basement, and in the *50% Off* basket. Harry had always thought those places were the end of the line, a kind of Potters' Field for *stuff*, but apparently not. Here it was, gasping its last, and stupid as it seemed, Harry found himself feeling sorry for all this dross, this unwanted *stuff*, this flotsam and jetsam of abundance. He felt obliged to buy something and picked up a package of ball-point pens – five for a quarter – and paid the silent, dull-eyed clerk.

She counted out his change in a slow, hopeless voice and Harry hurried out of the door, bumping into a woman who was passing by.

'Sorry,' he said.

The woman was compact, athletic but not sculpted, as if she got her muscles from work rather than a gym. Her head was too large for her body, like a child's disproportionate drawing, which somehow spoiled her otherwise pretty face. She was about Harry's age, but trying to look younger.

She stepped back, looked him over. She had a large, tantalising mouth which stretched, when she smiled, into a kind of cheerful sneer, revealing small teeth the color of skimmed milk. EDT, Clark always called teeth like that, Eating Disorder Teeth, discolored from puking all the time. The woman was wearing some kind of African or Indian cloth, a wildly red batiky kind of thing, wrapped around her body like a big bath towel. Kind of chilly for that, Harry thought, and wondered what would happen if it caught on a door handle. Or if he grabbed it; if he took a fistful of that bright red spiraling stuff and held tight as she passed.

'You're not from around here,' she said.

'Is it that obvious?' he asked.

She smiled again. 'I own the local dive,' she said, 'I know everyone up here.'

Harry stuck his hand out, and then remembered his mother telling him a lady should always offer her hand first. Too late, he thought, and grabbed her hand.

'Harry Butler,' he said.

'Any relation to Rhett?' she asked and he said yes, because he always did; because he'd been saying it since he was a kid and all the women at his mother's tea parties asked him the same question and they seemed so excited about it that he figured it must be a good thing to be, so he'd say yes and they'd giggle with delight, hug him to their various chests, and slip him one of the fancy chocolates from their plates.

'Aurora,' she said in return and Harry thought, Uh-oh. He was suspicious of people with only one name. One name was enough for a pet, or maybe a French actress, but a *person* should have two. For balance. For symmetry.

'Welcome to Helena,' she said. 'You homesteading or just passing through?'

'I don't know what I'm doing,' he said, sounding much more pathetic than he had intended.

Aurora laughed: a big, booming, fearless laugh, the laugh of a woman who didn't feel she needed to please anybody but herself. That was good. Harry like the Valkyrie type and what the hell, Brunhilde only had one name.

'I'm just opening up,' Aurora said, jerking her head toward a storefront across the street. Café Em. 'Come on in, I'll treat you to a cappuccino.'

'Em?' Harry asked as they paused on the curb, looking both ways for traffic. There was nothing, except a big white Cougar turning into the hardware store parking lot.

'My dog,' Aurora said, 'Emma.'

'As in Bovary?' Harry asked.

'That twit? No. As in Peel.'

Oooh, Harry thought, envisaging black-clad Diana Rigg taking out bad guys with a wicked kick from her wickedly gorgeous leg, this Aurora person could turn out to be interesting.

'You know,' Harry said as Aurora unlocked the door, 'I never did figure out just what those guys were avenging.'

Aurora shrugged. 'Beside the point,' she said and Harry guessed she was right, as long as you knew who the good guys were, it didn't matter what they were good *for*.

As soon as they walked through the door, Harry was assaulted by fifty pounds of brown and white fur, some kind of slobbering spaniel.

'Emma,' Aurora said, not particularly firmly, in Harry's opinion, 'get down. Leave Harry alone.'

The dog continued to jump all over him, wriggling not just her stumpy tail but her entire rear end in a some kind of dog-ecstacy.

'She's aggressively friendly,' Aurora said, 'I hope you like dogs.'

'Oh, yeah,' Harry said, 'sure. I *love* dogs,' but the truth was, Harry knew nothing about dogs, about animals of any sort, really. He had led a petless childhood, the only boy in his neighborhood without a dog or a lizard or a hamster. Cats were for girls so they were out of the question. His mother was not pet-friendly – 'Who would clean up the mess?' she always asked when Harry half-heartedly begged for a pet, 'Who would take care of it?' Not I, Harry had always thought and so there was no pet.

The café was very West Villagy: a combination trendy bar and coffee house. There was a long, gleaming mahogany bar running along the back wall of the main room, originally a soda fountain, according to Aurora. The place had been a pharmacy and Aurora had kept most of the fixtures – the wooden cabinets with their hundreds of little square drawers, the glass-doored cupboards where the drugs had been locked away, the old gas lamps that had been converted to electricity. The center of the room was filled with an eclectic mix of tables surrounded by motley chairs: wooden straight-backs, cane-seated ladder-backs, wrought iron candy-shop chairs, big heavy dining-room chairs and those plastic and aluminum ones, like Harry's mother had had in their breakfast nook when Harry was a kid. In the front corner, by the large window, Aurora had set up several over-stuffed chairs and a couch – covered with the same material as Aurora's bath-towel-dress – round a coffee table. Between the chairs she had end tables with reading lamps. This area was separated from the rest of the room by two large wooden display shelves, filled with old hardcover books, and placed at right angles, forming a large alcove.

'What's your poison?' Aurora asked, walking behind the bar, 'Espresso or cappuccino?'

'Cappuccino,' Harry said. He climbed on to a stool and the dog immediately jumped up, placed her paws in his lap, and began licking his crotch.

'Down, Emma,' he said and she looked up at him, full of spaniel adoration. '*Down*,' he said again, more firmly, and she lifted her lip and growled. OK, OK, Harry thought, this is a dog that is going to love you whether you want it to or not.

'This is a great place,' he said, 'You do much business?'

Aurora laughed. 'I do OK in the summer,' she said. 'In the winter, it's pretty dead.' She reached into a small refrigerator under the counter for a carton of milk and sniffed it warily. 'So where are you staying?' she asked.

'Kerley Corners,' he told her and she gasped.

Harry wanted to know what was wrong.

'Kerley Corners,' she said. 'It's the UFO Capital of the World.'

'No kidding?' Harry asked, 'You know, I woke up

this morning thinking I *had* been abducted.'

Aurora nodded. 'You probably were. Everybody up here has been. And more than once. The first few times it's not so bad, but wait until they start the experiments.'

'Experiments?' Harry asked and Aurora burst out laughing again.

'Oh,' he said, 'I get it.' *Everybody in Helena was a comedian, and Butler was getting tired of playing the straight man. He decided to change the subject.*

'What are you doing up here in the middle of nowhere?' he asked and Aurora told him she had had a restaurant in SoHo. She told him she got fed up with having to deal with creeps and yuppies and a waitstaff full of people who wanted to be doing something else. Break-your-heart wannabes. She couldn't stand seeing them defeated over and over again, couldn't stand having to deal with the fucking Mafia, with having to deal with the dirt of life.

'Up here,' she said, 'people are basic.'

'Basic what?' Harry asked.

'Basic people. What you see is what you get. The As-Is portion of humanity. They don't want to be anything other than what they are; they don't want to *be* at all, they just want to *have*. I find that refreshing. And honest. And real. Isn't that what America's all about?'

'Jeez,' Harry said, 'that's pretty cold.'

She shrugged. 'It's the way I see it,' she said, 'I mean, think about it. People don't become something in order to *be* that thing; they do it in order to *have* all the things that go along with it. Up here, people just skip the pretense.'

'So what about you?' Harry asked, 'What do *you* want?'

She said she was working on not wanting anything.

'Well,' Harry asked, 'what do you want in the meantime?'

Aurora threw back her head and let out her roaring laugh. She'd had a lot of dental work, Harry noticed, she must like sweets.

'I like you,' she said when she stopped laughing. 'What's *your* story, Harry Butler, relative of Rhett?'

What *was* his story? This was his opportunity to become a different person. He could sit here for hours, happily lying, without having to worry about being caught. He could tell her anything – he was prospector, heading up to Canada to reopen an abandoned gold mine. He was a bounty hunter, tracking a serial killer. He was a zoologist, hot on the trail of the last remaining Vermont rattlesnake. He could lie with abandon, but to his surprise, he just didn't feel like it.

'It's too complicated to begin,' he said, a little too mournfully.

Aurora glanced at his left hand; grimaced.

'Domestic disturbance,' she said.

Harry nodded. 'My wife doesn't understand me.'

'Oh, *please!*' Aurora moaned.

'No, really, she doesn't,' Harry said, not adding, 'she thinks I'm a murderer.'

'Look,' Aurora said, 'I don't care if she understands you or not. If you're looking for understanding, go look somewhere else.'

A tough broad. He knew the type. Bluster and bravado on the outside, all put-up-your-dukes, but you could knock 'em over, pulverise them, with one mean word.

'What are *you* looking for?' Harry asked.

'Nothing,' she said, spritzing some whipped milk into his cup, 'absolutely nothing.'

She handed him the cup. 'That's the point.'

He wanted to know what point.

'The point of *life*,' she said. 'To shed all worldly desires.'

He should have known. With a name like Aurora, she would have to be some kind of New Agey kook.

'I don't know,' Harry said, 'it seems to me the point of life is to accomplish something. To go out of the world feeling like you've left something of value behind.'

She made a kind of snorting noise. 'Accomplishments aren't interesting,' she said. 'The only thing that's interesting is *being* interesting.'

'Being interesting to whom?' Harry wanted to know.

She shrugged. 'To yourself,' she said.

Harry was baffled. Wasn't everyone interesting to himself? What was the point of living if you weren't even interesting to your own self?

He asked Aurora if she thought she was interesting.

'Of course,' she said. 'Don't you find me interesting?'

Less and less, Harry thought, but said, 'Sure.'

She nodded and picked up the thread he had made her lose.

'All those people in the City,' she said, 'wanting to *be*. And the ones up here, wanting to *have*. They're all miserable, because there's never *enough*. Better to not want at all.'

Harry felt as if someone had dropped a boulder on his back. The idea of sloughing through life, day after day, without a goal, without a desire, without a *reason*, was unthinkable.

It was too depressing to think about. He picked up his cappuccino and shuffled over to the alcove, the dog still clinging obscenely to his leg, to take a look.

'Emma,' Aurora said, again without the slightest tone of reprimand, 'leave Harry alone.'

Harry began looking over the titles. 'Most of it's junk,' Aurora said, 'I bought this stuff at auction. Twenty boxes of books for five bucks.'

'Wow,' Harry said, pulling out a slightly mildewed copy of *Tono Bungay*, 'How much do you want for this?'

Aurora shrugged. 'You can have it,' she said.

'You're kidding,' Harry said.

'Why would I kid? You want it, take it.'

'It's a first edition,' he said.

'It's your lucky day, then,' Aurora said. She came out from behind the bar, carrying a little polka-dot plate piled with biscotti.

'Are you serious?' Harry asked.

'This is the way I feel about it,' she said as she offered Harry the biscotti. 'Why should I stand between someone and something they want? Why not just let them have it, make them happy? All I ask is that you replace it with something else.'

'Fine, great,' Harry muttered. He'd bring in one of Bettina's bodice-rippers.

He couldn't believe his good fortune. A first edition *Tono Bungay*. If this couldn't get him back in Clark's good graces, nothing could, and the next time she complained about him not thinking about her when she wasn't in front of his face, he could just saunter over to the bookcase and wave Wells at her. Shame her into silence.

He laughed, grabbed Aurora and did a little dance.

'Thanks,' he said, planting a kiss on her forehead. 'Believe it or not, this may save my life.'

Aurora grinned. 'Maybe it's my lucky day, too,' she said as she pulled him over to the couch.

Twenty-five

She finally found the Chevette, in a parking lot next to a hardware store, but Harry wasn't in it. There was a bag full of insecticides lying on the back seat, but no blood, no signs of a body having been carted around. That was a relief. She rummaged in her shoulder bag for her own keys to the car, and opened the trunk. It was empty, thank God, except for Harry's free weights and the jack.

She walked into the hardware store and went to the front counter.

'Has a guy been in here – about six feet, black hair, pony-tail? Tortoiseshell glasses?'

The clerk – a lean, dusty-looking man, who reminded Clark of Eddie, the handy man who used to do odd jobs at her grandma's farm – was taking his time answering.

'E-yup,' he finally said.

'Oh thank God,' Clark said. He was alive. Alive and safe and shopping. Getting handy items. Thank God.

'Did you by any chance see which way he went?' she asked and the old guy shrugged and kind of nodded his head toward the door, as if to say, 'He went thataway.'

She went outside and looked up and down the main street. On the opposite side, there was a Chinese restaurant, a pool hall, a bar, an empty office with electioneering bunting falling down in the window. One of those ninety-nine cent places. On her own side of the street, there was a florist with a plastic fichus tree in the window, a Bible bookstore, numerous empty shop fronts advertising themselves for sale or lease. In the next block, she could see signs for a video arcade and a chiropractor. Food was her best bet: she'd try the Chinese restaurant first.

She dashed across the street and looked in – no Harry. The pool hall, perhaps. She and Harry had played pool a lot when they first started dating; they'd go up to Dan Lynch, shoot a few games, and then dance until Lorna came in and dragged Harry home. She felt rather daring as she opened the door and peered in – the pool hall had been the low-life center of Avoca, the farm-town equivalent of an opium den, filled with shady characters who might kidnap you and sell you to the white slavers – but this one looked pretty tame: a thin, white-haired man sitting behind the cigar counter, and a middle-aged couple playing eight-ball, perfectly friendly and nice when she asked if any of them had seen Harry. Which they hadn't.

She walked back outside. The post office! Perhaps he was sending her a love letter. Or reading through the WANTED posters; he loved finding felons to stick in his book.

But no, he wasn't there, either. Nor the bank. Nor the video arcade, crowded with school-skippers. She stood in front of the arcade, wondering where to go next. There was a little café she had missed, next to the florist. Café Em. She wondered what the Em was – a café for typesetters, perhaps? Short for Emily? Auntie Em from *The Wizard of Oz*?

Clark had spent her entire childhood believing that her grandmother was really Auntie Em; she looked like her, and sounded like her, and lived in a house like hers, so therefore, she must *be* her. 'My Grandmother's in the *The Wizard of Oz*,' she would announce to her little schoolmates and they all believed her because it was such a wonderful thing to believe.

She walked towards Café Em, remembering how, whenever she'd feel frightened or lonely, she'd madly click her heels together, wondering what was wrong, why she wasn't being instantly transported back to the safety of Grandma's, why, after she'd forgotten her homework, she was still standing in a corner of the classroom with a sign reading I'D FORGET MY HEAD IF IT WEREN'T ATTACHED pinned to her back. 'There's no place like home,' she'd chant, 'there's no place like home,' but it didn't help.

She looked into the window of the café, and there he was – Harry, her beloved, talking to the tablecloth woman who had tried to clobber the Cougar with her car door. Clark sized her up: late forties, big hips, big hair. Not terribly attractive; probably wore too much make-up. She was standing behind the bar, pontificating. Harry was slouched on a barstool, looking up at her. Clark couldn't see his face, but she didn't need to. His body said 'Bored'. Good. It was good for him to be reminded that not every woman was as fascinating as she, Clark, was.

Instead of rushing in and throwing herself in Harry's

arms, which was what she knew she *should* do, she scooched over to one side of the window, to get into a better spying position, where she could see but not be seen. It was wrong of her, but she convinced herself she needed a few minutes to collect herself. To calm down. And besides, this was an opportunity she couldn't pass up; she could, once and for all, shame herself out of her jealousy – she could watch how Harry behaved with another woman, see how true to her he was. She'd spy on them a while and then drive back to Paul's house, stop at a grocery store, if she could find one, get the fixings for a shrimp stir-fry, Harry's favorite. And candles. And a bottle of good Chardonnay. She wished she had thought to bring her negligée. She only had one, red, and it drove Harry bonkers. All she had to do was dig it out of her underwear crate and wave it at him and he would go wild.

Harry picked up his coffee and started walking toward a bookcase in a cutesy little reading alcove. A dog – a Springer! Clark loved Springers; her own Ada had been a Springer! – jumped up on Harry's leg and started humping. Clark watched, giggling, while he tried to nonchalantly push the dog away. He was so inept when it came to pets. She'd once brought a stray kitten home and Harry had been so terrorised by it that she'd had to give it to Martin. 'It *hates* me,' Harry would say when she'd come home from work, 'it peed all over my manuscript.'

She wished she could read lips. Harry took a book from a shelf and waved it at the woman, who was following him around with a plate, trying to weazle her way into his heart with food, no doubt. He'd better not start reading to her, Clark thought, but he didn't. He started laughing, and then he did a little dance, and then . . .

Clark couldn't believe her eyes. And then he grabbed her and kissed her! He waved the book again; kissed her again; and then she grabbed him and pulled him down on the couch with her! The whore! And Harry; he was too contemptible for words! All this time, she had been running all over Helena, sick with worry, desperate to find him, while he was going after the first female he got a whiff of.

Clark couldn't breathe. She was right; she had been right all along to suspect him, she had just suspected him of the wrong thing, this time. He might as well be a murderer, wasn't he butchering her heart, now, with this horrid woman? Adultery! Stoning was too good for them.

She supposed she should march in, confront them, do something dramatic like tossing her wedding band in Harry's face, and she probably would have, if Polly or Jana or Aggie were there, watching her watch Harry and that, that . . . strumpet. But she didn't. Although she had imagined just such a scene hundreds of times – every time Harry was more than a couple of hours late, in fact – and imagined herself blazing triumphantly in her righteous indignation, she never took the scene to its inevitable end. It wasn't the end she was interested in. She only liked the part about being triumphant and this didn't feel like a triumph at all.

She suppressed a sob and trudged back to the Cougar.

Twenty-six

'You want me,' Aurora moaned, but no, he didn't.

Harry had long since passed the point where he thought it was his duty to sleep with every woman who offered herself to him. This one was handy, and she was relatively attractive, and he was relatively horny, but she had Trouble written all over her and Harry had had enough of that for a while.

'Fuck your inkstand,' Flaubert had advised. 'Calm yourself with meat.'

How was he going to get out of this? She had wrapped herself around him and was leaning back, purring breathily, and squinting in that way that women think is alluring.

The dog saved him. As he was trying to edge himself off the couch, creating a little gap between himself and Aurora, the dog growled menacingly and lunged between them.

'Emma!' Aurora cried, pulling the dog back by the

collar, 'you stop that!' She turned to Harry apologetically. 'She's just jealous,' she explained as the dog barked and snapped at Harry. 'Don't mind her. She's harmless.'

But you're not, Harry thought as he backed away.

'That's OK,' he said, 'I've got to go anyway.'

Aurora looked rather crestfallen and, quite frankly, Harry didn't want to rule out the possibility of her for the future. What if he had to stay up here for weeks? Months? In a few weeks, he would be *looking* for Trouble, and now he knew where to find it.

He lowered his voice a notch. 'Raincheck?' he asked, huskily, and she shrugged sadly as he backed out the door.

He headed back up the street, to the Chinese place, his stomach grumbling. He feared the food would be bad – he was used to the real thing, in Chinatown, after all – but he was hungry enough to lower his expectations. He'd get Moo Shoo; always a safe bet as long as you didn't get pork.

The folks at the restaurant were real Chinese, which was a good sign. Harry felt unaccountably happy at seeing them, as if they were long-lost friends or something, and it took him a minute to realise it was because they reminded him of home, of New York. He hadn't seen anything other than white people since Albany and that gave him the creeps. Too much homogeneity made him nervous; it encouraged a form of Us-ness that could get real nasty.

He sat at a table by the window, where he could watch all the action. Or inaction, to be precise. How can people live here, he wondered, why don't they all move to New York? He thought about Aurora, how she had curled her lip and sneered when she mentioned 'the City', and he hoped he wouldn't have to stick around long enough to turn in his raincheck.

His food was brought out by a waitress, not Chinese. CRYSTAL, according to her plastic badge. She would have been damned good-looking if not for the bad perm and her dull, zombie eyes.

Butler was in the Town of the Dead, Harry thought. He was used to people being depressed in spirit, but this was more, a kind of deadness, a weariness beyond simple disappointment, which was why, at least in his estimation, everybody he knew was depressed. Life wasn't turning out to be what they had expected and so they got all mopey about it, as if they thought Life was letting them down, rather than the other way around. This girl, however, looked as though she'd never had an expectation in her life. Except bad ones. There was no fight in CRYSTAL's eyes, no interest, no hunger and it made Harry want to bundle her up in his arms, carry her out to the car, and take her back to New York, get her a job doing something fun – Clark could get her on the Make-Over team and she could begin with herself.

She plopped his plate in front of him and floated back to her chair beside the cash register. She was staring right at him, but Harry knew she didn't see him. Did she see anything?

He ate as quickly as possible. The food was surprisingly good; better, in fact, than the take-out place next to the laundromat at home.

'Check, please, Crystal,' he called and leaned back in his chair, picking his teeth. He broke open his fortune cookie. 'Doubt Whom You Will But Never Yourself.'

It had never occurred to Harry to doubt himself, but he imagined many people might find comfort in a fortune like that: there were a hell of a lot of lost souls out there, and, or so it seemed to him, lostness apparently was a way of coping with modern life.

He popped a fragment of the tasteless cookie in his mouth and let it sit there, softening to a consistency he liked. He vaguely remembered reading a story about a guy, a poet, maybe, who took a job in a fortune cookie factory, writing pornographic fortunes. Harry had liked the idea of it, but the story itself had been unsatisfying, hollow, not worth remembering. He smiled at the thought that after all these years he had proved himself right – the idea *had* been memorable, the story, not. He totted up another home run on his internal scoreboard. *Harry Butler, 5,357.*

But who was his opponent? 'The world' was too vast and besides, he had nothing against the world. Doubt. Doubt could be his opponent. Butler vs. Doubt. But where did doubt come from? It seemed to Harry that the tendency towards doubt was the kind of thing you were saddled with at birth; it was like an added appendage, a hump you had to carry round like a sack of rocks slung over your shoulder, making everything you tried to do that much harder.

Ugh, he thought, what could be worse?

He left CRYSTAL a five-dollar tip, hoping that might cheer her up a bit, and went back to the car. He drove through town, toward the outskirts, and found a strip mall with a K-Mart and a supermarket. A Price Chopper.

The store was vast, like an airplane hangar compared to the cluttered, overstuffed grocery stores of Manhattan. He pulled out a cart and rolled it up and down the aisles diagonally, luxuriating in all the space, filling the cart with comestibles: oranges, bananas, big green heads of broccoli. Cherries! He was surprised to find this much variety, this much choice, up in the middle of nowhere; he'd thought he would have to make do with Cheerios and wilted iceberg lettuce, but the Helena Price Chopper offered him all the imported booty he could possibly desire.

He sped through the aisles, grabbing packages of cookies, potato chips, all the junk food he wouldn't normally touch but seemed so enticing, for some reason, up here. Judging from the size of his fellow shoppers, junk was the food of choice. 'When in Rome!' he said, grabbing a Super-Economy box of Twinkies, which he planned to sneak upstairs and eat in bed, just like when he was a kid. He skidded to a stop at the meat counter, remembering Flaubert's advice, picked out pork chops, a package of cheery red hamburger, and two big old He-Man Steaks.

He heaved two twelve-packs of beer – Genny, when in Rome – into the cart. He'd have to give up his Bastille Day binge, the only one he had left this year, if he was going to get drunk up here, but he was willing to do it. He deserved it. He'd been through a lot.

When he arrived back at Paul's, he put the groceries away, made himself a bowl of cereal with bananas and sat down at the table to eat. He had the vague feeling that someone had been in the house; he couldn't put his finger on it, he wasn't like Clark, didn't claim to be able to sense molecule-wakes or whatever she called them, but he definitely felt that something was different.

Aliens, he thought, the alien possums had arrived to case the joint. Ghosts. A lot of people must have died in this house; it was ancient, over a hundred years old and God only knew who was buried underneath it, rumbling around a century later, still trying to avenge itself.

The kid. Maybe the kid's ghost had floated in, found a good place to hide, and was just waiting for the Witching Hour to start haunting him.

Oh well, he thought, and popped open a beer, feeling wickedly decadent – cereal and beer, if that wasn't a dinner that said 'Guy', what did?

Lonely guy, he thought.

Woodsy guy, he countered. A guy with no time for prancing around the kitchen in an apron.

Butler fixed himself a dinner of Cheerios, bananas, and beer. Genny. A real He-Man meal.

Harry glanced over at the blank computer screen. That was it – the computer was off! He knew he hadn't turned it off when he left – he never turned it off, that was Clark's job.

This time, he couldn't blame it on Clark. But *some*body had turned it off. He remembered writing the words *Butler had never thought about killing himself before* and then being so upset at even the idea of it that he had fled. But he had not, definitely had *not*, turned the computer off.

Could he have turned it off? Oh Jesus, was he getting Alzheimer's, was he going to turn into Mr Petrikas, taking a piss in the hall because he thought it was the Grand Central Men's Room?

Well, there was a way to find out. If *he* had turned it off, he would have saved his work. He reached over, switched the computer on, waited for it to boot up.

He finished off his Genny, grabbed another from the twelve-pack at his feet.

He pulled up the Directory, searched for 'Suicide'.

Nothing. Nothing under 'Country,' 'Gun,' or 'Death.'

He pulled up the entire manuscript, homed to the

end. He was back to the Mystery Woman, not even at Central Park yet, thanks to Clark.

Harry guzzled the beer, feeling slightly dizzy, and opened another.

Kids, he thought angrily, local mischief makers. Paul had said they were a problem, coming in and stealing all the booze, using the summer-people's houses for their orgies. That was it, Harry thought, local riff-raff, the kind of kids who thought it was a hoot to wipe out his, Harry's, work. He thought about the newspaper story. The kind of kids who thought it was a hoot to take someone out in the woods and gut them.

Better to think he was losing his mind. Or to blame it on ghosts; hadn't he read somewhere about house sprites, little trickster ghosts who got their kicks by moving your keys from the kitchen table to the refrigerator, rearranging the furniture in the middle of the night, stuff like that? Why couldn't this be a haunted house?

He seemed to recall that what one had to do was make friends with the ghost. He could do that.

'Oh, little ghostie,' he called in the cutesy voice people used for babies and pets, 'come out, come out, wherever you are! All ye, all ye, out's in free!'

He felt rather silly, wandering around the house with a beer, calling for ghosts, but he was giddy enough now not to care how absurd he appeared. And appeared to *whom*, he might ask.

Could he have turned off the computer without saving? Was he losing his memory? Was this the first clue, the first little whisper of the aging process, the sibilant hint that he was getting old?

'I will never get old!' he shouted. 'Harry Butler is going out in a blaze of blue light! Live fast, die young, before you mistake your neighbor's recycling bin for a urinal!'

'You'd better hurry,' a voice said.

Harry shook his head. He had heard a voice, there was no mistaking that.

'You'd better hurry,' the voice, a young, kind of dweeby voice, said again, 'if you're going to die young.'

An evil ghostie! An evil ghostie that wanted Harry to die so he could take over his body, corporate himself again in the shape of Harry Butler.

He followed the sound of the voice back into the dining room. There, sitting atop the computer, swinging his legs and waving, was Gordie Sheppard, in black and white, just as he had appeared in the yearbook photo.

'You!' Harry cried. 'Did you turn off my computer?'

Gordie grinned and shook his head.

'Not I,' he said.

'Well then, who?' Harry asked him, even if he was only a mirage. The truth was, he *seemed* real, and *looked* real, and if Harry's imagination was going to present him with a ghost, that was fine with Harry, even if it happened to be the very ghost that had brought him all this trouble in the first place.

'Not telling,' Gordie said.

Harry polished off his beer, tossed the can into the kitchen, pulled out another. 'Want one?' he asked Gordie. Might as well be neighborly.

I'm losing my mind, Harry thought, I'm developing Alzheimer's. I'm seeing things. I'm turning my wife's love slave into an imaginary friend. Oh well.

'I don't drink,' Gordie said. Or Harry imagined him saying. It really didn't matter, did it, whether he was real or not, whether he was a real ghost or a real hallucination. Whatever he was, he was there.

'You ever have an imaginary friend when you were a kid?' Harry asked him.

'Sure,' Gordie said, 'doesn't every lonely kid have one?'

Harry had never thought of himself as a lonely kid before and the thought made him feel all weepy and sad. I shouldn't drink, he thought.

'So,' Harry asked his hallucination, 'what's it like, being dead?'

Gordie shrugged. 'I can't tell you that,' he said.

'Why not?' Harry wanted to know.

'It's the only mystery left,' he said. 'Would you really want to lose that?'

Harry pondered. It was true, mysteries were good. They kept you guessing, and most of the time, guessing was better than knowing. It was certainly a lot more interesting. Once you knew, the quest was over and what was life without a quest?

Harry asked for a hint.

Gordie sighed. 'You don't get it, do you?'

Harry was offended. 'Of course I get it. I'm not asking you to reveal the secret; I'm just asking for a hint.'

Gordie shook his head. In a patronising manner unflattering to Harry. 'OK,' he said, 'here's a hint. It's not what you think.'

But Harry didn't know what he thought.

'Will I know what's happened?' he asked. 'Will I still be me?'

Gordie grinned. 'Once you're dead,' he said gleefully, 'there's no more Harry Butler.'

Oh God. That was horrible. Worse than anything he could have imagined. Harry loved being Harry. He didn't want to be anybody or anything else, he didn't want to come back as some tree or something, not even as a person. He wanted to be himself, Harry Butler or no one. What if he came back a hundred and fifty years from now and read his book and didn't even realise he had written it? He'd be reading away, thinking, 'Gee, this sounds oddly familiar,' even though he was the King of Saudi Arabia or something, an Estonian hockey player perhaps. And he'd think, Maybe I lived in New York in a previous life, never knowing that he had not only lived in New York, he'd lived the *book*, that he was *he*! That he was Harry Butler, alive and breathing and getting into hockey brawls with a bunch of burly brutes who could be anyone – the goalie he was beating to a pulp could be Lenny or Paul or even Clark!

Clark! He missed her; she would get a kick out of this – 'Harry! Hurry up!' she'd call and he'd say, 'I can't, I'm talking to a ghost,' and she would laugh, come over and sit on his lap and join right in the conversation, introduce Gordie to her imaginary brother, Bobby or whatever his name was, and they'd all sit gathered round the computer, the quick and not-so-quick, having a little soirée.

Clark! He imagined he smelled the memory of her perfume, 'Dawn to Dusk' or something like that, lingering over by the computer. When was she ever going to relent? *Was* she ever going to relent? He loved her. He needed her. As infuriating, unreasonable, and downright crazy as she could be, he couldn't bear the idea of being without her. Who else could he read *The Anatomy of Melancholy* to in bed? Who else would laugh at his silly songs? Who else would wake him up in the middle of the night, demanding to know what his favorite word was and then rewarding him, when he said, groggily, the first thing that came to his head – inevitable – with a little screech of delight and an incredible tongue-bath? Who else? Nobody else. There was no one on earth like Clark, and he missed her so much he could feel his heart shrivelling up inside him, deflating, as she huffed out of her place in it, leaving a big, empty sac.

'It's all your fault,' he growled at Gordie, but he had disappeared, crawled back to whatever corner of Harry's imagination he had burrowed into.

Harry felt a heaviness, a kind of dullness, descend over him like a wet, gray cloak. He tried to lean over to grab another beer, but the box seemed too far away, it was too much effort to push himself forward a few inches on the chair so he could reach.

Why bother? he thought miserably. Why bother about anything?

Wifeless. Homeless. Friendless.

'Come back,' he called to Gordie.

Ghostless, too.

He felt the same cold shiver of aloneness he had felt when Clark kicked him out. Loneliness was something he'd never had to deal with before. 'I don't *get* lonely,' he'd brag to the Lornes, 'I have my imagination for company.' Not to mention his string of girlfriends.

He tried to get himself interested in the feeling of it. He'd had this feeling once before, when he was taking a physics exam. He had skipped most of the classes, and had barely opened the book, but he had a wild notion that if he just thought hard enough, he could come up with the answers and pass the class. He had sat in his little wooden desk chair, straining valiantly, but much to his own surprise, his brain didn't come through. He had left the room, feeling defeated for the first time in his life, and the feeling he was having now was like that. A straining to grab a hold of something, anything, but coming up empty, with only a handful of air. Looking at that empty hand, feeling baffled and somehow cheated, and then the sickening realisation that you'd been beat, that for whatever reason, you just weren't good enough or lucky enough or smart enough or, in his own case, studious enough to win whatever prize you'd been chasing after.

But what had he done? Or not done? Could one stupid, tiny lie have brought down his entire empire? Could one little droplet of doubt have poisoned his entire life? How could that be? It was so unfair! It was one thing for life to be unfair for the Vermont rattlesnake, but for him? For Harry Butler?

He imagined all the people and things he loved, dropping away from him, as if the walls of his life were crumbling down, leaving him exposed, naked, unprotected. Clark. His apartment. New York – the world he loved! Lenny. Raptor Music.

Butler still had himself, he thought, but even that didn't cheer him.

This is what depression feels like, he thought, but he was too miserable to make use of it.

'Why bother?' he said aloud. 'Why bother about anything?'

Twenty-seven

'It serves him right,' Clark told Polly as she emptied another milk crate of Harry's clothes into a box.

'Serves him right for what?' Polly wanted to know.

'For what! For crawling into bed with the first skirt he met! Oh, excuse me, tablecloth. With the first tablecloth he met. She was wearing a *tablecloth*, Polly! What kind of a woman goes around wearing nothing but a tablecloth?'

'Clark,' Polly said, 'calm down. You don't know he was sleeping with her.'

'That's generally what comes after making out on couches.'

'You don't *know*,' Polly insisted. 'It could have been completely innocent.'

'Believe me, I know,' Clark said as she tossed a bagful of Harry's underwear into the box. 'I know exactly what it leads to.'

'Why didn't you go in?' Polly asked. 'Why didn't you confront him?'

It was another secret she tried to keep from herself. Clark was not adverse to making scenes, and she adored confrontations with any sort of symbol of authority. Enemies? Who cared? She'd duke it out with them any day. But she had a shameful and deadly fear of rivals. She had, at one time or another, had a good, healthy fight with every single one of her friends, but she wouldn't, couldn't, confront a rival. It wasn't that she was afraid, exactly, it was just that there was something so dangerous about it, deadly almost, as if she were frightened not of the rival but of herself, and so she would go to any lengths to avoid them. Of course she couldn't admit this to Polly, it was news she could someday use, for although Clark loved her friends, she didn't trust them, at least not as far as men were concerned.

'Women should stick together,' she snapped at Polly. 'Men couldn't push us around if we'd keep our hands off other women's men.'

'What do you expect?' Polly asked, 'You *did* kick the guy out.'

'I didn't kick him out! I sent him on a vacation.'

'Clark . . .' Polly said.

They'd been friends for decades; since their temping days. They'd always be the last two sent out on jobs and they'd sit at the coffee table, accessoriless, unmanicured, reading Virginia Woolf and talking about Art. It was at that Tempo table that they'd formed the idea for *Bad Ass Girls*. First as a nickname for themselves, later, as the band, and lastly, the magazine.

'Clarkie . . .' Polly said.

'I only *kind of* kicked him out,' Clark said. 'I just needed to be alone.' She picked up the clothes hamper and dumped it: the clothes tumbled out, a jumble of her things and Harry's, all mingled together, a striped sock of Harry's wrapped around one of her bras, two tank-tops – his and hers – intertwined. Just like our lives, she thought and started to cry as she began separating her dirty clothes from Harry's. 'I was going to give up my apartment!' she sniffled. 'I was going to go out and *buy* a co-op so I wouldn't have to kick him out the next time I needed to be alone.'

'It's not too late,' Polly said but yes, it was. Too late, too late, too late.

'He couldn't even make it a *day*,' she told Polly. 'Not even one measly little *day*.'

'You don't *know* that,' Polly said again but Clark knew what she saw. Harry in the arms of a tablecloth. It was revolting.

She sealed up the box and addressed it.

'Come on, help me with this stuff,' she said to Polly as she lifted one box in her arms. 'The UPS place is open now.'

She hadn't slept. She'd driven straight back, arriving around eleven p.m. She had parked the car in front of Rent-A-Wreck, picked up a few empty boxes from in front of D'Agostino's, and come home to pack. It had been a dreadful night – she had raced through the apartment, pulling Harry's books off the shelves, his clothes from the milk crates, all his little odds and ends from various drawers and cupboards, tossing it all in one big pile in the center of the apartment, making a little mountain of his stuff. The larger it grew, the harder Clark cried – 'What am I *doing*?' she'd sob as she rifled around in the desk drawers – but she felt powerless to stop. There were times, during the endless night, when she felt possessed, as if she, Clark, was not doing this – she, Clark, would have more sense; she, Clark, was a woman of the world, a grown-up, self-confident enough to overlook a little indiscretion; she, Clark, knew Harry loved her and her alone – but she couldn't *find* herself, she was lost in the madness.

What had happened to that invulnerable fortress of love she had thought about while driving up north? Crumbled. Rotted from inside.

She had begun sobbing afresh when she emptied out his side of the desk, dumping his personal private items into a banana box. In the other drawers she found the wooden Gettysburg pencil box he'd been carrying around since grade school; the green Miss Liberty headband she'd given him; the watch she'd never been able to get him to wear. His old wire-rims. A shriveled-up chestnut, a keepsake he'd brought back from their one camping trip. Little pieces of Harry. Of her. Of their life together.

She loved him. She *did* love him. But then she'd find some scribbled note – 'Mystery Woman: Polly + Odette,' and she'd hate him. Odette? Who was Odette? Some little chicklet he met at Theatre 80? At DoJo's? Love, hate; love, hate; love, hate, all night long. She felt as if she were on fire, as if she had stuck her finger in an electric socket, as if every hair on her body was standing on end, straining to get away from her body, to escape her fury.

She cried herself raw. It hurt, now, to speak, even to breathe.

'You're making a big mistake,' Polly said, hoisting the other box into her arms, 'I'm telling you, Clark, you are going to regret this.'

Clark grunted as she manoeuvered around Mr Petrikas, who was sitting on the landing, singing 'Chattanooga Choo-Choo'.

'Clark,' Polly said from behind her, 'you can't *do* this. You love Harry. He's your husband.'

'I can't trust him,' Clark said, 'I can't let him out of my sight for five minutes without his running off after someone else.'

She hoped Polly wouldn't try to analyse her, chalk it all up to the abandonment fears of an orphan. Of *course* that's what it was. She *was* an orphan. She *did* fear abandonment. It *did* make her insane, so what? Everybody who had spent more than five minutes in her life *knew* that about her, it was a given, and what good did it do to trace the cause when it was the effect that was the problem? She'd been in analysis; she knew it was because on some childish level she still blamed – and would for ever blame – herself for her parents' death, so what? So what, so what, so what? She was who she was and that was a person who couldn't tolerate being abandoned. And who saw abandonment everywhere she looked. So what?

'For God's sake, Clark,' Polly said. 'What if he *did* sleep with someone else? It doesn't *mean* anything. He loves *you*. He's married to *you*.'

'Not for long,' Clark said.

They had reached the UPS place. 'I want these to arrive today,' Clark told the clerk. 'How much will that cost?'

The clerk, a young, red-headed boy, looked at the address.

'Kerley Corners?' he said, 'Where the heck is Kerley Corners?'

'Upstate,' Clark said, 'near the Canadian border.'

The boy shook his head, said it was impossible.

'Tomorrow, at the earliest.'

'I'll pay extra,' Clark said.

'No can do,' the boy said, taking a computer list out of a folder and showing it to Clark, as if all those letters and numbers meant anything to her. 'Tomorrow. By noon. That's the best we can do.'

'OK,' she said and paid.

Polly was standing outside, leaning against the plate-glass window and smoking.

'Can I have one?' she asked.

'No,' Polly said.

'Come on, just one.'

'No. You made me promise, when you quit, that I would never give you one if you asked, even if you got down on your knees and begged.'

'Some friend you are,' Clark moaned and Polly laughed and put her arm round Clark's shoulder.

'Clarkie, I'm your friend, no matter what stupid thing you do. And this is really stupid.'

It probably was. The minute Harry's things were loaded in the truck, she would probably want them back, but now, while they were still retrievable, she wanted them gone.

'You know why I never wanted kids?' she asked Polly.

'Because you're too selfish,' she answered.

Clark shook her head. That was what they always said, but the truth was just the opposite. She didn't want to saddle some poor kid with her genes, sentence him or her to a life of perversity.

'Not in the obscene sense,' she told Polly. 'It's just that I'm so . . . so . . .'

'Perverse,' Polly said. 'You're the only person I know who literally *would* cut off your nose to spite your face.'

'Ah, but it's a curse, it is,' Clark said in a fake Irish accent, 'the bane of my life.'

Polly laughed and hugged her.

'Are you OK?' she asked, 'I've got to get to work before they give my job to some Tempo girl.'

Clark nodded. 'I'm OK. I probably should go to work, too.'

Polly headed west; Clark stood in front of the UPS place, dazed, wondering what to do. Polly was right, of course, she *would* regret this, it *was* the biggest mistake of her life. Life without Harry would be horrible. 'There's always someone else,' her grandmother used to say when she'd come home from school brokenhearted because Fergus O'Sullivan didn't 'like' her, and up until she met Harry, Clark thought that was true. But there was no one like Harry, and after Harry, no one else would do.

She'd become an old maid. She supposed that wouldn't be so bad; after all, if there was no one to leave her, she wouldn't have to worry about being abandoned, and she could go back to being her cheerful, good-natured self.

But what good was being cheerful and good-natured by yourself?

It wasn't too late. She could turn round and reclaim the packages, reclaim Harry.

But what if he wasn't reclaimable? What if he'd already moved in with the tablecloth woman?

How *could* he? she thought, How could he run off with the first woman he set eyes on? She was right to send his things off – she couldn't live with someone she couldn't trust.

But she couldn't live without him, either.

Damn him and his inability to be alone. Damn her and her insane jealously. It was hopeless. Impossible. She loved him; she knew in her heart he loved her, but how could they stay together when she couldn't trust him? 'It's almost as if you want him to betray you,' Polly had once said, and Clark could see how it could look that way, to someone on the outside. And, she had to admit, Harry was on the outside, and there was no way to let him or anyone else know it wasn't what she wanted at all.

What *did* she want?

A cigarette, she told herself. She wanted a cigarette. A drink. Chocolate. Quaaludes. She felt an overwhelming sense of disappointment – in life, in herself, in Harry. I haven't turned out to be the person I wanted to be, she thought. On another day, even in another hour, perhaps, she would think, Well, there's still time; I can still tinker with myself, but right now everything felt hopeless.

She wanted to obliterate herself, but since she couldn't do that, she might as well go to the office. She could figure out what to do while she worked. She wondered how Peggy was doing. Fine. Peggy would be doing fine. She would be covering Clark so well no one would notice her absence and she suddenly wished she could bequeath her job to Peggy, trade places with her. Peggy could be Clark and Clark could go back to being Peggy, which was, really, the happiest time of her life.

Too late, she thought sadly, too late.

'Ms Clark?' a voice called.

Clark turned around and saw O'Donnell standing behind her, beckoning her.

'Ms Clark?' he called again.

'You can skip the Ms,' she said as she approached him, 'everybody just calls me Clark.'

'I'm glad I ran into you,' he said. 'The Sheppard kid's parents are coming in to town today, to pick up his effects. I've asked them if you could have the photographs.'

'Oh, thanks,' she said, 'I guess.' His 'effects'. It sounded so brutal, as if he had never been alive, never been a human, just some creature that had shed its skin, its 'effects'.

'Don't you want them? You had expressed interest . . .'

She nodded. The Mohawk. She *would* like to have that one to tuck away in some safe spot where no one could find it but her. And she'd take it out, when she was old and gray and all alone, having chased off everyone who had ever cared for her, and remember how daring she had once been, daring and full of life.

'I really only wanted the one,' she said, 'you know, the one where . . .'

O'Donnell grinned and nodded. 'I'll see what I can do,' he said and Clark thought he wasn't such a bad guy after all, cop or no cop.

As he walked away, Clark realised she hadn't thought about Gordie even once since she had left his apartment.

Oh well. She would just have to feel bad about that later. There was only so much she could feel bad about at one time, she thought as she picked up her shoulder bag and headed uptown, and feeling bad about Harry took precedence.

Twenty-eight

Harry hadn't slept. He had stumbled up the steep stairs at some point, groped in the dark for a bed – why bother to turn on the light? – and collapsed, waiting for oblivion. It didn't arrive, how could it with all that racket: the trees scraping against the windows like claws, some industrious form of critter scampering across the tin roof, back and forth, back and forth, building its nest in the middle of the night, some crazed bird singing its obnoxiously cheerful song, over and over again. And, just as he was falling into that semi-numb state that precedes sleep, the blood-curdling screech of some kind of cat, a panther, perhaps, something huge and hungry and very, very angry, roaring in the woods not fifty feet from the house, from him, Harry.

He lay in bed, watching the light grope its way into the room, slowly at first, like a child testing the water with her toe, and then, blam! She jumped in, cannonballing the room with her bright glare. Harry pulled the pillow over his head.

His stomach rumbled. Why bother? he thought. He had to pee. Why bother? he thought, but that was going too far, he wasn't going to wet the bed. He felt a wave of shame wash over him, as the memory of spending the night at Wally Bradley's started bubbling up from his Hall of Humiliations. 'Do I really need to remember that?' he asked himself, but apparently he did, and there he was, twelve years old, sleeping over at Wally's while his parents attended a Perfumers' Convention, waking up in a puddle of his own pee. He'd been in a panic, not because he had wet the bed but because he was afraid Wally would tell. That he'd have to spend the next couple of years beating people up for calling him a bedwetter. He had done the only reasonable thing: he had jumped out of bed, run into Mr and Mrs Bradley's bedroom, got down on his knees and begged Mrs Bradley to save him. 'I'm sorry, I'm sorry, I'm sorry,' he had sobbed and Mrs Bradley had been wonderfully cuddly and kind, getting up and changing his bed quietly, without waking Wally, laying thick blue bath towels under the clean sheets.

Harry groaned and went downstairs.

When you wake up in the morning
And you wish you were dead

Did he wish he were dead? He had never, in his life, awoken without a sense of excitement, of wondering what the day would bring. Even when things were going badly, which they occasionally did, he would awaken joyfully pugilistic, telling Life to go ahead, give him its best shot, knowing that he, Harry Butler, could take it.

Even when he awoke in a panic, he at least felt alive, but this, this was awful, terrible. It was as if his spirit had been sucked out of him, and he wondered if maybe, in the middle of the night, the aliens had come hovering about in their flying saucer, seen him lying in bed, and inserted some kind of straw in him and just vacuumed up all his energy.

He shuffled into the kitchen, opened the cupboard. There were fresh turds scattered round the boxes of cereal, but he didn't care. If the critters wanted his cereal, they could have it, he wasn't going to fight for it.

But if he were dead, he remembered, he wouldn't be *him*. 'No more Harry Butler,' the kid had said, and while last night that had seemed horrifying, this morning it only seemed slightly more tragic than an ordinary person's demise. He took an orange, cut it in half, bit in. 'That's disgusting,' Clark always said about the way Harry ate oranges, nibbling away at the pulp first, then sucking the juice and then finally and messily scraping out the rest of the pulp with his finger, but it was the way he had always eaten them, a method he had devised himself and found satisfying to all his senses.

Or had done. Now, the juice dribbling down his chin just seemed tasteless and kind of sticky. He tossed the orange in the trash, wiped his chin, and shuffled over to the table.

Butler was a man of action, if only in his own head, he thought as he waited for the machine to chug its way to life. It didn't excite him. Harry had the sinking realisation that this was going to be a day of firsts, and none of them pleasant. By the time the computer had worked itself up to Word Perfect, he had lost interest in his thought, could barely come up with the energy to remember it.

Why bother? he thought as he listlessly typed the letters in. *Butler had never thought about suicide before. But if he was going to do it, he was going to do it right. He was a man of action, if only in his own head.*

Suicides. How do they come up with the energy? he wondered. Right now, he didn't care enough about his life to end it. Why bother? It would happen soon enough, without his having to lift a finger. He could sit right here, staring at the screen, doing nothing but watching the computer suck up electricity, and Death would come along, tap him on the shoulder, say 'Time's up, Butler,' and that would be that, he'd grab on to Death's big shepherd's hook, heave himself out of the chair and follow along, peaceably, to his next life, as a tree.

His legs grew heavy; he felt his feet expand, rootlike, as if he were in one of those frolicsome animated cartoon movies of his youth. Wagner boomed in the background, the overture to 'Tannhauser', perhaps, as his feet grew larger, barky, and burrowed into the floorboards, seeking the cool, damp sweetness of the earth below.

He guessed it wouldn't be so bad, being a tree. He could do worse. He could be a Vermont rattlesnake, for instance, the last of his race, trying to slither away as his final foe, a woodsy, bearded kind of Butler in a plaid flannel shirt and camo pants, came after him with a cudgel.

Being a tree, he wouldn't have to move. He would just stand there, majestic, benevolent, ruggedly handsome, shading lovers at picnics. And when Mr Picnicker pulled out his jack knife and began carving away at

Harry's trunk, trying to carve himself into immortality, Harry would drop a big, spikey chestnut on his head.

But what if there wasn't a next life? What if there was no tree in his future, but just a big, deep hole in the ground, full of hungry, slimy things? What if this was it, his only chance, and he was wasting it away, leaving absolutely nothing behind, nothing to indicate he had ever been here in the first place?

He jumped up, shook the bark out of his legs, paced.

He had to do something. He had to leave something behind. He either had to finish *B by B* or impregnate someone. His wife, for example.

His wife who suspected him of being a murderer. His wife who was probably rolling around in bed, at this very instant, with that fop of a detective. *The fop cop. Butler's wife was in bed with a fop cop. He'd have to kill them.*

But maybe she was over it by now. Harry had been away over forty-eight hours and Clark never stayed mad longer than twelve. The truth was, he needed her. To tell her that was out of the question. He doubted he could get the words out of his mouth, but even if he could, they would make Clark despise him and that was the last thing he wanted.

He could call her and hang up, that always worked; he'd call, heave a few deep sighs, and the next thing he knew, she'd be on her way up to rescue him.

There was a general store and post office up the road, in Kerley Corners. He took a can of insecticide in each hand and went out into the battlefield. The flies bombarded him instantly, but he was ready for them.

'Take that!' he cried, spritzing the air. 'And that!'

The phone outside the general store was broken. Might as well be in New York. He walked inside and it was as if he had walked into his own youth, into Barney's

Neighborhood Sundries – the wide, painted floorboards, the erratically stocked shelves, the center rack stuffed with loaves of Wonder Bread in their packages decorated with balloons. The big red slide-top Coke cooler next to a candy display: Mallow Cups! Pixie Sticks! Oh my God, they had Buns! Harry hadn't had a Bun in thirty years! He couldn't help himself: he felt, well, like a kid in a candy shop. Buns! The maple ones! Of course, the best thing about the Buns of his youth had been the thrill of slyly stuffing them into his pocket and savoring the sweet taste of petty theft.

He sighed, and added Barney to the list of invitees to his execution.

The guy behind the counter wasn't Barney – Barney had had all his limbs, and this guy was missing an arm – but he was a close facsimile. A little gray guy, in black rimmed glasses, with this morning's stubble still clinging to his cheeks.

'Help ya?' he asked. Not unfriendly, but wary. Alert. With a never-can-tell-about-these-strangers edge.

Harry picked up a maple Bun and walked over to the counter.

'Is there another phone around here?' he asked.

'Nope,' the Barney guy said.

Harry glanced at the wall phone behind the counter.

'Could I use yours?' he asked, 'I'll pay for the call, of course.'

'Local?' he wanted to know and Harry said no, but he'd pay. 'I'll give you ten dollars, if you'll let me use your phone for five minutes. You can time me.'

'Ten dollars?' the guy asked, 'Where you calling, Timbucktoo?' He laughed happily at his own joke.

'New York,' Harry said, pulling a twenty-dollar bill from his wallet; twenty dollars was probably more than he makes in a week, up here, he thought as he waved it tantalisingly in front of the guy.

'Be my guest,' the guy said, grabbing the twenty and making room for Harry behind the counter.

Harry tried her office first; got her voice mail. He wasn't above grovelling, but he didn't particularly want to leave a public record of it. He'd try the apartment.

'We're not here, but leave a message for Beatrice Clark or Harry Butler after the beep,' her voice said cheerfully. At least she hadn't taken him off the tape, that was a good sign.

He waited for the beep, took a deep breath.

'Huh. Huh. Huh,' he breathed into the mouthpiece and hung up.

The old man was staring at him. 'Twenty dollars for "Huh. Huh. Huh"?' he asked.

'It's a code,' Harry said and went back to Paul's, to wait.

He gave her eight hours. Two to get the message; one to pick up a rental car; and five for the drive.

He went to his bag of books, pulled out Jack London. He'd eat his Twinkies and read *White Fang*. The abuse part wouldn't be so unbearable, if he imagined Emma as the dog.

Ten hours later, he sat stupefied in the armchair, the floor littered with cellophane wrappers, halfway through his second tin-foil thriller. Somebody was going to blow something up, but he wasn't sure why. There was an exploding clock that reminded him of Oscar Wilde or Graham Greene or Joseph Conrad, he couldn't remember which.

The old exploding-clock trick, Butler thought as he addressed a package to the fop cop, works every time.

She wasn't coming. She wasn't going to save him. She wasn't going to relent. She wasn't going to come take care of him.

He thought about getting in the car, taking a little trip into Helena to see Aurora, but although it was raining, in Harry's poor heart, it wasn't raining *that* hard. He stood up, feeling dizzy and queasy from all that sugar, and stumbled into the dining room.

'She's not coming!' Harry cried.

The only thing that could save him now was *Butler*. He switched on the computer, leaned down and pulled a warm beer out of the twelve-pack that was still sitting under the table.

He brought up *Butler by Butler*, pressed Home-Home and the down arrow, and waited. Hunka chunka, the computer groaned, making its way to the end, hunka hunka chunk. It took a while; there were a lot of pages for it to scan, or whatever it did, to get to the end. One thousand seven hundred and thirty-eight, to be exact.

One thousand seven hundred and thirty-eight pages of what? he asked himself.

'Of me!' he shouted, 'Of my life,' but what was that? Harry didn't like to think in terms of value; that kind of thinking could mess you up, make you question yourself, stop you, God forbid. Every once in a while, when he was reading something really spectacular, *Master and Man*, perhaps, or *The Judgement*, he'd feel a little queasy, guilty almost, as if Tolstoy or Kafka were trying to tell him something, something apart from the story, something about himself, something a little too personal. 'Stick to the story, Franz,' he'd say; 'Mind your own bee's wax, Leo.' 'Who are you talking to now?' Clark would call from the kitchen, where she'd be sitting with a stack of almanacs, soaking up facts, and he would ask her if she thought there was something missing from his work. 'Silly,' she'd say, coming in and standing behind him, kneading his shoulders, tickling his neck with kisses, 'of course there's nothing missing. You're brilliant. Just keep going,' and her words were like a dose of Pepto Bismol, calming his queasiness into oblivion.

'Please wait. Please wait. Please wait,' the computer politely flashed.

If he waited long enough, Clark would come to her senses.

Wouldn't she?

Hunka chunk, the computer said.

There it was: page 1738. Harry was afraid to look at the words. He felt as if he were standing on a precipice, teetering unsteadily, and if he looked, he would lose his balance and all would be lost.

He closed his eyes, and tried to remember the great idea he'd had in the car. What was it? Something about Achilles? The Trojan War?

No. Dialectics. Butler vs. Butler.

Ugh, he thought, how stupid. How could he ever have thought it was brilliant? How could he ever have thought *any* of it was brilliant? How could he have ever been so stupid? Who was he trying to kid? He was just a fraud, a big fat phoney, living off his wife's largesse, taking up space, breathing air someone else might need, someone who might do something *useful* with his life, something for the good of mankind. What was he, really? A forty-seven-year-old parasite, a loser, a nothing.

You're not going to start blubbering, are you? Butler asked but yes, he was, he was going to sit in that chair and cry like a baby, he was going to sit there until he starved to death and Clark would come up and find nothing but his skeleton, poised in front of the computer while it flashed 'Please wait. Please wait.'

Clark. All this was her fault. If she hadn't sent him away, he'd be happily working at home, feeling great, never doubting for a minute the importance of what he was doing. But he would forgive her, if only she'd relent . . .

It was too late. He might as well give up. Without Clark, he was nothing; he might as well toss the computer out the window and go and join the Peace Corps, go and do something worthwhile. He could join the French Foreign Legion, if it still existed. Or maybe he could join some expedition, go and study penguins on the South Pole and die of frostbite. They'd bury him in the Polar Ice Cap and a hundred years from now, when the Ice Cap melted, he'd thaw out and get to begin life anew . . .

Science fiction! Now there was something he'd never tried before, he could put Butler in a rocket, have him darting through space, dodging asteroids, battling alien possums, colonising galaxies . . .

But he didn't want to dodge asteroids or battle aliens or colonise galaxies. All he wanted was his old life back. Too late. He switched the computer off.

'Why bother?' he asked and climbed upstairs. As far as he was concerned, the alien possums could have him.

'I'm yours for the taking,' he called, and lay down, waiting for them to carry him off to their lair.

Twenty-nine

Clark went to the office and pretended to work. She felt like Scarlett O'Hara, having kicked Rhett out one time too many, sobbing in the doorway while he disappeared into the fog.

Rhett *Butler*! Harry *Butler*!

But she wasn't like Scarlett. Scarlett was selfish and greedy and cruel; Scarlett deserved to be left, while she . . .

While she deserved it, too. She picked up the phone and tried her answering machine again. Nothing.

She called Information for the number of the 9th Precinct.

'I was just wondering,' she said when she got O'Donnell on the phone, 'I know it was a joke, and everything, but by any chance did Harry call you to check in?'

He asked her if anything was the matter.

'No, no,' she said. 'He had to go out of town for a

few days and I forgot to tell him. About the joke part. He thought you were serious.'

'Not serious enough to check in, apparently,' O'Donnell said.

What had she done? Polly had been right; she shouldn't have jumped to conclusions. She wanted to get Harry's things back, but by the time she called, it was too late to stop the delivery and now they were bouncing around in a truck somewhere on the Thruway.

She looked through her In-box, trying to find something in which she could get lost. Breast implants. A profile of a female astronaut. Pets that saved their owners' lives. Computers that talked. Electric cars that could travel a hundred miles without recharging. A hundred miles? What good was that? What good was any of it?

Aggie opened Clark's door and stuck her head in, wanting to know where Clark had been for the past two days.

'I was sick. Flu, I guess.'

Aggie grinned. 'I thought maybe you sneaked off to check up on Daniel Boone. How's he doing up there?'

'Fine,' Clark said. She picked up a sheaf of galleys and started scribbling. 'Can't talk now, Aggie,' she said, 'I'm way behind.'

'What have I done?' she moaned again as soon as Aggie closed the door. She picked up the phone to check her messages again.

'Huh. Huh. Huh.'

Harry! It was Harry, letting her know in his caveman way he needed her.

What could she do? How could she get a message to him?

'You could try Sam,' Paul suggested when she called

him, 'He's got the General Store up there. Is everything OK?'

No, no, no, everything was not OK, but she said 'Yes,' took Sam's number, and hung up.

She called all afternoon, but there was no answer.

'He's probably out fishing,' Paul said when she called again, 'Try him again in the morning.'

The morning! How was she going to get through the rest of the day? The night? The idea of returning to her ransacked apartment made her feel like a malefactor who was being forced to revisit the scene of her crime.

She had Hotline duty from six to eleven tonight, but how could she face the women there? Most of them were survivors, women who had endured unspeakable acts of brutality and cruelty from their spouses, their boyfriends, their girlfriends in some cases. Women who had been locked in closets, gagged with duct tape, bludgeoned with a baseball bat, harangued into a state of paralysation.

How could she have done it? How could she have packed his clothes up and sent them away? If she had just waited, like Polly kept telling her, she would have reverted to her usual semi-reasonable self, given Harry the benefit of the doubt, taken the bus up this weekend and they could have made up, come back home together, and gone straight to a real estate agent.

Now it was too late. He'd get the boxes, think it was over, and run straight back to the woman in the tablecloth.

She'd behaved despicably. She should have just barged into the café, confronted him, made him squirm a while and then dragged him back to the Chevette, stuffed him in and said, 'Home. Now.'

Once, when Clark was little, she had said something

horrible to her grandmother, something so vile that even now she wouldn't allow herself to form the words, and later, after crying herself sick for half the day, she had apologised, but her grandmother refused to comfort her. 'I will never, so long as I live, forget those words,' she had said and Clark had begged her and begged her to forgive her. 'I take them back! I take them back!' little Beanie had cried, and her grandmother had said, 'You can't take them back, Beatrice. There are some things you just have to live with.'

And now she'd have to live with this.

But she couldn't. She couldn't live with 'this', if 'this' meant living without Harry.

Harry. Who had never lifted a finger to her. Whose idea of brutality was not speaking to her. The meanest thing he had ever said to her was 'You're getting flabby, Clark.' Harry. Dear, sweet, infinitely tolerant Harry.

But there was a limit to tolerance. She had kicked him out before, but never for long, and he never went very far. She always knew where to find him – Theatre 80 or the bookstore – when she cooled off. He would pretend to be angry, force her to say 'please' and then 'pretty please,' and then come happily home. But this was different – he wasn't just browsing through the stacks at St Mark's – he was hundreds of miles away, unreachable, alone.

Or maybe not alone. Maybe with that woman . . .

'Stop,' she told herself.

Maybe she should go back to her shrink. Maybe, if she worked a little harder, she *could* do something about her perversity, her contrariness, her tendency to fly off the handle first and regret it later. 'You're addicted to drama,' Jana was forever saying, 'and I don't mean the stage.' Jana was always try to drag her with her to one of her Anger workshops. 'But it isn't *me*,' Clark tried to explain to her, 'It comes from somewhere else.' 'Yeah, sure, that's what they all say,' Jana said, but the point wasn't where it was coming from, the point was it was ruining her life. As much as Clark loathed the idea of spending an evening sitting in a room full of guilt-ridden hot-heads, whining about how rotten she was, maybe she should try it. It couldn't hurt. The worst thing that could happen was it would piss her off.

She felt like calling the Hotline, saying she was sick, but she wouldn't. She would go, and be ashamed, and figure out how to get Harry back.

Thirty

He was awoken by the sound of someone pounding on his door. Harry had no idea what time it was; he hadn't thought to pack an alarm clock, but it was well into the day. He walked over to the window overlooking the driveway, opened it, and stuck his head out.

'Delivery for Harry Butler,' a UPS guy said cheerfully. 'You have to sign for it.'

Harry told him he would be right down. A delivery? For me? Harry loved deliveries, even though they were almost always for Clark, still, there was the possibility someone might be sending him a surprise.

This had to be from Clark; who else knew he was up here? Nobody, not even O'Donnell, whom he had forgotten to call with his whereabouts. He wondered if he could get in trouble for that. Oh well, didn't matter. What mattered was that his call had worked after all: Clark had received his message and although she hadn't been able to get up here herself, she was sending him something, a little gifty to tide him over until she arrived.

'Up here for the duration, eh?' the UPS driver, SCOTT, asked.

Everybody in the City of the Dead wore their names in capitals, Butler thought. To make up for being dead, probably.

Duration of what? Harry didn't ask. He just shook his head, said he was going home any day now.

SCOTT raised his eyebrows, shrugged and headed back to the truck. He took out a hand lift – what would he need a hand lift for? – and disappeared into the back. She must be sending him something big. A TV! Harry thought, she was sending him a TV so he wouldn't get bored and lonely. A TV would be good; he could get back up-to-date with what was going on in the collective unconscious, see what it was the rest of America was needing to catharsise these days. He hoped it was color. Harry had never owned a TV, probably the only person in America who hadn't. Of course she would get the best. That Clark, when she did something, she did it right. She went all out. She was generous to a fault.

Harry could hear the packages scraping around in the truck. SCOTT reappeared, laid a big cardboard box on the hand lift and then disappeared again.

Two! Harry thought, she sent me two presents. If the first one was a TV, what could the second one be?

'Let me help you,' he said, rushing over, too excited to wait, and he wheeled the packages up to the back porch. They were definitely from Clark, but they weren't TV's. Too light. Too rattly.

Harry ripped the tape off and opened the first box.

His *stuff*. The box was full of his *stuff*. He dug through his dirty clothes, looking for a note, ripped open the other box. More stuff. His books. His records. His foam rubber Miss Liberty sun shade, the one Clark had won for him at a street fair. His Ophelia wig. And at the bottom, shattered into pieces, was his gold-painted copy of *Bongo Boogie*, which Clark had presented to him on their first date.

She was kicking him out, for real. She really *did* suspect him; she really *did* think he had something to do with the kid's death. She really *was* having an affair with O'Donnell.

He sat on the top step, waiting for the UPS guy to pull out of the driveway. If he was going to start blubbering he at least wanted to do it in private. Go on, go on, get outta here, Harry kept thinking while SCOTT sat behind the steering wheel, making endless notes on a metal clipboard. Scram, why don't you? What was he doing, writing *War and Peace*?

Finally, SCOTT put down the clipboard, waved happily, and backed the truck out on to the road. As soon as the taillights slipped behind the bushes, Harry started to cry, quietly, at first, but then with more gusto, collapsing halfway into a box.

'Clark!' he wailed.

'What are you?' Butler demanded. *'A man or a mouse? Get up! Are you going to let some GQ detective steal your wife? You, Harry Butler? Not on your life. Go get her, Butler. Win her back.*

But how? He'd never had to *do* anything before; women came to him, he won them by just being himself but apparently being himself was the problem, in this case. He was more than happy to be someone else, on paper, but in real life?

And what was his 'real life', without Clark? What was anything without Clark? He thought about Aurora, tried to imagine what she'd say if he woke her up in the middle of the night, asking what her favorite word was. 'Words aren't interesting,' he imagined her saying and he shuddered. He thought about Polly, imagined himself handing her *Butler by Butler*, imagined her wrinkling her little nose and saying, 'You want me to *read* this?'

Butler was only half a man without Clark. No. *Butler was only nine-tenths of a man without his wife.*

If this were a novel, he'd have to change and change was something Harry hated. But if he wanted his life back, something would have to change.

Maybe he could get Clark to change.

'No, Butler,' he imagined Gordie's voice saying, 'it has to be you.'

'Why me?' he asked, 'what's wrong with *me*?'

'Do you want her back or not?' the voice asked.

He asked the voice what he was supposed to do.

'You could start by thinking about her for a change.'

Wasn't that was he was doing, for God's sake, hadn't he been thinking about her almost constantly for the past three days? He felt that uncomfortable, queasy feeling again, the feeling that something was trying to get through to him that he didn't want to let in.

Well, he wasn't going to sit around, crying and arguing with imaginary voices. He was going home. It was his home, as well as Clark's, even if he wasn't on the lease.

He ran into the house, unplugged the computer and loaded it into the car. The rest of the stuff he could come back for later.

Thirty-one

Clark felt better; almost herself again. It was amazing what taking an action, any action, could do; it reintroduced the concept of possibility and, right up to the final heart-crushing instant when one realises the possible isn't, it gave one energy, excitement, life.

These ups and downs were killing her, though. She wondered if there had been any mood disorders in her family. There was no way to find out – everybody on her mother's side of the family was dead and neither she nor Dee Dee had spoken to any of the relatives on her father's side in decades, not since the Christmas their grandmother packed them up and sent them out West to spend the holidays with their other grandparents, the Yukky Grandparents, who believed in some kind of weird religion that didn't countenance Christmas presents.

She had called Sam – what a nice man he seemed! – who had promised to go over and give Harry a message:

'Big mistake. Love you. Call me. Clark.' She went to work; cleaned up her In-pile; delegated to the ebullient Peggy; made an appointment with Greta, her old shrink; made it through lunch with Aggie without once growling at her. And now, she was going home, to await word from Harry.

She hadn't thought to give Sam her telephone number, in case there was a problem, so she had no way of knowing her message had never been delivered. Sam had gone – he never missed an opportunity to get a buck or two from tip-happy New Yorkers – but when he arrived, there was no one there. Just a couple boxes of clothes on the back porch.

Clark felt almost joyful, not because everything was 'all right', at least not yet, but because she felt hopeful that it could be. Hope. Normally, she thought it was dangerous, something tossed to the despondent so they wouldn't revolt, but today, today she saw Speranza in a better light, in all her full-blown glory, and she felt so happy she wanted to hug people on the street, she wanted to laugh, to buy up all the freesia at the Korean deli and hand them out to everyone she passed.

She glanced at herself reflected in a deli window. She looked happy, like a happy person very much in need of a hair cut.

She laughed, turned around, and headed for Freida's. Who says one can't change? she thought. When I go up to get Harry, I'll be a blonde.

Meet me at the Duelling Grounds, Butler told the Fop Cop.

'What do you want with a woman who thinks you're a murderer?' he asked himself around Yonkers, and the truth was, he didn't know. But he would forgive her for suspecting him, if she would forgive him . . . for what?

He hadn't done anything. The only thing he'd done was been present in his own home when a body fell past the window.

It seemed as if it had all happened weeks ago, months ago, as if, in fact, it hadn't happened at all, in real life, but rather in some nightmare, some memory of an old movie.

Harry had often experienced the feeling of unreality in his life, but in the past it had been pleasurable. He had been so happy with his eccentric life, living most of the day in his imagination, taking an occasional break to become Tarzan or Frankenstein's Monster or Blotto the Clown. He'd walk home from a delivery, feeling like the luckiest man alive because unlike the people he was passing – the day-to-dayers, the Suits, the squares, the conformists – he was living in his very own fantasy of what his ideal life should be.

And his very own fantasy of what his life should be included Clark. For better or worse. Whether she suspected him of being a murderer or a free-loader or a two-timer or anything else. It was just Clark, being one of her hundred different selves – one of the least likeable of them, but still, the ninety-five delightful Clarks were worth the five shitheads. He'd just have to go home, convince her of his innocence, and get back to the business of being the luckiest man on earth.

That is, if she hadn't gone too far with O'Donnell. There was one of those not-so-nice Clarks who was fully capable of falling in love with someone else and completely forgetting how much the other ninety-five loved Harry.

He took the Major Deegan, drove by Yankee Stadium and over the Willis Avenue Bridge, into the South Bronx, where he was bombarded by squeegee-guys.

'Go ahead,' he said, choosing one old guy who the young ones were trying to beat off, handing him a dollar when the light changed.

'How does a guy get to be a geek?' Tyrone Power asks at the beginning of *Nightmare Alley*, one of Harry's favorites. 'How does a guy sink that low?'

How does a guy get to be a squeegee-man? Butler asked himself as he plowed through the hovering group of bums, waving their squeegees menacingly.

Harry always gave them money. He felt it was his duty, after being in a line of traffic on Houston one day, stopped behind a guy in a Mercedes. The guy had his window down, smoking a cigar, and when the bum came up to the window and held out his hand, the rich guy tapped his ash in it. It had outraged Harry, outraged him to the point of tears, it had taken every ounce of his willpower, and many reminders that he didn't have collision insurance, to keep himself from bashing his Chevette right up that Mercedes' ass.

Even now, he got tearful, just thinking about it. He didn't know what it was about that particular incident – he'd lived in New York for nearly thirty years now and seen enough to break every heart in Dublin, Ohio ten times over – but there was something about the way the rich guy tapped the ash, the way the bum just stood there, holding it, as if he thought he might get a tip for being an ashtray.

Harry drove down Second Avenue, sniffling, to 5th Street, usually the best bet for getting a parking space this time of day. The cops were in and out of the spaces all day and chances were pretty good of finding one empty.

He turned the corner, slowed down to prowling speed, and began watching both sides of the street for a spot.

He recognised O'Donnell first, standing on the steps, talking to some compact blonde. It took Harry a minute to recognise the dress, the new blue one, and the grubby WNYC bag slung over her shoulder. Clark! Clark, in disguise!

Oh shit, he thought. There was a cab behind him, right on his tail. The only thing keeping the cabbie from blasting his horn was the precinct house, but Harry could see, via his rear-view mirror, that the guy was ready to take his chances anyway. Harry stuck his arm out of the window, tried to wave the cab around, but there wasn't enough space. The best Harry could do was to pull in next to the fire hydrant, hunker down and hope that Clark wouldn't come his way.

He sat there, peeking over the steering wheel, watching them. O'Donnell was gesturing, speaking intently, and Clark was leaning in, head cocked, listening and looking up at him. She had a kind of dazed expression on her face. Love sickness, Harry thought miserably, my life is over.

O'Donnell reached into his inner jacket pocket, pulled out an envelope, and handed it to Clark.

'Oh no!' Harry moaned, 'A *billet-doux*!' It was worse than he thought – if O'Donnell could write, if he had even the most rudimentary sense of language and rhythm, Clark was lost for ever.

Oh shit. Oh shit, oh shit, oh shit, they were coming his way. He scrunched himself down in the seat, knowing it was useless to hope she wouldn't see him. Clark wasn't at all like Harry, she noticed everything: she could tell where he'd been running by the scuffmarks on his shoes; what he'd been eating by the tiniest pin-prick of sauce he'd slobbered on his shirt; tell by the heat of the computer how long it had been since he'd stopped working. She was a regular little Sherlock Holmes and there was no way she would walk by without noticing the Chevette.

They were smiling now – Clark kind of wistfully, as if O'Donnell had just told her a sad story featuring his childhood puppy. She nodded, waved the *billet-doux* at him and slipped it in her bag. O'Donnell nodded as well, confirming their rendezvous, no doubt.

'What will your husband say, if he finds that?' O'Donnell was saying as they approached the car.

'Oh, he'll never see it,' Clark said emphatically, 'I can guarantee you that.'

They were right next to the car. It was over; Harry's life was over. Any second now, Clark would see him and demand to know what he was doing there. She might even have O'Donnell arrest him.

O'Donnell was laughing as they passed by. 'I guess he doesn't snoop, then,' he said.

Harry could barely hear Clark as she said, 'Not any more.'

He couldn't believe it. Clark had walked right past him and not even noticed him. And some detective O'Donnell was – Harry had been right there, under his nose, and he hadn't seen him.

Well, that was that. His life, as he had known and loved it, was over. Done. Kaput. He might as well go up on the roof of the squatters' building and jump off, end it all where it started, at least it would be symmetrical.

Why not? he thought. Life without Clark would be dull beyond belief, now that she had filled up every part of his being. No other woman, not even Polly with all her Best Friend allure, appealed to him.

What would his life be, without Clark? He'd have to get a job, buy a suit, join the day-to-dayers, give up

B by B. And what would his life have been *for*? He would, in the end, turn out just like Ivan Ilitch, stuffed in the sack with all the others, carried off to the boneyard and dumped in a heap. But unlike Ivan Ilitch, Harry wouldn't even have the consolation of having been rich, having had a little power to lord around, he'd never have the satisfaction of sending someone off to Siberia.

He laid his head on the steering wheel. 'Oh, God!' he cried.

Thirty-two

Clark walked into the apartment, plopped the groceries on the table, and raced to the answering machine. Polly, Jana, Dee Dee's garbled voice, echoing across the Atlantic.

She pulled the envelope out of her bag and opened it as she listened. Martin wanted her to dog-sit – was he *mad*?; there was a meeting at the Red Cross tomorrow; she had a dental appointment at four.

She pulled out the photograph of herself in the Mohawk. Had she ever been that young? she asked herself as she pushed the skip button at the sound of Aggie's voice, had she ever been that wild? She guessed she had, tucked the photo back in the envelope and walked over to the bookcase. She'd hide it in *The Sound and the Fury*; Harry hated Faulkner.

The machine clicked and rewound itself.

But where was Harry?

She listened again, thinking she might have missed

him, but his voice wasn't there. Could Sam, who had sounded so accommodating, not have delivered the message? Did that mean Harry was sitting up at Paul's, all alone, surrounded by all his things, thinking she had officially kicked him out? They had agreed, when they got married, that if either of them ever wanted out, the other would let them go. *Nolo contendere.* 'Swear,' Clark said. 'I swear,' Harry said.

Butler had never thought about killing himself before.

Oh God, what had she done? It would take too long to drive back up there, she had to reach him, *now*, but how?

Paul! She would have him send a telegram, a real one. He was in the business, he would know how to get one through now, tonight, this instant.

She picked up the phone and dialled.

Harry stood near the ledge, a few feet behind the yellow police ribbon, watching the apartment.

She had come home alone, that was good, but practically the first thing she had done was take out the love letter, read it, and tuck it away in some book. Probably Faulkner.

She looked so different, with the new hair-do, younger. More like her young self, the Clark he had fallen in love with that night at the Where?House.

He watched her as she paced around the apartment, apparently agitated. She kept walking over to the answering machine, probably listening to a message from her paramour, over and over again. But she was upset, he could see that. Maybe her detective was getting cold feet. Clark was, after all, a married woman and hard as it was to believe, adultery was still a crime.

She picked up the phone. Harry was amazed at what

he could see, standing up on the roof. His apartment was a mess. It looked as if it had been burgled, which in a sense it had. Clark had cleaned him out, stuffed him in a couple of boxes and carted him off to the UPS, but he wasn't angry, not any more. He was too empty to feel any emotion at all.

Clark put down the phone and walked back into the kitchen. She started unpacking the groceries, walking to the fridge with a half-gallon of milk, then back to the bag for a two-liter bottle of soda. She opened it, took a swig straight from the bottle, wiped some dribble with the back of her hand. She opened her mouth, probably letting out a belch, and then recapped the bottle and stuffed it in the fridge. There was something so sweet about watching her go about her little domesticities, completely unaware that she was being observed. She seemed so vulnerable and Harry felt a love for her that was different, somehow, from what he had always felt before, something more tender, almost fatherly, although he could never describe it that way to her. Not that he would ever get a chance to.

He felt the sting of tears building up behind his eyes. His heart, he realised, was like the apartment. Rifled. Burgled. Robbed.

He could see not only into his own apartment, his own life, but into Martin's as well. He was sitting on the couch, a dog on either side, the light from the TV illuminating his face. He was either laughing or crying. He leaned over, kissed the black and white dog on the head. Yuck, Harry thought, how does a guy end up like that?

But at least Martin had his dogs to love him. He, Harry, had no one. Not any more.

He looked back into his ex-apartment and wondered

how much of his own life the kid had seen, what his life looked like from up here. He blushed, thinking of the times he had masturbated while he was working. Not often! Not a lot! Just a couple of times, when he was so excited by his own ideas he couldn't wait for Clark to get home. Had he watched Harry and Clark in bed? Had he watched Harry alone, during the day, pacing the apartment, working out, eating his lunch, putting on his apron to clean the kitchen?

Not that it mattered. Harry's secrets were safe, but, he had to admit, they were pretty tame in any case. Boring, even. From up here, you couldn't see what was going on inside, inside Harry, inside Clark, and that was the only thing that was interesting. The rest was all just plot.

Butler had come to the end of his plot.

Had he, Harry, come to the end of his? Had he been deluding himself all this time? Was the only thing that kept *Butler* going Clark's belief in it, in him?

Butler 5375: Doubt 1. One big one. One that could wipe Butler out.

Should he jump? He looked down into the courtyard. Beer cans. Shopping bags full of garbage. A broken bicycle. A charred mattress. He tried to make out a chalk outline of Gordie, but all he could see was a whole lot of hard, gray concrete.

What was going on inside Clark now? Harry looked back into the apartment. She was sitting at the kitchen table, with her head buried in her arms. Crying. Oh, Clarkie, Clarkie, he thought, don't cry. He wished he had a vine he could grab on to so he could swing across the courtyard, on to his own fire escape and into his apartment. He'd sweep her into his arms, comfort her.

But who was she crying over? Him, or that malnourished detective with the quivering nostrils? She stood up, walked to the door, and began slowly pounding her head against it.

Clarkie! It was ripping him apart to see her in so much pain and he didn't care who she was crying over, he just wanted to take her in his arms and rock her tears away. He felt light-headed, dizzy; his love for her had never seemed so pure, so untainted. He'd never felt love like this for anyone, ever, not even himself.

I've changed! he thought, I've changed! And it didn't kill me!

He felt a warmth envelop him, as if some goddess had leaned down from her cloud and placed a kiss and a wreath on his head. Oh joy! Oh happiness! Harry had always wondered what grace felt like, and now he knew. It felt like this. It felt as if every cell in his being had suddenly come to life, was dancing about in ecstacy.

Harry was not a dancer, but he couldn't help himself. 'I've changed!' he sang as he did what he thought was a pirouette, 'I've changed!'

He picked up one of the yellow police ribbons and waved it in the air. 'I've changed!' he shouted.

He walked back over to the ledge, holding the ribbon, and looked down, thinking about the kid. Gordie had been right; Clark was a woman worthy of worship, and Harry, for the first time, felt sorry about the poor kid's death. He felt tears welling up again – could he be feeling grief? Grief for someone he had never even met, except in an hallucination?

He remembered the body, lying helpless down there, and he wept: for the kid, for wasted life, for himself, for not having even tried to help, for not having had the humanity to care.

He knew now he could win Clark back; and he knew

how to do it. He looked round, to see if perhaps Gordie's ghost was hanging around, nudging him, reminding him that the way to recapture Clark's heart was through his own adoration of her. It made perfect sense – after all, wasn't that how she had won him, Harry, in the first place? With her fandom? Her praise of his work? The way her eyes would sparkle when she'd watch him sauntering towards her? He could do that! Why not? It was only what she deserved. Maybe he'd even put aside *B by B* for a while, go to work for Paul full-time, make a few bucks and let Clark get back to her own work for a while.

Yes. He'd go home, sweet-talk his way into the apartment, and once in, he would overwhelm her with his love for her. She'd have to give in; his love was irresistible. *He* was irresistible. He was going home.

As he waved the police ribbon and did his little dance, he didn't notice as Clark approached the window, a look of curiosity on her face. He couldn't hear her thinking, Some nut is standing on that ledge again, couldn't hear her gasp when she recognised him.

'Harry!' she screamed, 'Don't jump!'

Harry turned, and saw the face of his beloved. She was calling to him. As he danced toward her, the ledge began to crumble and the last thing Harry saw was the streak of Clark's blue dress.

The Shadow of Desire
REBECCA STOWE

At the age of thirty-eight, Ginger has spent most of her life running away from her alcoholic mother, Virginia. Now she is on her annual pilgrimage to her parents' house for Christmas, anticipating the usual tensions and tantrums, knowing she will revert to teenage behaviour, hoping that this year will be different. And it is, but not in the way she expects.

As Ginger and her older brother humour their father's delight in the season's rituals, she turns an honest, ironic eye on herself and her family, tracing the roots of her sense of inadequacy. But she cannot clearly recall Virginia before her breakdown, before the childhood death of a second brother. Nor does she foresee the revelations that Christmas brings, giving her a startling new perspective on her mother and her past and, finally, the courage to follow her own desires.

'Secrets, lies, and indelible memories from the past are brought into focus through the medium of her glistening emotional prose to create a bittersweet tale of a damaged household'   *The Sunday Times*

'Exuberantly written, Stowe's novel is crammed with observation. A striking voice'   *Scotland on Sunday*

'Rebecca Stowe can't write a boring sentence . . . The affection, sadness, reproach and sheer intelligence which infuse the book make it memorable and powerful'
Fay Weldon in the *Mail on Sunday*

'Mad and witty'   *Marie Claire*

SCEPTRE

Eating Cake
STELLA DUFFY

Lisa's life seems perfect in every way. In her early thirties, she has a loving husband, a comfortable south London home, and a successful management consultancy. But she wants more. In fact, she wants to have her cake and eat it. So she embarks on a passionate affair with her best friend's boyfriend, and then seeks further gratification in the arms of a woman until, finally, Lisa is burnt by the fire she thought she was playing with.

'Duffy is deadly, and very funny, on the narcissism and self-delusion which seems to keep coupled love going'
Independent

'It's a credit to Duffy's sometimes unbearably honest prose and devastating observational eye that this speedy descent into selfish narcissistic pleasures remains both funny and compassionate . . . a sassy, frank and wickedly convincing page-turner'
List

'Duffy doesn't take the regular route of chronicling how the spouses find out and react. This is an altogether more subtle look at the effects of adultery . . . With typical assurance, Duffy examines the thirty-something IKEA generation and finds hidden strengths within the self-delusion and hypocrisy'
Gay Times

'A witty, candid tale'
New Women

'Duffy proves to be a chilling social observer'
The Times

SCEPTRE

A selection of other books from Sceptre

The Shadow of Desire	Rebecca Stowe	0 340 67189 0	£5.99 ☐
Eating Cake	Stella Duffy	0 340 71563 4	£6.99 ☐
City of Light	Lauren Belfer	0 340 74842 7	£6.99 ☐
Gorgeous	Lynne Bryan	0 340 73969 X	£6.99 ☐
Kissing the Pink	Jane Holland	0 340 73856 1	£6.99 ☐

All Hodder & Stoughton books are available from your local bookshop or newsagent, or can be ordered direct from the publisher. Just tick the titles you want and fill in the form below. Prices and availability subject to change without notice.

Hodder and Stoughton Books, Cash Sales Department, Bookpoint, 39 Milton Park, Abingdon, OXON, OX14 4TD, UK. E-mail address: order@bookpoint.co.uk. If you have a credit card you may order by telephone – (01235) 400414.

Please enclose a cheque or postal order made payable to Bookpoint Ltd to the value of the cover price and allow the following for postage and packing:

UK & BFPO – £1.00 for the first book, 50p for the second book, and 30p for each additional book ordered up to a maximum charge of £3.00.

OVERSEAS & EIRE – £2.00 for the first book, £1.00 for the second book, and 50p for each additional book.

Name _____

Address _____

_____

_____

If you would prefer to pay by credit card, please complete:
Please debit my Visa/Access/Diner's Card/American Express (delete as applicable) card no:

☐☐☐☐☐☐☐☐☐☐☐☐☐☐☐☐

Signature _____

Expiry Date _____

If you would NOT like to receive further information on our products please tick the box. ☐